Birch

The One and Only

A Worldwide Cataclysmic Occurrence
Leaves an Alaskan Alone in the Arctic

Garry Chandler

Publication Consultants
Since 1978

PO Box 221974 Anchorage, Alaska 99522-1974
books@publicationconsultants.com—www.publicationconsultants.com

ISBN 978-1-59433-582-2
eBook ISBN 978-1-59433-583-9
Library of Congress Catalog Card Number: 2015953305

All drawings, maps, sketches–personal by author.

Manufactured in the United States of America.

Dedication

To my family.
To all who I have met, loved, and learned from.
To all whom I have yet to meet.

Contents

Chapter One .... Haul Road 7
Chapter Two .... Pushing On 16
Chapter Three .... What The. 31
Chapter Four .... The Eagle Has Landed 42
Chapter Five .... Grave Yards and Ghost Ships 51
Chapter Six .... A Whale of a Good Day 79
Chapter Seven .... The Search 89
Chapter Eight .... Freezeup 103
Chapter Nine .... Friends or Foes 112
Chapter Ten .... The Leader of the Pack 128
Chapter Eleven .... Exiled 138
Chapter Twelve .... Downriver 155
Chapter Thirteen ....
Playing in the Snow—Surviving the Storms 165
Chapter Fourteen .... Boredom, Breakup, and Bear Hugs 180
Chapter Fifteen .... The Kobuk 189

Illustration

Alaska State and Haul Road 8
SASSY 37
Prudhoe to Kaktovik. 62
Before—Barrow-Teshekpuk 76
After—Barrow-Teshekpuk 77
Pt. Hope to Kotzebue 87
Before—Kotzebue-Selawik-Kobuk River Area 92
After—Kotzebue-Selawik-Kobuk River Area 93
SASSY—oil painting by author 192

Chapter One
Haul Road

Birch asked CG, "What do you mean you have to work on the trucks? What's wrong with them?"

"It's complicated, and you know you always get bad headaches when I try to explain complicated things to you. But don't worry. Why don't you get some sleep while me and the mechanic take care of everything, and then in the morning you can turn the big wheel in the cab. By the way, do you remember which pedal is which?" teased CG. "There is a clutch, a gas pedal, and most important of all, there is a brake pedal. I should label them for you. Don't worry about a thing now. Oh! I almost forgot. I need your credit card."

"You want my credit card, and then tell me not to worry?" As Birch handed CG his Birch Construction, Inc. credit card, he commented, "Right, I won't worry about a thing." But he couldn't keep from smiling, "Besides, it's only got a thirty-six-dollar limit."

"Thirty-six dollars won't even buy good whiskey," CG muttered.

* * * * *

5:30 a.m.

Birch wakes up and thinks, *Today I'm going be drinking my coffee when CG rolls out of the sack. Of course, this will be a first. There is always a first time for everything, me being up before CG, that is. Well, anything is possible.*

Guess I better get up and see what's going on. CG should have the rigs checked, repaired, and ready to roll. He said last night he would be ready this morning right after I bought him breakfast.

"It's your turn to buy CG!" Birch reminds him.

"That's not the way I remember it," just as he had said every morning for the past two weeks.

I'm feeling a bit peaked this morning, too peaked, otherwise I might argue with him. I also might have to slap him around a little, Birch thought. *Lucky for him, I'm feeling so peaked. Maybe tomorrow I will have more energy to slap someone around who is twice my size. Yup! It's just lucky for him*.

Birch will be driving one of the heavy-duty semi-tractor rigs, pulling a trailer with his cargo consisting of *SASSY* (Safety and Satellite Survival Ship/Yacht), an eighty-foot survival boat built to tend one of the major oil company's offshore drilling rigs and pads, which will be on a lease/purchase trial basis. Because the load measures sixteen

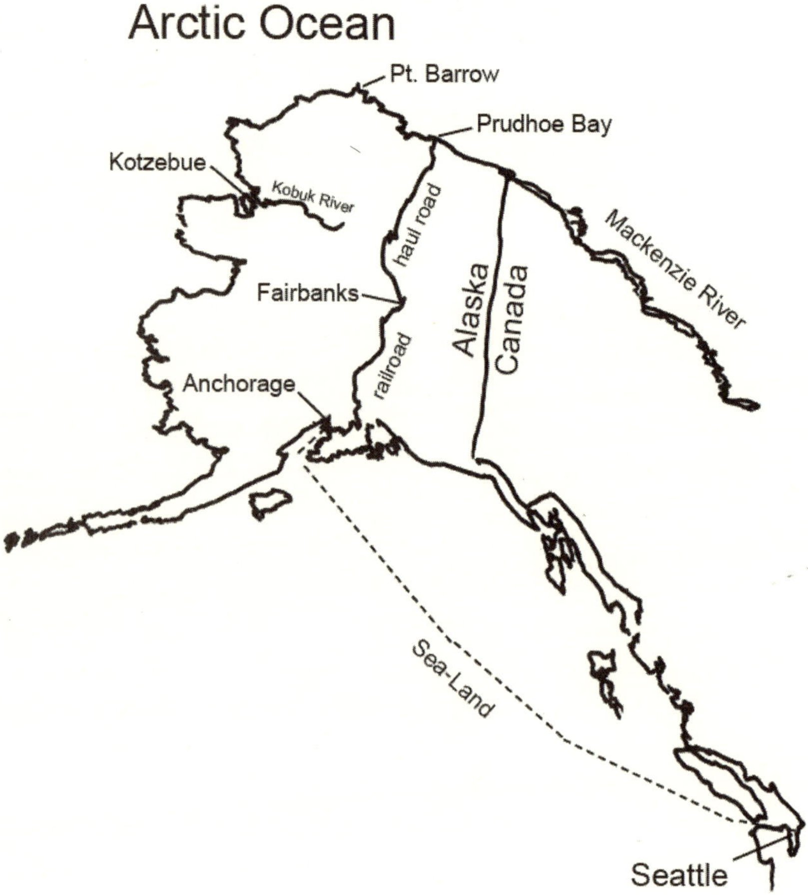

feet wide, and because of the height, length, and width of the load, having a pilot car in front and one in back with beacons, radios, and wide-load signs to warn approaching traffic is required.

Birch's load is too heavy and too large for any one rig to haul alone, which will require an additional truck to push the trailer hitched to Birch's rig. CG is driving the push truck that will help push Birch's truck and load so he can make it up some of the steeper hills and mountains. Both of the rigs have sleepers and are cozy and comfortable. After picking up the load in Fairbanks, it took them two days to make it to and down Beaver Slide and on up to Coldfoot Lodge without any major difficulty, but after coming down Beaver Slide, CG thought it best to check both rigs and make some minor but important repairs. They still had a ways to go and some difficult miles ahead.

Birch remembered picking up a semi driver walking down Beaver Slide some years ago. Beaver Slide was a long, downhill section of the haul road to Prudhoe Bay. Birch told the driver to hop in and warm up, as it was not too cold but still below zero. Birch spotted a semi rig up toward the top of the hill off in the side of the ditch. Lucky there was a ditch. In some places along the road it was just over the side of the road and straight down.

Birch asked the fellow he just picked up, "I assume that truck up ahead is yours?"

"It is."

"What do you want to do."

"I want to be taken to the nearest airport."

Birch mentioned to him that he might have noticed passing no airports since leaving Fairbanks several hundred miles south.

"I just want to fly back home to Oklahoma."

"What about the truck and load?"

He said he didn't care; he just wanted to fly back home.

Poor fellow was just petrified and scared to death, having survived the crash into the ditch. He was thankful that the load straps and tie downs did not break loose from the trailer during the sudden stop, allowing the load of materials to slide forward off the trailer and crush the truck cab and everything else inside, including him. At this point he didn't know which would come first, being killed on the haul road or freezing to death.

The haul road is no place for amateurs and flatland haulers. Even during the summer some of the professional drivers have lost control and ended up in the ditches or over the side. There have been some with deathly consequences, with most happening during the winter.

Birch dropped him off at the Coldfoot Lodge and arranged a ride for him with a trucker heading south to Fairbanks and wished him luck, as he probably wouldn't get paid and had lost his truck since he was an operator and owner. He also would probably get billed for the loss of material. Hope he had good insurance. The state would also probably bill him for cleaning up the wreckage; possibly confiscate his truck and trailer. Didn't look like he spilled any fuel or there would be another charge, and pocket change wouldn't cover that bill.

Birch had *SASSY* shipped via Sealand from Seattle to Anchorage, where the Alaska Railroad had freighted their load to Fairbanks, and where Birch and CG took delivery. From Fairbanks they headed north to Prudhoe Bay on the Arctic coast.

CG and a mechanic at Coldfoot had been working on the drive trains, breaks, and Jake breaks on both the push truck and on Birch's rig for the past couple of days after receiving parts from Fairbanks. The Jake breaks, when engaged, use the engine compression to retard the speed so they wouldn't need to ride the brakes as much and burn them up on some of the longer steep grades going downhill. With what lay ahead of them, CG and Birch wanted everything working top notch, especially the Jake brakes, going down the steep grades still ahead.

They received the parts the night before last from Buddy, one of the haul-road truckers going north to Prudhoe Bay. Just in time too, as one of the other drivers following Buddy had lost his cargo on the bridge crossing the Yukon River, significantly damaging the bridge and putting the Trans Alaska Pipeline in danger. But thankfully, no damage was done to the pipeline, which hangs over the side of the bridge. Alaska Pipeline gets lots of attention if it is affected or might be affected in any way. The pipeline company goes to great lengths to keep the pipeline safe and well-maintained. Much more so than they ever get credit for.

The bridge will be closed down for an indefinite time until everything has been repaired and inspected. From what Birch heard, a couple of structural braces had been damaged, so it could be several days or a week or more before any traffic would be catching up with them. That would be good for them, as they would not have any traffic to contend with, and they also wouldn't be holding up any traffic traveling north.

Birch wanders over to the Coldfoot restaurant and runs into CG standing just outside the entry drinking a cup of coffee.

"Where's my coffee?" he asked CG.

"Inside, in the pot where it will stay hot for those who have a tendency to sleep the morning away. Besides, you don't need any coffee. It's almost lunch time."

Birch looked at his watch and noticed it was 5:45 a.m. *Sure is lucky for him that I'm feeling peaked and poorly*, he thought. "What do you mean sleep the morning away? I ate breakfast two hours ago, but if you're going to eat something, I'll just have a piece of toast while you have breakfast."

"Sure you will," smiled CG, both of them knowing that the kitchen didn't officially open for a few more minutes at six o'clock.

Coldfoot is the last privately run business where you can get a hot meal, fuel, shower, or room until you arrive in Prudhoe, unless you were hauling loads for the pipeline, or had business at one of the few pump stations still in operation. Several pump stations have been downsized or bypassed completely due to the exploration and development companies' activities being curtailed by certain groups who are adamant about completely shutting down any development at all and wanting "to bring the third-world countries up on par with the USA." As has been publicly stated, "One way to do that is to bring the United Stated down to their level, and everyone should do their part," for a better world, in their minds, he guessed. Congress and the present administration seem to be going out of their way, doing their damnedest, intentionally or unintentionally, to accommodate.

Birch finished his breakfast and sat there drinking his coffee while looking in amazement at CG, who was still working on his breakfast. Birch was thinking that a guy has to have a rich uncle to fill CG up. "Well, should I come back in a couple of hours? You might be done by then."

"By the time you clean up, I will be ready. I don't know how someone who is just having a piece of toast can make such a mess and get all that syrup and egg yolk all over his face, CG said. "Hey Judy," he calls to the waitress, "can I buy a bib for the kid here?" Then he says to Birch, "Here, you got some on your face right there." He grabbed Birch's ear and damned near pulled it off.

Birch thinks, *Oh man, he is so lucky I am feeling so tired, yep, really lucky.*

"CG, I was just thinking."

"Oh no, not again—you know how dangerous that is. You remember the last time you did that, we almost got arrested."

"As I was trying to say," Birch continued, "we should have the whole road to ourselves."

"Does that mean you want to go back to bed and sleep in?" CG asks.

"No! What I mean is, with the bridge down, there will be no loads or traffic moving north, and I heard last night there was no traffic moving south. The truckers will stay in Prudhoe Bay until the bridge is open. And that is really a great stroke of luck; especially with the way you drive. By the way, have you seen Carol?"

CG looked around and said, "She was here awhile ago. She and her partner probably went back to bed since you were sleeping in this morning."

Carol was one of the two pilot car drivers required by the state to accompany large or wide loads like they were hauling.

After Birch paid the bill they went out and found Carol and her partner in the pilot cars, beacons rotating on the roofs, and steaming cups of coffee on the dashes.

"I'm going to do a walk around and do a last equipment and load check to make sure all the tie downs are secure," Birch said.

Birch also knew that CG would also be keeping a close watch, a very close watch on Birch's payload while following close behind his rig as they made their way north.

The Coldfoot community consists of the truck stop and a road maintenance camp and a few miners spread out in the area. From here on out to Prudhoe, the only other residents would be at the road maintenance and the pipeline camps. No other truck stops until they reached the Arctic Coast at Prudhoe. Birch and CG made sure everything was in working order and tied down as help might not be ready available.

"I'm heading out, Carol. Any traffic coming or leaving the turnout?"

"Not a thing in sight," Carol replied.

"Okay, time is right at seven. Hopefully we will make Slope Mountain around 12:24 p.m." Slope Mountain is a DOT road maintenance camp along the haul road.

"Twelve twenty-four! Give me a break!" A gravelly voice barely comes through the CB radio.

CG will be driving the push truck, another heavy-duty semi-tractor rig with a long wheel base, carrying a large concrete block over the drive wheels, giving it extra weight and traction to push and assist Birch's rig up steep grades and long pulls up and down hills, such as Atigun Pass. They will chain the push truck to the trailer load to help with braking when going down the steeper hills, especially Atigun Mountain Pass.

Birch knows CG is probably in his late sixties, but he is still one of the best around for hauling the heavy stuff up the haul road and is always in demand. He should be hauling *SASSY*, and Birch should be on the push truck. But CG was adamant that Birch drive the lowboy with the multi-million-dollar load, telling Birch, "You need an annual refresher course, if the truth be told. But don't worry, you will get the hang of it, if not this year or next, then one of these years, for sure."

Birch and CG have been close from the day Birch was born. Birch's dad took CG under his wing years before Birch was born and tried to watch over him like a mother hen, and for the most part he was successful in keeping CG out of serious trouble. That's not to say that the two of them didn't get in non-serious trouble, mainly in the bars. Finally, Birch's dad married and settled down. Wasn't long after that CG married Birch's mother's younger cousin, and he, too, settled down. CG and Birch's dad worked together on various projects over the years during the summer construction seasons, then later on during the winters. As winter working technologies allowed winter exploration up north along with the prospect of oil discoveries, they continued to work together off and on. Especially after oil was actually discovered in the Prudhoe Bay area

Birch's mother and her cousin were extremely close. The two families (CG's and Birch's) stayed near and shared every holiday, even after Birch's dad was killed in a plane crash while Birch was still in high school. CG was never really asked to be Birch's Godfather, but he was the closest thing to being one. He tried to help fulfill the duties without even realizing he was stepping into that role.

After the plane crash CG tried to keep Birch under his wing. But that was difficult, since CG, like Birch's dad, was usually called to work in remote areas or bush jobs. Both of them had developed reputations as being reliable, not needing any guidance, and would get the job done regardless of any setbacks, including weather or delayed supplies.

That left Birch without any guy-type guidance for long periods of time. During that time Birch ran wild and carefree, eventually dropping out of school. But he would work where he could: paper routes and later on when he was a little older, he hustled freight for the airlines and got good enough to hustle a few bucks at the local pool halls. At times he would just disappear and end up wherever his interest at the time took him. He would spend time with his friends in their villages, sometimes Indian villages in the Interior and sometimes Eskimo villages on the Arctic coast. Sooner or later, at each new locale, it seemed he would have to prove himself to one or more of the local toughs in his age group. Fortunately, he did have a little experience on the Fairbanks city streets and pool halls. Once the locals and Birch introduced themselves to each other, he usually had friends for life. Turns out Birch was really good at these local introductions and got better and better. No one was ever really hurt during those altercations other than some bruises, puffy heads, and black eyes.

As he got a little older and after a stint of waiting tables, checking IDs, tending bar, and trying to make it up to his mother for nearly giving her nervous breakdowns every time he wandered off, everyone (even one of the local judges) thought it would be a good idea that he join the army.

In looking back, Birch was always glad he did not go in the army when he was seventeen or eighteen like a lot of kids did right out of high school. If he had, he would probably still be in a brig somewhere, as he was not prone to taking orders from anyone, and it didn't matter who they were, either. When he went in the army he was in his early twenties and had started to wise up. During his enlistment he made good rank and had a good job in communications and enjoyed the challenges of being a paratrooper and dropping in unexpectedly on folks. He actually enjoyed his time in the service, had no regrets, and realized the three years were good for him and had kept him out of trouble. But three years were enough.

Chapter Two
Pushing On

Carol was ahead in the pilot car with a wide-load banner fastened to the grill of her pickup with the amber, rotating beacon. She would warn Birch of approaching traffic and warn the approaching traffic over the CB radio of the wide loads coming their way. She would also advise Birch of any other conditions or any other road hazards that he should be aware of. Her partner, following the semis, was doing the same.

The roads out of Fairbanks were in fair shape. Fairbanks to Fox is nine miles on the four-lane Steese Highway. From Fox it's sixty miles on the Elliot Highway to Livengood, thirty miles plus of which was paved in just the past couple of years. Before the pipeline and haul road were built, it was always called the Livengood Road. It wasn't much more than a mining road full of hairpin turns barely wide enough for compacts. Now the pavement ends at Livengood. Good old washboard, rutted gravel, and pot holes from there on up to Prudhoe. From Livengood it's another fifty-five miles on up to the Yukon Bridge, and another 185 miles to Coldfoot from where Birch and his crew are just leaving. They hope to be over and well beyond the Atigun pass and the big mountains of the Brooks Range while they still have daylight. Losing about ten minutes a day of sunlight this time of year, up north of the pass in midwinter you won't see the sun for a couple of months, since the sun will be just below the horizon. South of the pass the sun will only be above the horizon for a couple of hours at these latitudes. Midsummer will be just the opposite. The sun will not drop below the horizon for a few weeks. In Fairbanks some will go watch a midnight baseball game on June twenty-first. Others might read a book outside. The farther north you go, the more or less light you have depending on the season and month.

From Livengood on the Dalton to Atigun Pass is usually well graded, as the Department of Transportation (DOT) has several maintenance camps along the way. On the south side of the pass there are good material/gravel sites every few miles where the maintenance crews can get material for grading and pothole fill as needed. On the other side of the pass is a whole nother story. There are material sites, but the material is mostly mud. No good gravel sites. Not having much to work with, the DOT maintenance crews are left with putting the blade down into the ditch along the side of the road, rolling up the rocks to shake the dust off, and then rolling the rocks back off the road into the ditch. The gravel that was there at one time has been rolled back and forth so many times it has been worn down to almost dust. Makes for a very bumpy ride in the summertime, especially after heavy rains when lots of big potholes appear, shaking some of the rigs and vehicles to pieces.

Later that afternoon and prior to climbing up on what is called the Chandalar Shelf, Birch and CG checked the loads, tie downs on the loads, tires, air, gauges, and fluids on both of the trucks at a pullout at the bottom of the climb going up the shelf. The shelf was just at the foot of Atigun Pass and was only five or six miles long before actually starting up the climb and going over the Atigun Pass, the highest point of the haul road.

When they got to the bottom of the pass they would stop at the pullout made for the truckers and double check both trucks and pilot cars, just as they did before climbing up onto the shelf.

The pullouts were primarily where truckers chained up during the winter when the roads were icy or had snow on them. They were also a place where the truckers could wait while the DOT maintenance crews plowed snow drifts, clearing the road for passage.

If the truckers did not have to chain up during the winter, they would normally make a run to get as much momentum as possible, hoping to not spin out. Drivers did not want to spin out and come to a stop on this steep grade. It's real tough trying to put chains on, even on a flat grade. If the truckers spun out and then jackknifed, sliding backwards, they would be in big, big trouble. Any other truckers going up or coming down would more than likely be held up and ticked off until the DOT crew brought up a road grader or their front-end loader to straighten the blockage and clear the road.

During the summer the truckers would also make a run for the hill, trying to get as far up as they could before downshifting. In order to not lug the engine, the driver would continue to downshift to their lowest gear on some of the longer grades (depending on the loads they were carrying), keeping the rpms up and providing power. At times they could be just crawling along in their lowest gear before going over the top.

When Birch and CG got ready, they would coordinate and make a mini-run at the pass. With the load they were hauling, they were not moving very fast anyway, even on flat ground.

Birch remembered a time when he worked for the pipeline company and was making a trip north, had passed Coldfoot just before ascending up the shelf right about where they were now driving along the Dietrich River. It was in the fall of the year, real nice out, fifty or sixty degrees above, sun shining, fall colors on the trees and brush as he was climbing up on the shelf. Once he got to the top it was like someone had thrown a switch from fall time to arctic time—just like that. Near and on top it transitioned to a foot or more of snow, barren of trees, extremely bright. There must have been a thousand different shades of white, but at the same time it was also stark white with no contrast, as there are no trees in the arctic, just tundra, brush, and willows along the creeks and rivers, all covered in snow. But on that trip everything was covered in fresh snow. He also remembered trips when it was sixty-degrees-below zero or more through here.

On a different trip, one of the pump station technicians told him that one time while he was monitoring the pump stations' airport and reporting the weather, when the pump station manager made him come back to the pump station because the temperature had just passed eighty degrees below and was still dropping. He wanted to stay, as the record low of minus eighty-two degrees was down near the Alaska-Canadian border at Snag in the Canadian Yukon Territory. But he was ordered back to the pump station, since the manager felt it wasn't safe. Sometimes during the summer in the valleys, depending on the elevations you can see temperatures in the eighties. From eighty degrees above to eighty-degrees-below zero, a person had better keep an eye on their tomato plants.

With Carol in the pilot car on ahead and on top of the shelf, Birch was watching CG as he crept up with the push truck and made contact. Birch picked up the CB radio mike, smiled, and called him. "CG, you can come on up and start your push, but be careful. I got some whiplash from the last hill. You know the idea is creep on up and make contact. Crashing is not allowed. We're not playing bumper cars, you know."

"You really like the sound of your voice, don't you? Pushed you up and over, dropped on back, poured myself a cup of coffee, and you're still jabbering away. Carol, you see anything up your way?"

"Not a thing. I'll wait for you at Chandalar DOT camp."

"Okay, I'll check the tie downs on *SASSY* when I get there before we go up the pass."

"Carol, you see that stunted little spruce tree sitting out there all by itself? That's the last firewood we will see until we come back this way."

"Yeah, I see it, and it sure looks lonely."

Birch teased Carol, saying, "If I had my axe handy, and if it wasn't so far away, I would go get that tree. You never know when you might need some firewood."

"You cut down that tree and I'm going to call the FBI, EPA, Alaska State Police, CIA, IRS, and the Alaska Fire Marshal and give them your home address. I might even call the president of the Mafia. Heck, I might even call the President, and he will tax you to death and take away your axe," laughed Carol.

A low, deep, gravelly voice was heard over the CB. "Go get him, Carol."

Carol was just coming out of the Chandalar DOT camp at the base of the mountain pass as Birch and CG pulled in off the road. Birch walked around, tightened up the slack on a couple of straps, took a leak, and walked around to the pilot car and asked Carol, "What are the guys up to here? I didn't see any of them working on the road anywhere."

"They are changing out the rubber and cutting edges on the blades, getting ready for winter."

"Well then, let's saddle up. Carol you go on up to the top, and when we start up I'll let you know, and then you hold up any traffic. There shouldn't be any traffic other than possible pipeline pickups coming over the pass. No big rigs expected until the Yukon Bridge opens. We won't be able to stop, pull over, or back up once we start, as you know, so don't let anyone get past you. I'll have my hands full keeping an eye on CG so he doesn't get lost."

"I heard that."

"Okay, I'll see you on top," she giggled and replied, as she got into her car and drove ahead.

"We are coming up, Carol. How are things going up?"

"Road's good all the way to the top. If you have your camera, you can get some good pictures of the sheep."

"Hope they're not on the road?"

"Nope, but they could be by the time you get here. Got your gun? We could have lamb chops."

"What! You'd want me to shoot them little fuzz balls? What kind of guy do you think I am? Just because I hang around with bad influences and shady characters, I get a bad rep."

"I heard that," a low, deep, gravelly voice is heard from the radio.

"Carol, did I tell you when I found out I was coming up here for the first time, and I mean right about where we are now, just below the summit where you are, I bought a good Nikon camera and a big zoom lens to bring with me. I came up some years ago for the pipeline company and traveled with the dig crews that were contracted to the pipeline company doing maintenance on the pipeline. At that time we had a big camp right next to the DOT camp there at Chandalar. So, the first time I drove up the pass I got the camera out, put the big lens on, and started up. Sure enough, about three-quarters the way up there is a ewe and her baby lamb, just on the other side of this guardrail. As I was in a crew-cab pickup and with no other traffic around, I stopped and took a picture. Thinking to myself, I hope this turns out okay. It should be a great picture along with some others I took. Maybe when I grow up I will be a famous photographer."

"So how did they turn out?"

"Well, when I got them developed, half of them were this great big eyeball staring back at me. But I went ahead and framed one of them and hung it on the wall in my office. It wasn't hanging there very long before this fellow came along with one of my clients and said that it was a really a nice piece of work, very artistic. He had a certain flair about him, if you know what I mean. He seemed to be taken by the colors of the eyeball veins. He asked how this radiation outwards was accomplished. I guess I stuttered a little bit, and he said, 'I know, I know, trade secrets, right? Tell you what, I will give you five hundred dollars and split fifty-fifty any copies I make and I sell, okay?' I said, 'Well, okay, I guess.' He did make some copies and sold quite a few, and that's how I got enough money to buy this truck."

"Carol, have you ever noticed," asked a deep, gravelly voice, "how everything the kid has is the best, most famous, fastest, strongest, shoots the straightest or is top secret, even though it's sold all over the world?"

"I did notice something to that effect," Carol responded. "He does have a tendency to go on and on at times."

"Yeah, and he hasn't even got to the starting line yet."

Birch replied, "Well, facts are facts. Besides, I don't go around telling just anyone those kinds of things. I keep those kinds of things just among my friends and family because it might give other people the impression that I'm arrogant."

Carol heard CG laughing so hard she cautioned him to pull over to the side before he drove over the bank and killed himself.

Carol heard something barely audible over the radio, couldn't really make it out, but it sounded something like, "God forgive him."

Everyone who traveled the haul road except for tourist has and monitors the CB radio for entertainment but mainly to become aware of anyone who might be in trouble and need help for one reason or another. This far north assistance and ambulance service is a long ways and a long time off.

But at this altitude anyone on the south side of Atigun Pass, even as far back as Cold Foot, was probably enjoying the banter over the radio.

"How are you doing, CG? It's awful quiet back there. You have any trouble coming up?"

"Not a bit, Carol, not a bit, even when Kid Clutchless missed all them gears. Good thing I had a hold of him, though. Do you think I should get in front of him going down the other side of the pass? I might be able to hold him back so he don't kill himself or scratch up the paint on *SASSY* there. That would give him a heart attack and kill him for sure if he got a scratch on *SASSY*."

In reality, missing a gear going up or down the pass could be disastrous. Not much room for error. Birch and crew were making good time, and everyone was on their toes, checking everything over from time to time, and there was no push on time. He had to get *SASSY* up to Prudhoe and off the coast to the west near Olitok where a new gravel island was put in last winter. Birch's dad had once hauled gravel over the ice from an island eight miles offshore to three miles south of Olitok, a DEW (Distant Early Warning) radar station, to construct a gravel drilling pad and an airstrip. Because of the lack of roads, equipment and camps were hauled in over snow- and ice-roads during the winter so the tundra would be protected rather than during the summer when it would not be protected by the snow cover. Now it seemed they were hauling gravel back out over the ice to locations offshore, constructing and building drilling pads for exploration. More than likely to the same place they got it from during the late sixties, when all the oil companies were drilling exploration wells all over the North Slope so they would be in position to know how much money they wanted to risk and on which of those sections the state would eventually put out for lease.

His dad once told him that Birch's mom wrote, telling him they made a mistake on "her" paycheck, not his but hers. Since she picked up his paycheck each week at the Fairbanks main office, logically that made his check hers, right? Absolutely. Of course it did. The whole camp got a kick out the letter, which his dad had to show to everyone, of course.

His dad and CG had been all over the North Slope for different oil companies, building and installing small drilling camps. In a frenzy to find what lay underneath the tundra, they worked sixteen or more hours a day. They considered the first fourteen hours like everyone else would consider a standard eight-hour day. Anything over fourteen hours was considered real overtime. It wasn't uncommon to work sixteen or eighteen hours a day. Anything over eight was time and a half, and anything over twelve was double time. His mom wrote to his dad telling him to go farther north and send more money. He wrote back that he and CG were driving out over the ice to an island and couldn't go any farther north, as the next place to get fuel would be in Australia.

No problem going up and no problems going down the back side of the pass. No problem at all, when you hire the best. *I should give myself a raise*, thought Birch. *I may give CG a raise when he gets a little more experience under his belt. Maybe a couple more years will do it*, he chuckled. *CG would just skin him alive if he heard that.*

Once they got to the bottom you could almost hear the sighs come over the radio. They all relaxed a little. It was a nice summer day, and they all could enjoy the view while still paying attention to the road that was next to the headwaters of the Sag River. The sheep were down off the mountain feeding on the grass at the bottom. The sheep were white against the white snow on the mountain but were blending in with the straw-colored high grass at the bottom.

Birch remembered being right here some years ago. He was actually driving along the buried portion of the pipeline right of way. He could cross the river in places more like a stream at this point and was checking the right of way for any serious erosion or possible concerns. He stopped and got out of his crew cab to get a fresh drink of water. He wasn't worried about beaver fever, and the water couldn't taste any better, but he did see beavers just on the south side of the pass. He didn't like their chances of surviving on the shelf valley, as there were no trees or brush to speak of to build dams or beaver houses with. They wouldn't last the winter unless fish and game moved them downriver in the valley.

He had filled a root beer bottle and was sipping and savoring the water, looking down the valley to the north, when he saw the eagle dropping out of the sky. Soaring and dropping, until it was over the river and about a thousand feet from where he was. Birch knew the eagle was watching him all the time as it got nearer and continued to watch him as it passed about fifteen feet over his head. The eagle watched him momentarily over his wing while still following the river, which was running right next to the mountain on the east side of the valley. When the eagle was close to the bottom of the mountain, Birch could see it starting to rise and continue to rise until it floated over the mountain several thousand feet and was out of sight.

It was a magical moment. Magical, because during the time he watched the eagle drop out of the sky, ride the winds up the valley following the river, and then catching and riding a thermal off the side of the mountain, floating up and over to the other side, and out of sight, never once did it flap its wings. Not once.

Next stop will be the DOT camp just south of Pump Station 3. Birch wants to fill up the water tanks on *SASSY* at the DOT camp. *SASSY*'s tanks are considerable as the water might have to last a good while until they could be refilled. That will be the last chance to get good clean water, non-chlorinated water, that is.

On the way they will pass Pump Station 4 (PS 4) of the Alaska Pipeline sitting up on a rocky hill in the middle of the valley at the head of what is call the North Slope, a gradual slope from here to the north coast of Alaska. The altitude next to the hill at PS 4 is right at 2,650-feet-above sea level. From PS 4 it is 144 pipeline-miles due north to PS 1 about thirty-five-feet-above sea level. That's about an eighteen-foot drop per mile on the average over some rolling hills from the PS 4 valley to the coast. Dropping down out of the hills to PS 2, it really flattens out to the coast, but is still dropping six hundred feet at about nine feet a mile, but looks absolutely flat. That's where the name "North Slope" is derived.

Birch looked at his watch as he pulled into the Slope Mountain DOT camp. It was high noon. "CG, what time do you have?"

Birch asked, smiling, since CG knew full well that he not only had his own wristwatch but the truck and radio had the time also. He also wasn't surprised when he didn't get a rise or response out of CG from his inquiry of the time.

"Carol, I think we would have been right on time if old what's his name didn't have to go to the powder room every twenty minutes or so. But I'm not one to mention any names or point fingers. That really goes without saying, wouldn't you say?"

"Oh, for heaven's sakes, some people just love the sound of their own voice," the mystery CB voice whispered.

"I'll meet you two inside. With some foresight, I packed a lunch, boys and girls. I would like to share, really, but I'm starting to feel faint," Birch said. "What do diabetes symptoms feel like?"

The DOT guys were sitting in the camp kitchen listening to the CB radio and heard Birch carrying on with CG and Carol, whom they had all known very well for a long time. When Birch walked in the door, he was peppered with a bunch of stale, hard donuts.

One of the guys said, "Here, these donuts are diabetes antidotes."

"Donuts my butt, those were rocks. Now I got to go get X-rays or an MRI."

CG and Carol walked in and heard the laughter and asked, "What's going on?"

"I just got stoned," groaned Birch.

Some time ago, CG was a little surprised by the fact that one of the DOT operators had made the mistake of trying to bully and put Birch down. CG had warned the operator that Birch had whipped bigger and better men than him (the operator) and he had better back off. He would have better luck tangling with a wolverine. Unfortunately for the DOT operator, he did not heed CG's advice because Birch was not a big man and was much shorter than the operator. After one of these occasions and remarks, Birch got up close to the operator and told him he should keep his comments to himself. The operator tensed and started to swing or grab Birch. Birch hit him two or three times before the man hit the ground and before he'd even got his arm raised high enough to hit Birch. Birch also hit him several times after he hit the ground. Birch was not one to let someone bigger or who out-weighed him grab hold of him. If you got Birch mad enough to hit you, he would make sure you were out cold, you quit, or until you gave up. If not, then he made sure you wouldn't get up very easily.

CG went over and picked the operator up and dusted him off and whispered "I tried to warn you." Birch walked up and handed CG and the operator each a cup and poured out coffee from his thermos and started talking about the road conditions like nothing even happened.

After that the operator would tease Birch unmercifully about this and that but he never again laughed at Birch or tried to put him down. Since then he also never let anyone else put Birch down or say anything bad about him.

"I think you three have earned a well-deserved safety nap while I fill *SASSY*'s water tank. It shouldn't take too long. The guys here have the hoses all laid out for me. I'll give you a call when we're done. Heck, I might get a few winks myself."

Birch set his brain clock for thirty minutes, and thirty minutes later he woke up and looked out the windshield and saw CG getting out of his truck. CG, Carol, and the follow-up car driver should have gotten almost an hour's rest. Driving right after eating lunch with the sun blazing through the windshield, making it all nice and cozy, would just knock you out. Lots of people just fall asleep on the straight stretches and drift off the side of the road. Birch was not a full-time line hauler or trucker, but if CG was tied up someplace else or for someone else, Birch would haul his own equipment and heavy loads from job to job. Good truckers like CG do not usually fall asleep and run into a ditch. Trailer vans were one thing when you ran off the road. Trailers with loads strapped and chained down were another, like steel drilling pipe. Running off the road into a bad ditch, stopping the truck in its tracks would not stop the load until the load got to the same point that stopped the truck. Driver's puny little bodies aren't much deterrence in stopping cargo; they just make smudge spots.

They had one more grade at Ice Cut to overcome: a slot cut out of a hill next to the Sagavanirktok River. Not many could pronounce Sagavanirktok, so naturally everyone calls the river the Sag. Like most everything under the tundra, it was frozen solid; hence the name Ice Cut. When they first built the road it took a few big dozers with ripper shanks on the back of the dozers and lots of ripper teeth. A lot of fill also had to be placed ahead of the slot in the hill to build it up and even out the grade where the trucks could get up and over. Wasn't too long of a grade, and heavy loads could generally make it, especially when they could get a run at it. All but the extremely heavy loads, that is, like Birch was pulling. Then it was necessary for assistance by a push truck. Same thing in the winter, but then if conditions were not good, everyone chained up. The distance between PS 3 and PS 2 is approximately fifty-five miles. Half way between is Ice Cut, followed by Oil Spill Hill, the last notable feature before PS 2, which lies right at the bottom of the last hill on the haul road going north.

Birch had arranged to have a tanker-trailer pup of diesel fuel staged at PS 2 ahead of their arrival. The five thousand gallons were needed to fuel up *SASSY* and the trucks. He staged the fuel because he did not want to take a chance on the diesel fuel processed in Prudhoe Bay. Sometimes it lacked the quality that Birch wanted for *SASSY*'s small diesel engine. The rest of the number one fuel would go in the trucks. What was left, if any, CG would haul back to Fairbanks. The reason the fuel was staged at PS 2 rather than fueling *SASSY* up in Fairbanks was that it saved thirty thousand pounds, give or take, to the weight Birch would have to haul over mountains and hills. But from PS 2 it was all flatland, gently sloping to the coast, and Birch's rig and the especially modified lowboy trailer for hauling *SASSY* could handle the fuel along with about the same amount of water. The extra weight would be substantial, but it was manageable.

Once they arrived at PS 2, the push truck would no longer be needed. Carol, partner and CG would head on back. Birch had arranged to have two pilot cars from Prudhoe meet them at PS 2 in the morning. He had called them from Slope Mountain DOT camp earlier and told them they would arrive late in the day, transfer the fuel, overnight, and he would be ready to head out in the morning as soon as they arrived from Prudhoe.

While he was sitting in the truck, a big raven landed on the hood of his Kenworth. “Don’t you be scratching up my hood, grease ball! Birch continued to talk to the raven, and the raven listened, hoping to get a handout. For the most part, Birch did not feed the animals. The people who know frowned upon feeding animals, as it made them less reliant on themselves and more dependent on humans.

“So what’s for dinner, and as far as that goes, what’s for breakfast? Let’s see, what we have here in my Boy Scout survival bag. I can make some of my famous gourmet Nalley’s Jalapeno Hot Chili or Stagg Dynamite Hot Chili. Can’t think of anyone who could complain about that, other than a passenger maybe. And then there are others who have made slanderous accusations about my gourmet cooking. Take my mother, for example, who would tell me from time to time when I was cooking, ‘They arrest people for assault, you know.’ I don’t really know what she meant by that. And at times my girlfriend would say the cruelest things. I have never needed help making toast. I don’t care what she says.” My ex-girlfriend, that is.

Decisions, decisions, what’s for dinner? Is it going to be jalapeno hot chili or dynamite hot chili? Decisions like this give me a headache. And to further complicate the decision-making process, the question is, hot or cold?

Look at that raven. Now it’s trying to stick its head in the window. “Here birdie, birdie. Stick your neck in just a little bit more, and I’ll have some chicken to mix in with the chili.” Birch rolled up the window. Next thing you know, the raven will probably want to take a nap in the sleeper. Yeah, give them an inch.

CG and Carol chose to head on back and overnight at Slope Mountain camp, stopping in tomorrow at Coldfoot for a hot meal on their way back to Fairbanks.

The next morning Birch started cleaning out the truck and transferring everything to *SASSY* that he would want to take with him during the trial and training period. Things like a few CDs, handheld GPS, satellite phone, and odds and ends including pistols, rifle, and shot gun, since he could be isolated and stranded alone for extended periods of time during the shake-down trial periods while being in grizzly and polar bear country this coming winter. He transferred everything but the thermos for the drive to the coast.

SASSY was already loaded for the duration with everything conceivably needed for the trial run, including food stockpiled for his personal taste and survival rations for three months for up to twelve people. The trial and training period would take three months offshore. The exploration company would provide four people with rotating shifts. Two on for two weeks and off for two weeks, then their alternates would come on for two weeks and receive their training and familiarization with *SASSY*. That would be a total of four personnel the second and third month coming aboard for training and familiarization.

One last thing he needed to check while he was waiting for the pilot cars from Prudhoe to arrive: that everything was laid out to install when they got to the coast. That included the mast and sail he had insisted on during design and construction. He liked the idea of being able to sail from location to location rather than burning up the diesel and having to fuel up in open waters.

SASSY did have a built-in antenna, but Birch would also mount two vertical antennas once the boat was launched for maximum range and reception. That would amount to plugging in the connections and bolting the antennas poles down to the top turret. Same with the radar and radar pole mount. It shouldn't take more than a few minutes to mount each one.

As Birch finished up and was heading back to the truck after securing the access doors on SASSY, he felt like he might be getting woozy; his equilibrium was off. Then he saw the rig and trailer swaying. *Wow, that's not me*, he thought, *that's the ground moving*. He jumped in the truck and turned off the working lights and backup lights and tried to raise the Prudhoe pilot cars on the CB. It was just now 5:30 and they should be on the road by now, but there was no response from the pilot cars. Like all line-haul trucks, his CB was as powerful as they come, and it was a straight shot to Prudhoe. He had the range.

"Anyone out there? Anyone out there? Come back." Birch should be able to raise someone out there in the Prudhoe Bay area, as there was always someone around twenty-four hours a day. Mechanics servicing equipment before the crews started work. Lots of activity was always going on in the Prudhoe Bay oil fields. Oil companies all had their own security as well as the pipeline, and they all had roaming security patrols. Security at the airstrip, PS 1, BP, and Arco were all secured areas. He couldn't raise anyone, and knowing his CB was working, he was becoming alarmed. Next he tried the Alyeska Pipeline FM microwave radio with the pipeline frequencies and voice called PS 1 security. Getting no response at PS 1, he raised the local repeater, located on a high hill to the south of him and called PS 3.

* * * * *

PS 3 came up right away. "PS 3 Security."

"This is Birch and I'm at PS 2 and have been trying to raise PS 1."

"PS 1 is down and the pipeline has shut down. We are in the fact-finding mode trying to find out what is going on. Give me a report on what you see at PS 2."

"The only thing I would report is I felt some tremors fifteen minutes ago and I see no visible damage. It is still dark and no steam visible anywhere. If you hear anything about PS 1, give me a call and I will do like likewise."

The eight hundred miles of pipeline starts at Pump Station 1 at Prudhoe Bay on the north coast and terminates at Valdez on the south coast of Alaska. About one half of the pipeline runs above ground, sitting on support members where the ground is permanently frozen in what is called permafrost, and the other half is buried where the ground isn't frozen. With the throughput down from just over two million barrels to just under six hundred thousand barrels per day, several pump stations have been taken offline, and a few have been dismantled like PS 2, as it is just a pass-through now and unmanned.

Birch tried the CB again with no luck when he felt a shake that rocked and rolled the truck and gave him a good scare. He decided he would strike out for Prudhoe without the pilot cars, and forget about getting a ticket.

Chapter Three

What The. . .

Birch hadn't gone a quarter of a mile when a jolt almost turned the rig over, and a rift in the earth opened up in the ditch alongside the truck and ran down and cut across the road right in front him. And there wasn't anything he could do about it. Birch hadn't yet been doing fifteen mph, and it just gradually opened up underneath him and swallowed the truck whole. "What in is going on?" he said, as he watched the rift widen and become a little deeper. Now he couldn't see over the edge of the rift. He wasn't worried that the sides would cave in on him, because except for the road base material itself, everything below was permafrost and frozen solid down to depths of two thousand feet in some locations on the North Slope.

Now he became frantic as he saw water pooling up ahead of him in the bottom of the rift. Where is the water coming from? He knew immediately of two possibilities: one being the water along both sides of the road in the ditch, which grew wider and deeper from the disturbance of the road and the accumulation of the dust from the traffic as it passed by. The darker material of the dust held the heat from the sun and thawed the material around and below the dust, and since water is also a heat collector, causing the water surface to spread and deepen, becoming ponds during the summer months. The oil pipeline and river paralleled the road, as did the gas line running in the ditch alongside the road for most of the way from PS 1 to PS 4. More ponding accumulates over the gas line side because the soil and permafrost were disturbed during installation of the gas pipeline. He didn't think the water entering from the ditch would amount to enough to concern him if it continued to run downhill along the trench.

The other possibility was groundwater where the ground was thawed out at or near the river, which wasn't that far away, and that did concern him. With the earthquakes the river could channel to him, and the truck would be submerged in short order. There was only one thing to do. He turned off the truck and grabbed the thermos and what else he could carry and made his way to the trailer. With everything else going on now, the wind started howling overhead. It was bad enough that it almost blew him off the trailer as he went from strap to strap, cutting them as he went, until he cut the last one and got to one of the access ports where he threw everything ahead of him and ducked inside *SASSY*, closing the port door behind.

When Birch opened the port door, it activated the emergency light, which also had a motion detection switch and would stay on for fifteen minutes. Birch secured the door and went to the command controls and powered up the ship and the ship's computer. Next he went to the helm and raised a periscope very gradually until he could see over the edge, did a 360-degree view and saw nothing except for a glimpse of what appeared to be a forty-eight-foot van trailer hurtling by above the ground. From seeing that trailer/van go by, Birch knew he had never seen winds like this, and he had been through several bad typhoons at sea in the Asian Pacific and hundred-mile winds on the Alaskan coast. He quickly lowered the periscope before it became damaged and turned the radios on and calibrated the single sideband/short wave (SSB). *SASSY* was equipped with several antennas, one for single SSB that ran full length and on top of the ship, buried just below the skin. Just about every frequency had nonstop traffic, most of it Russian, Korean, and Japanese with some Australian or New Zealand thrown in. And all of it was in international panic, so far as he could tell, even if he didn't understand Russian or Korean. What he could pick out were screams of high winds and on other frequencies people's screams of inland flooding.

All the access doors, portholes, and ramp had been dogged down with camloc latches before leaving Seattle, and he had just closed and secured the man door above after he entered. But Birch checked each and every one, including the ramp door again. They wouldn't leak even underwater for twenty or thirty feet. They were, in fact, designed for pressures of forty feet deep because of the rough seas, waves, and conditions where *SASSY* would be operating.

While listening to the radio, the earthquakes and shock waves kept coming and increasing in intensity. They were getting so bad that Birch had to strap himself into the control seat. The seat belt shoulder-harness straps were designed for the roughest of North Slope waters. Now, even through the foam insulated hull, the noise from the winds was like standing next to a jet engine. The thought crossed Birch's mind that if it wasn't for being sandwiched in between the side walls of the rift, giving *SASSY* the protection from the hurricane winds above, he would not survive being blown to heaven only knows where. He could not move for what seemed like all day but his watch showed 11:00 a.m.

He had been strapped in for nearly five hours when the winds subsided, and he decided to take another look through the periscope. Behind him to the south, PS 2 had now risen eight hundred to one thousand feet higher than he was. A ridge had developed, running east to west, or his position had subsided by that amount. What he was looking at, according to what he had read about geology, would have taken millions of years to form in what had just taken place in a matter of hours. To the west some miles away, he could see what appeared to be volcanic eruptions and venting taking place.

Birch's mind could not logically grasp what was taking place as he tried the short wave again. He got no response calling out over different channels. So far, from his search through the channels, it appeared that radio traffic had completely ceased. Finally he heard two ham radio operators talking, but they were not responding to or could not receive him. One operator, along with six others, had survived in a concrete structure in the high desert, but the outlook was not good. The facility, probably military, was completely buried from what he could determine. They couldn't get the doors or windows open, and they could not see out of the windows. He and the others were probably lacking oxygen, as he said the others appeared to be drowsy, and he was starting to slur his words. It did not sound very good for them.

The other operator, from what Birch gathered, was somewhere in Asia. Although he spoke better English than Birch did, he was definitely not American and had a heavy accent, and the radio reception was about 4 x 4, which means it was fairly clear. The Asian sounded like he, too, was resigned to not surviving and was saying that his time was probably very limited. He said that reports of people all over the world in the coastal areas and miles and miles inland were in the process of being buried, submerged, or drowning, and he had no prospects of escaping.

Birch had started to conclude, as did the two ham operators who were talking, that some kind of impact or polar shift was taking place. The ham operators had picked up reports, before communication was lost with others, of radio and satellite reports describing winds over three hundred mph and of new island chains in the Caribbean, Mediterranean, and additional Hawaiian islands appearing, along with many other changes worldwide, including entire population losses in the coastal areas.

The realization that people the world over were being lost due to the wind storms and surging waters was starting to sink in. Birch was having a hard time coming to grips with the loss. He tried calling out to the ham operators, but could not speak right at that moment nor could he see as his vision blurred when the two ham operators said goodbye to each other and signed off.

He just sat and stared at the radio for the next two hours before he started to come out of the daze he was in.

Birch knew he had to shake this off and concentrate on what he could and needed to do to survive what was happening around him. Then he felt *SASSY* sloshing around like a rubber duck in the bathtub. He had been aware that the water had been rising in the rift and went to the helm to see what he could see. And what he could see was not good. The water level in the rift was about half full.

What really bothered him was a tidal wave in the near distance, a wall of water that appeared to be a couple of hundred feet high was fast approaching and would be upon him before he could buckle in if he didn't hurry.

Suddenly he felt like he was being flushed down a toilet upside down, and just before he passed out *SASSY* was shot out of the rift like a canon ball. Birch did not know how long he had been out, but it was only a few minutes or less. When he came around, the first thing he thought was that he needed to check for damage and leaks, as violent as that tsunami wave was. Although the violent tossing had subsided, he decided he'd better wait before he tried to move through the ship from end to end until it calmed down some more, since they were still being tossed around like a cork. Later, he looked all around him from the turrets at each end of the ship. He also had a rear camera with the view showing on an overhead monitor. What he saw was rough seas typical of stormy arctic waters and bluffs far to the south. I assume that is to the south and the sun is setting. It's not even five o'clock yet!

How can that be?

Where am I?

Okay—damages, any damages? He saw nothing that concerned him throughout the ship along the passageways, including cubbyholes, storage areas, and cupboards. Now the engine room: Looked like it had just came off the show room floor, spotless. He murmured, "*SASSY*, you make me proud. So far you have come through like the pro you are."

* * * * *

Birch had every reason to be proud, as he had the original concept and was the primary designer. Designing *SASSY* to take the roughest seas anywhere in the world and crashing into and taking everything the arctic ice could throw at them. He saw the need and had the idea for what was necessary if there were extreme emergencies for offshore drilling rigs or small islands built for drilling rigs with no access in the summer except by air or water. During the winter access was by air or ice roads, constructed when the ice grew thick enough to support heavy equipment and dump trucks full of gravel. The building of the ice roads could be expedited by spraying water along the route where the ice was too thin to thicken it.

Access at times could be delayed for several days or more at a time, both during the summer and winter due to the extreme arctic storms that were common in the area.

SASSY's primary design was for response to explosions, fires, or protection from severe weather, and for helping personnel constructing the gravel pads and constructing the camp housing. One of the main features that Birch demanded was a rear ramp that could be dropped where the injured could be brought in on a stretcher. The ramp is secured in place by cam locks, and the more outside forces or external pressure on the door, the tighter it becomes. Providing safety and shelter for a limited number of the personnel at that location until rescue staff reached them was a primary purpose. And that might not be right away since there was always a storm there or close by.

The waters of Prudhoe Bay were very shallow. Most freight came in by barge, as there was no deep portage. High winds and rough water during the summer at times made travel impossible. High winds, ice at various stages and thickness, pressure ridges, and drifting snow with whiteouts, where you couldn't see your hood ornament, either made travel impossible or unsafe during the winter. Too many have lost their lives trying to go from one building to another during a winter arctic storm and letting go of the rope that had been strung from building to building, only to be found between the buildings frozen solid the following day or the day after the storm let up. Blowing snowstorms at times were like trying to find your way while in a milk bottle. Because of these conditions, Birch also incorporated the best navigational systems available at the time, including sonar and depth indicator.

Drilling rigs usually crewed up around thirty people, including cooks and housekeepers, and *SASSY* could strap that many in at one time and could house, sleep, and feed half that many (one of the two shifts) somewhat comfortably for a couple of weeks.

* * * * *

SASSY was ten feet across the very bottom with the sides at a sixty-degree angle for five feet, then thirteen feet nine inches at the widest spot then angling up to the inside sixty degrees. Overall height was sixteen feet three inches, eight feet of each end served like a conning tower, three feet wide at the very top and was five feet higher than the middle deck. The mid deck was eight feet wide. If you were looking at it from the end it would look like a hexagon that was a little wider at the bottom and the top portion pulled or stretched upwards. Flat across the bottom, but for the outside two feet on each side was six inches deeper than the middle four inches, like small pontoons. Each side had two two-inch solid stainless steel runners or skegs on the bottom as snow machine skis have a steel rod running down the middle. These skegs run the full length of the ship and are part of the structural cage to protect the bottom and tankage above from damage if the ship runs aground. Tankage included water, propane, and diesel fuel. In lieu of holding tanks for sewage and waste, there was also below deck a process to burn off any waste.

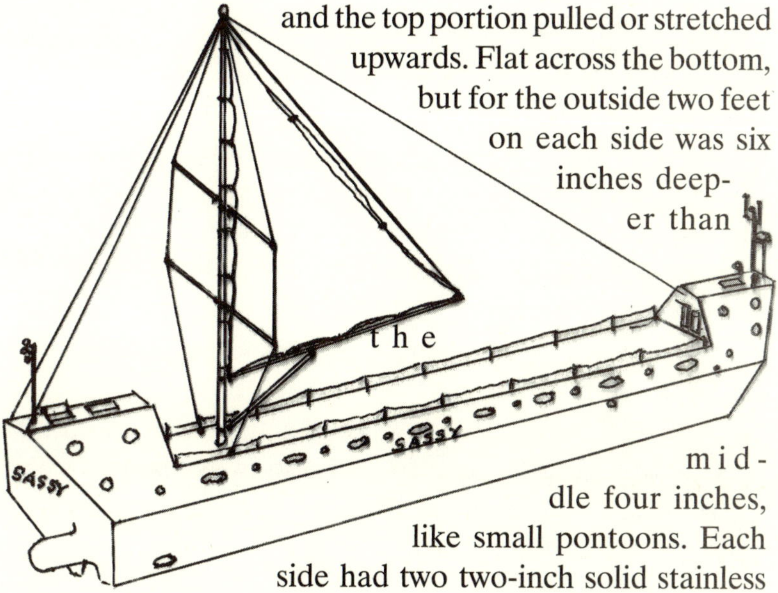

Originally Birch wrote up the general specifications and drew up some working drawings and got together with an engineer, Billy Phelps, who designed and built yachts in the Seattle area. Birch showed Billy what he had and explained to him that he wanted to incorporate some of the new technology utilized by the boating and aviation industries in the hull of *SASSY*. Billy had been working with Kent Duval of the aerospace industry, and after Kent reviewed the material, the three of them came to an arrangement, developed, and finalized the design and made a mock-up of *SASSY*. They sold their product to the first oil company they approached. Consequently, a company was formed, and work on *SASSY* became an obsession until they had a product to put on the Seattle dock for shipping to Anchorage. From there it would go by Alaska Railroad to Fairbanks.

The exterior hull consisted of high-strength multi-layered fabric overlaid and epoxied to both sides of extruded foam three inches thick. Compartment walls and interior doors were fabricated the same with three-quarter plywood cores for strength, except foam was one inch thick. Cabinets were constructed of three-quarter-inch plywood faced with vinyl. Along with the caged bottom, as earlier described, a continuous two-inch solid stainless steel rod ran around the entire waist of the ship. The ship was light-weight, strong but somewhat flexible and could take a pretty good punch.

One of the other features they had specified and installed was the best air and gas filtration system available.

Birch was traumatized and was just staring off into space when the winds started to pick up again. He had the forethought to launch a sea drogue and to strap himself in as soon as the winds became noticeable. And pick up they did. The winds today were beyond anything he had ever experienced before. Unknown to him, they were beyond what any living person had ever experienced before. He did have a wind velocity gauge good up to 200 mph. In other words, the gauge was useless. By the noise and howling of the wind, he surmised that the velocity was not quite as much as he experienced earlier. The velocity was such you would never ever want to be caught out to sea in any kind of ship or liner. But here he was. He knew he was being blown along at an unbelievable pace and had even tumbled several times and had been momentarily upside down.

"You don't like that one bit do you *SASSY*?" *SASSY* did not hesitate to roll upright again and again when she was blown over. But he could tell the sea drag, so far, was still holding. Without it there, no telling what would become of him and *SASSY*.

The winds diminished to a gale force between fifty and sixty miles per hour by the next morning, and Birch had still not slept and was out on his feet. He just could not fathom what had happened. Why the time shown on clocks, his watch, or computer was not agreeing with sunset or sunrise. Most of all, he was in deep denial about the human life evidently just disappearing. His friends, relatives, and everyone he knew were probably lost. It is just not possible. He spent the rest of the day staring at the wall. He could not yet deal with what was taking place. At sundown he crawled into a bunk and put up the guardrail webbing.

He woke up in a cold sweat, and had no idea how long he had slept. He also knew that he was grungy, starving, and smelly and felt like he had a champagne hangover. Then he had a hurtful but strange image of CG telling him, "Hey, stinky, quit feeling sorry for yourself and get moving." In reality it did not really occur to Birch to feel sorry for himself. He was in state of deep depression from thinking about what appeared to have happened all over the world.

Oh! Yes, now concentrate and get with the program, Birch thought. No observable damages that I can see. Now, let's see if I can determine a fix or location. Where in the heck am I? To be or not to be, that is the question. Where I be? That is the big question. At the COM desk he determined the Loran System was out, but the GPS was working. He took the coordinates and attempted to plot them on the north coast Prudhoe Bay area chart, but the coordinates were off the chart. By locating a map of Alaska on the ship desktop, Birch determined he was way west of Tahiti, give or take a few thousand miles.

"Let's take a look around and see what we can see."

Not a damn thing as far as the periscope could see. What was noticeable was thick haze in all directions, which did hamper visibility in all directions. It looked like ash or dust on the surface of the boat. Birch saw the sun low on the horizon. Should still be out of the east, so he set a way point forty-five degrees west of the where the sun was presently at fifteen miles out. He then set the depth alarm for fifty feet on the depth finder, and since he was not in any hurry or had any place he really needed to be anymore, he engaged the autopilot to steer with the wind as it was in his favor for the present.

Priorities for Survival:

Head for land
Find land
Follow land
Find firewood

Next, he needed to calibrate the on-board system controls and set the alarms. Humidity was high, which he adjusted along with the temperature. Refrigeration and freezer temps right on. Fire alarms and carbon monoxide testing completed. Bilge pump functioning but not needed, as the bilge compartment camera channel was showing the bilge area dry, not even any condensation. Winds were blowing at twenty-one knots to the southwest. Exterior temperature was reading in the sixties. Maybe he was getting closer to Tahiti than he thought.

What's up with dat? he wondered.

Everything was fine-tuned and/or checked out to the positive. Birch couldn't remember when he last had a good meal but knew he needed to fuel up. He then remembered the chili and offered his sincere apologies to the manufacturer. How about a mountain of Birch's world-famous-known-throughout-the-world pancakes?

"That's what I'm talking about. I'm getting faint."

He also got out a couple of eggs and some bacon while he was at it. Put the skillet on medium, after turning the propane on at the main tank and then the stove. He got out a measuring cup and opened the brand new package and poured one cup of Snoqualmi Falls old fashioned pancake and waffle mix into the mixing bowl, and instead of pouring three-quarters of a cup, he poured seven-eighths of a cup of water, and that's what made all the difference in his secret recipe and had become a treasured recipe.

While the eggs and bacon were cooking, he whipped up the pancake mix and poured a small glass of orange juice, got a plate out and dished out the bacon and eggs. Poured the grease off into a small cup, and only then did he participate in the second part of the pancake procedure, and that was to pour the batter in a circular motion into the skillet and wait until the exact moment when the bubbles told him the pancake was ready to flip—just before the top hardened up. Since the top is still pretty rare, you have to slop it over gentle-like or you can get batter clear across the room.

"That's what I'm talking about," he said, as he dug in and realized he was famished.

* * * * *

While he was eating, he remembered telling his mom what this trial period entailed for the lease/purchase agreement. How he would be by himself for a month and then training personnel for a while.

"Who is going to cook for you?"

"Well, it will be just me for awhile, so I'll have to cook."

His mom came over to him and gave him a big hug.

"What's that for?"

"Because, you're going to die."

That gave Birch a sense of déjà vu when later his girl friend suggested he probably had a honey that was going to cook for him. "Absolutely not. I am going to cook," he told her.

She gave him a big hug.

"What's that for?"

She said, "Dead Man Walking."

Those two are just too much alike.

Chapter Four
The Eagle Has Landed

Birch cleaned up and put away the dishes, washed his face and brushed his teeth. He looked into the mirror and started to comb his hair, paused, looked again and thought, *Why*? Still facing the mirror, he said, "Let's go topside and face the world." *Or what is left of it*, he thought. He turned aside and walked down the passageway, strapping on a harness, and went up to the turret and opened the hatchway and stepped outside.

He was surprised that the winds were no more than a good breeze. He had to shield his eyes from the bright sun as he looked out to the sea, slowly looking, hoping to see something, anything, on the horizon. Still turning, he stopped suddenly as he spotted a big ratty ball of feathers lying on the other end of the mid deck. He made his way to the other end and looked at the ball of feathers at his feet and wondered what it was. He bent down and gently straightened what was a wing back out of the way and saw a bird's head lying on the deck.

Wondering if it was alive, Birch looked into the bird's eye and said, when he realized the bird was looking back at him, "Well, what do we have here? Are you a stowaway? One very large golden eagle. I see you left a deposit of eagle crap and vomit. I'll tell you right now that is not going to pay the fare on this ship, "chicken of the sea." And if you can't pay your fare, and you are messing up my deck, then it's into the soup bowl with you. Maybe I will fatten you up a little, and then you can be the main entrée on the dinner menu. Come to think of it, those feathers you're wearing will make a good dust mop."

The bird was alive, all right, but it was near dead with exhaustion. More than likely it had been blown out to sea and landed on the first thing it had spotted. It was so exhausted it could not hold its head up. Birch wondered if it would drink water. He wondered if it could even drink water. He had never seen or noticed large golden eagles or any large birds drink water before. Birch made his way down below and rummaged through the kitchen utensil drawer and found what he guessed was a baster, wondering where that came from. He filled it up and ran back up on deck. He picked up the eagle's head and the eagle tried to get away for a minute but didn't have the strength to move. He waited a second until the eagle calmed down, but the bird watched Birch intently as he gave him a small squirt of the water. It looked like the eagle swallowed the water, so Birch gave him the rest, sip by sip, and petted the eagle's head for a couple of minutes. Birch rubbed the bird down, checking for injuries and broken bones and found none. The eagle did not like that one bit, and at first tried to fight Birch off but was not strong enough. He gave up, and endured this uninvited assault by this stranger. Birch was thinking that it was probably good that the bird was feeling peaked. Yeah, real good for me. Then they continued to look at each other for a few more minutes while Birch was thinking. What am I going to do with you? He thought there would be no problem carrying the big bird down below in the condition the bird was in, the problem would be when he tried to carry an energized eagle up from below. I probably wouldn't survive the battle.

Birch's mind wandered off momentarily as he thought that if this eagle made it through whatever just happened to the world, then other animal and human life could have also survived. Birch knew he was in denial and did not really want to give more thought to the possibility that his family, relatives, friends, and acquaintances could have been destroyed since they were all unprotected. From what he heard in the last few moments listening to the ham operators, Birch surmised that those that could have survived would not last long, as they would have no shelter, food, or water.

After a lost minute or two, Birch set about raising the thirty-two-foot mast. But first he had to open the eight-inch-wide hatch covers along the top of the deck, raise the mast, then close the hatch covers after the mast was upright and secured The mast served several purposes, one being for extending communications. Another purpose the mast served was for raising the canvas sail, but right now the mast was going to serve an unintended purpose. Birch opened a side hatch and pulled out a storm sail. A small sail that he thought he could fashion around the eagle to give it some protection from being blown off or washed overboard.

After he finished he looked at his work, cinched up one of the tie downs, looked at the eagle and asked, "Well, chicken soup, what do you think of your new home?" The eagle raised its head for a few minutes, watching Birch. "Don't look at me like that. It's not my turn to cook, and I'm all out of birdseed. What do I have in the pantry that you might find delectable? I need to fatten you up for the pot."

First I'm talking to myself, and now I'm talking to animals, and we are not even friends.

Birch started below and remembered the sea drag. He needed to retrieve and stow the drogue. But first I have to see to our guest; first things first. Looking through the cupboards and storage lockers, he came across one of several cases of Spam. *Just the ticket*, he thought. He dished out about half a can on a saucer and went back on top.

"Here, 'chicken-fried steak,' try this." The bird watched him approach and set down the Spam but did not move and ignored the food. "Boy, you have really been blown off course, haven't you?"

It was a wonder that the bird was alive at all. How could it even breathe with all the dust and ash in the air and all over the ship? Its throat had to be raw.

He would need to clean the filters on the filtering system ASAP.

Evidently, the filtering system worked great and did its job automatically, as there was no difficulty breathing down below nor did he see signs of dust below like he did topside.

It seemed to be touch and go for the bird over the next several days. Lucky the weather was holding with no strong winds yet, or the bird could be blown over the side. Birch continued his limited nursing skills, feeding and watering the bird.

"Big bird" even seemed to enjoy Birch scratching his head and petting him. Birch thought it might be worthwhile massaging the bird's muscles so they didn't atrophy. At first it didn't take kindly to Birch's attention.

One day Birch thought he heard the bird chirp while he was scratching its head.

Birch warned the bird, "If you start purring, I'll make you walk the plank."

* * * * *

A few days later, Birch turned to business and started the backbreaking process of retrieving and bringing the sea drogue aboard, which he knew would be a two-man job. He had left it in place until now, just in case those high winds or storms blew in. But now he would try to make headway. No more procrastinating.

When he finished storing the drogue, he had an idea he wanted to try and went below. He had packed fishing gear on board mainly to while away some time when things were slow. Plus fish was a favorite with Birch. In Fairbanks, being so far inland, the restaurants did not serve much in the way of seafood, mostly just battered, deep-fried frozen fish. When he was in the Seattle area, seafood was a first priority with him. Birch's fishing experience was entirely around inland rivers. No experience in deep sea or ocean fishing, except for a half-day charter for halibut out of Homer, south of Anchorage. The charter had landed a 195-pound halibut the day before. From the picture it looked like it would cover a Volkswagen with no trouble. The charter captain had asked, "Wouldn't you like to catch a halibut like that?"

"If I did, I would cut the line real quick. These small ones are just right, even if they don't put up much of a fight." Pulling a 195-pound, or larger, halibut off the sea bottom would be about as much fun as pulling up a barn door through the water flatways. He had heard the smaller ones were better eating anyway.

He did purchase some gear for this voyage, or he should say the original purpose of this voyage. He wouldn't mind landing a small halibut or two. He wondered if they had anything like cod in these waters. One of Birch's favorites was cod, but he didn't know what one really looked like when it wasn't in a sandwich or on a plate. He took both rods topside, and baited the ocean tackle with a piece of the Spam. He cast the lure out and fed out more line. Tied the rod off and went below, got a small, rubber shower mat out of the head, got a small bowl of water, the rest of the Spam, and went back up on deck and set the water and Spam on the rubber mat in the small enclosure next to the eagle.

"Here you go, 'chicken gizzard,' now get off my back."

Later on he noticed that the bird hadn't moved but the Spam was suspiciously gone. He looked at the eagle and stated, "Hey, 'chicken wing,' you got a real guilty look on your beak. Get up and get busy. I'm not serving you in bed. Get up and earn your keep. I wonder if you need some more water. And don't be giving me the evil eye, that it's just a small piece of Spam. I don't want you throwing up all over my shiny new boat."

Birch thought he heard a tiny little screech, but he wasn't positive. Might have been his imagination.

No more hand feeding. If Big Bird gets anymore strength, I could lose a hand.

Birch got a bucket and washed away the eagle deposit as best as he could. He would get the hose out later.

He looked at the eagle and said, "You better not be crapping on my deck anymore or your life span will be incredibly shortened. I'm researching eagle recipes, you know. You would be amazed at how many dishes I can make. Wonder if I got all the ingredients for hot wings. You know, I'm giving you a second chance here."

When Birch was below last time, he looked at the depth finder and it showed 185 feet deep. He looked at his halibut rig, and he knew he couldn't tell what, if anything, had happened. Birch reeled it in and decided to put a float or bobber on and add some weights so he could tell when the line hit bottom. The hook was still baited. He re-rigged the rod and recast. Then he took the spinning rod he used on the river for grayling and put his Top Secret lure, a white grub with a long thin tail, and slipped it over a red-headed hook with a white eye and also added some weight to feel the bottom, and then he cast it over the side. Birch had used this Top Secret lure in lakes near PS 2, 3, and 4 and caught grayling and lake trout, and some good-size lake trout in Paxson Lake before taking a canoe down the Gulkana River and hooking a monstrous six-inch rainbow.

On the Kobuk in western Alaska, he landed a thirty-four-inch sheefish, a twenty-four-inch pike, a fifteen-inch grayling, and a twenty-seven-inch salmon in less than thirty minutes with this Top Secret lure just upriver from Kiana. He needed the light-weight rod in order to set the hook with these smaller fish when he felt a fish taking the lure.

While Birch jigged his line, he watched the bobber on the heavy rod and also scoured the horizon. After a while he looked over and noticed the bird moving around, getting a little closer to the Spam. Birch smiled and went back on watch, and he also looked skyward, hoping to see any possible sign of jet contrails.

Two days and six cans of Spam later, standing in the same spot and still hadn't caught a thing. Birch looked over at the bird and said, more to himself, "Who invented this stupid game anyway? What are you looking at, 'chicken butt'? You think you can do better? I'm going to try something different." He reeled in his Top Secret lure off the bottom, replaced the heavy weights with a small weight just to get it down a few feet, and cast it toward the opposite end of the boat, and reeled in.

Birch heard this awful squawking and turned around, and Big Bird was up walking round just carrying on like all get out.

"What's with you? You got any better ideas?"

Squawk. Squawk.

"I got a nibble." Get ready to set the hook, Birch said to himself. "I'll show big mouth over there. Where did you go?" Jesus! Big Bird washed overboard. "Whoops, got a bite!" He set the hook and went back to looking over the side behind him in the wake, looking for loud mouth, when again he heard, Squawk. Squawk. Birch looked up, and there was Big Bird perched above him on the turret. "Are you cheerleading or bitching? I know, I know, it's about time I caught something, right?"

Birch reeled the fish up to the side of the boat, and since he did not even think to bring a net—it never even occurred to him—he wanted to tire the fish out before he tried to haul it up on the boat. After all that effort and noise he had been through lately, he did not want to lose the fish.

If I did lose this fish, can you imagine the carrying on I would have to put up with? Squawk. Squawk. It would probably never end. Okay, let's haul this big baby up and see what we got. Well, now that we have it on deck I still don't know what we got. It ain't real ugly, looks like a fish. Doesn't have any spines. It's probably poisonous. "Here birdie, birdie. Take a bite and tell me what you think. Come on, 'chicken noodle,' try this out. What's your preference, grilled or sashimi?"

Birch brought up a little grill, a potato, and an onion and hooked the hose to an exterior propane deck connection and lit the fire. Boy, did that set off a series of five-alarm squawks. Next he set about filleting the fish and put a piece of the raw fish down for the loud mouth and backed away. That's when Big Bird attacked. In less than thirty seconds Big Bird had devoured the fish, and that was no small feat, as the fish was probably four or five pounds, and Birch had given him a fairly good-size portion, and he was now worried. In the bird's condition it might have been too much. The bird ate so much, it probably hurt itself.

Birch sliced up the potato and onion and put it on with the fish and let it cook while he took care of some chores.

Thirty minutes later, after making sure the big bird was still moving, he devoured his large share of the fish and potato. "I think I hurt myself," he said aloud, "that was a darn good fish, and we are still alive."

After cleaning up, Birch proceeded to haul up the big rod's gear from the sea floor and put it away and stow everything else for the night. When he was done with the chores, he noticed Big Bird was back in the nest.

"Hey, 'chicken feathers,' you still alive? How are you feeling?" Big Bird waddled out to Birch and put his beak under Birch's hand for some head scratching.

"Well what's with this? Yeah! If you survived, my fine feathered friend, I probably will too. Besides, this Spam is getting old." When he closed the hatch door and went below, he heard Squawk! Squawk!

A few days later Birch woke up a little later than usual and went up to the top deck. "Bird brain" was just carrying on and on.

Screech! Screech!

"Well, I see you got your voice back, and you seem to have made a full recovery, and now we know what gender you are. Don't know how old you are, but we know you're either a teenager or an old crone by the way you're always bitching and nagging about something. Regardless, we are going to set down some ground rules."

The eagle stopped screeching and cocked her head to one side and just stared at Birch. "First of all, you are old enough to lay eggs, and I want to see some eggs laid or no breakfast. You got that? No egg. No breakfast. Secondly, you crapped on the mast again, and I'm going to slice you up and use your guts for crab bait, and the rest of you I got plans for. You got that, chicken-fried steak?"

Screech! Screech!

I guess I scared her. He could tell right away he scared Big Bird by the way she went right back to screeching at him.

One week later.

"Okay, okay, so I slept in for a few minutes." He looked at his watch and said. "Well, maybe an hour or two. So what's it gonna be, leftover fish or Spam?"

After Birch cleaned the dishes from breakfast, he went back on deck and scanned the horizon and sky for any signs of anything. The weather had been holding steady, and Birch had hoisted the main sail, and *SASSY* was just clipping along. He was just chasing the sun to the southwest, hoping to see a coastline. He knew he had been blown and washed offshore and should either be looking at a coastline or the ice pack or both. One or the other, but he saw neither. Seems cooler today than yesterday, he thought. He adjusted the sail and again set up the parameters and alarms for where he wanted to go. With the curvature of the earth he could only see to the horizon twelve to fifteen miles away. So the depth alarm at fifty feet would, or should, warn him if he was nearing a shoreline. Providing the coastal waters are shallow like Prudhoe Bay.

Meanwhile, with the good weather, Birch opened some hatch covers on the sloping sidewalls that protected the solar panels to charge up the batteries and heat up the water tank for a shower and to do some cleaning and washing. While the solar panels were hard at work, he got out the fishing poles and turned to Big Bird and said, "Let's go fishing."

Screech. Screech.

"Yeah, I know you could do better." Birch baited the hook and took care of the heavy rod first, and then cast over the side and bounced it on the bottom a time or two then tied it off.

"Let's get to work," and Birch landed three nice fish from right under the ship. A papa, mama, and baby one, like the first fish that they caught. He tossed the little one to Big Bird to see what she would do. It didn't take long to find out. "Big gulp" took care of baby fish right away.

"You big pig, you didn't save any for later? No dessert for you. I'll cut a couple of pieces from papa fish for supper and put the rest with mama fish in the freezer. "

When he came back up on deck he heard Big Bird, who was sitting on top of the mast, screeching away and looking out to sea ahead of them. Then Big Bird dropped off the mast, and it looked like the eagle was diving into the water but swooped on out ahead of the ship just a couple of feet above the water. I thought Big Bird was going to take a bath for sure. Big Bird started gaining altitude, climbing and climbing, till she was almost out of sight, and then she started circling over a stationary area about fifteen degrees to the west, guessing about five miles out. Birch could just make the eagle out without the telescope, and with the telescope Big Bird was a joy to watch as she was soaring lower and lower down to the sea and then rising again, way above the ocean without moving her wings once. Back at altitude, she glided to her perch atop of the mast. What was she circling? Yes, there is something in the water, I am sure. But what?

Chapter Five
Grave Yards and Ghost Ships

Flotsam. From where? From what? Birch dropped the sail and went to the forward bow turret and started the diesel and throttled forward, carefully watching the water ahead so he wouldn't sail or run into a sunken Connex, or container, and put holes in *SASSY*. With the diesel engine engaged, he had more control than when the sail was up, if he had to stop suddenly. From the turret he could also operate bow and helm thrusters to push bow and helm to one side or another. He could spin *SASSY* 360 degrees within her length if he had to, and going through this flotsam the bow thrusters could be handy. Birch was a little uneasy as he maneuvered through what seemed like a ship's wheelhouse cabin and deck that had been through an explosion. A life preserver and clothes floated amongst pieces of the superstructure. It just dawned on Birch that there was not even a breeze, and the sea was flat calm; even the eagle was silent. He did not like this at all. Felt like a graveyard, going through the debris. Because that's what it was, a graveyard, and he didn't like spending anymore time in the area then he had to. He throttled ahead and slowly made his way through the area and beyond.

A couple of days later Birch went top deck to feed Big Bird, and there she was prancing around just outside of the door hatch. He had made the eagle wait for her breakfast. He had some leftovers from his breakfast that he wanted to give her as a treat and see what other foods she would eat or wouldn't eat. The eagle had absolutely no fear of Birch anymore, if she ever really feared him. Yes, wary at first but no longer. Fear?—he didn't think so. She could probably whip me in a fair fight anyway. If I fought fair, that is.

Birch didn't fight fair; he didn't know how.

Birch went about studying the horizon and sky while the bird ate. The only thing notable he saw was the dark clouds in what he assumed was north.

Screech.

"What's that, my fine feathered friend? Is there too much Tabasco sauce on the corned beef hash?"

The eagle circled the ship and landed on top of the mast, looking at Birch for a minute or two and said something, then dove off and headed out to sea, climbing as she went. Birch watched her climb until she came to what he assumed was a thermal, because she started rising and not using her wings anymore.

He continued to watch her until she made a large circle and disappeared on a heading close to the heading Birch had been following. Now that the eagle had gone, he turned back and studied the clouds on the north horizon.

"They're getting bigger and closer, aren't they? Better watch that." Talking to a bird is one thing, but talking to yourself is another, especially when you ask yourself a question and you just stand there like you're in a trance, waiting for an answer. "They'll put me in a home and lock me up for sure."

The wind was picking up, and Birch had already set about dropping the sail and closing the hatch covers on the solar panels. He next checked the drogue anchor in case it was needed. He hoped not. He hoped that he could keep the bow into the wind under power. He hoped that if the approaching clouds were a storm front, the storm would just be your ripsnorter, typical Arctic storm, which *SASSY* could handle. He hoped it wouldn't be anything like the last one.

After scouring the horizon and the sky, and especially his heading one last time and double checking that everything was secure on deck, he went below. He reset his course a few degrees to the west as the crow flies, or as the eagle flies. Not that the eagle is any smarter than me. She just probably knows something I don't.

He had left the mast up, and checked the radar from time to time. Birch still could not get his mind around what the GPS and the compass were indicating compared to where and when the sun rose and set. Nor could he adjust to the temperatures he was experiencing at this time of year. Should be much colder for where he thought he might be: somewhere on the arctic coast.

Birch updated the ship's log on weather, activities, performance, trial checklist, statistics, and noted visitors' arrival and departure dates and times. The depth gauge had been bouncing between 150 feet and 250 feet. For no real reason, he thought he was following the coastline not all that far offshore. Just far enough he couldn't see it.

Feeling a little faint, he made some soup and a sandwich while paying attention to the radios. After he cleaned up, he started a serious search for radio contact. Birch called out over all the CB channels and different short wave frequencies with no results. Same results with the computer Web search, same error message stating: Server down or busy Please try again later.

SASSY was getting bounced around somewhat in the winds with her pontoon-type flat bottom, though not too bad considering she wasn't made to go cruising and cutting through the rolling seas or waves. She was made to survive, and so far she's done that real well. *This weather doesn't appear to be anything other than a squall*, Birch thought, while checking the weather from the forward turret. *Of course I could be wrong, I've been wrong before. I thought I made a mistake once.*

There was one thing he hadn't done yet that might help in staying on the direct course he had set. He could lower the two keels that were tucked up between the two pontoons. One forward and one aft, both of which were long and narrow like the racing yachts used. Lowering them was easy enough, as they were hydraulically operated. He didn't know why he hadn't dropped them before. Probably fear of the unknown closing in on him again? Also, I just forgot. Birch was still getting familiar with the ship.

"Wow! What a difference when you're keeling."

SASSY was still rocking side to side but not nearly as much, and the wallowing was no longer noticeable.

As *SASSY* was going through the "car wash" and getting all the bird crap washed off, Birch was thinking of the eagle and where she could have been going. He had left the small canvas up in case she did come back. That was another reason he had left the mast up, as the little hut he had made for her was tied off to the turret and the mast. He was sure the mast could weather just about any normal arctic blows. Maybe not those horrendous initial winds they experienced. No one anticipated anything like that.

Birch checked his heading against the compass points he set and plotted his position against the last position, and he was right on course to his next waypoint—at a crawl. What fuel he had on board was all he had, and all he was going to get, he figured. Not like he could just pull into some port or harbor and fuel up, so he was using the wind and currents to propel him toward where he wanted to go. *Wherever that is*, he thought. "What else do I need to do? I know I had to do something real important. But first things first," he said to himself, as he headed for his bunk to take a nap. "Have to get your priorities right."

"Whoa there!" said the man who woke up as he was thrown out of his bunk. Better go see why we are rocking and rolling. Looking out the portholes in the forward turret to see the white caps and the dark skies, he thought it might be a little more than a squall, while not quite admitting that he might have been mistaken. He checked the ship from one end to the other, also looking through each of the portholes, and then he went to the rear turret and checked the ship from that end, making sure he didn't miss any blind spots. Nope, no sign of Big Bird, but the canvas hut was still holding. Birch checked the ship several times a day over the next several days until the storm let up to a steady light rain where he could go top deck without getting blown off.

Although he had used hardly any water, he went up and opened the rain gutters to the leeward side, which funneled clean rainwater into the water tank below. Once the tank was full, a float closed the valve until it was manually opened again. Birch had decided to charge the tank every chance he got for the same reason he was conserving fuel. He hadn't seen any service station signs in the vicinity. No place to fill up or check the oil.

Birch also did not open the gutter when the winds were blowing, or he would be drinking salty water.

Birch closed the gutter to the rainwater, then went up to the top of the turret and scanned the skies and horizon. Went below and checked the depth gauge and did a couple of sweeps with the radar. He got a faint reading on the radar a few degrees off the starboard bow. Twenty minutes later he was getting a constant reading. Depth was getting shallower, varying around 100 feet to 125 feet. He adjusted the steering rudder a couple of degrees toward the radar contact, then went topside with his binoculars to take a look.

The rains had let up, and the winds were blowing a nice ten knots. He put the sail up and fine-turned it by taking all the slack out of the sail, then took a good look at the horizon where the contact was suppose to be. He so hoped that it would be a ship sailing his way. Well, he could see something on the horizon, but he could not make it out. If it was a ship, and it was not sailing in the same direction or heading for him, *SASSY* would never catch it. *SASSY* was built for comfort not for speed. "Right, *SASSY*?" he said. Birch went below and tried all the CB channels but got no response. He checked depth alarms and went back on top and looked through the binoculars again. It looked like a short shoreline with something else on one end. It was still too far away to make it out. By now he had determined whatever it was, it appeared to be stationary. An hour later he could see that it was an island and a ship that was beached high and dry.

Birch dropped sail, raised keels, and fired up the diesel and engaged hydraulics for the bow thrusters, in case they were needed, and slowly made his way the last few miles toward the ship, watching the depth getting shallower. When he was within a quarter of a mile out, he started circling the island, watching for reefs and seeing none. He turned around and went back to the backside of the island near the beached ship to be on the leeward side rather than windward side, where the waves were breaking in the surf. He inched up on shore. The waters were clear. No sign of any type of reefs. The beach seemed to be sandy, for the most part, with pockets of pebbles here and there. He would be able to come right up to the beach and tie off if there was anything to tie off to. Which he didn't see at the moment. He would grab a screw anchor and drop the main anchor where she beached, and then take a pole and screw an anchor in up off the beach and tie off. He hoped the tide didn't leave him high and dry. He could have anchored offshore a little bit and got the zodiac out. He put *SASSY*'s system on standby, then went to his bunk area and got dressed for outside.

He strapped on his .44 Ruger, although he had scoped the island out and hadn't seen a thing that should worry him, he took it anyway. He thought, You never can tell if a polar bear is out there hiding in a foxhole somewhere. You just can't be too careful now days with polar bears and gangs about. He grabbed his coat and headed topside. The island was about a half mile long, a quarter of a mile wide at its widest, and maybe fifteen feet high at its highest with a little bit of brush here and there, high enough to hide a bear.

Some years past, soon after he got out of the army and back to Alaska, he was working on a crew constructing a drill pad, runway, camp, and drilling platform on the slope. The second evening he asked some of the guys if they wanted to go with him over the hill to the south of where they were. It wouldn't be much of a walk. The previous month he and others on a different crew put in the first section of a much larger camp that could house a couple of hundred personnel compared to this small thirty-man camp. By now the camp should be close to being, if not already, completed.

It turns out that the other camp was close to this new site. It must have been a hot spot for drilling. Most of the exploration camps were miles and miles apart. Since they did not yet have heat in any of the sleeping trailers, bathroom trailers, or the mess hall in the small camp where they were now working, and it was below zero, Birch said he was going to this other camp to get a shower, hot meal, and sleep in a warm real bed. He along with others had been sleeping in the generator trailer next to the big generator. Warm, but sure was noisy. There were no takers.

So, he took off alone walking on the hard packed snow, since there were no roads. Early the next morning he walked the mile and a half back to the smaller camp, having had a big breakfast, feeling all warm and clean. Fat, dumb, and happy, he got back just as some of the guys were waking up.

Everyone was pissed. Sometime before midnight someone noticed that Birch was not there. Everyone was up looking for him around camp before someone remembered, around two in the morning after a futile search, that he had said he was going over the hill to another camp for the night to get a hot meal and a warm bed.

Everyone lost a few hours of sleep and got madder than blazes every time Birch burped and rubbed his belly, complaining about how much he ate that morning and talking about the hot meal he'd had the night before. They did not want to hear about the hot shower or talk about the nice comfortable bed he slept in. He just didn't understand some people at times, begrudging others of their comforts.

About midmorning a couple of Eskimo hunters on snow machines pulled into camp. The crew invited them in for a cup of coffee inside one of the trailers that now had heat and a coffee pot going. They also gave them some pancakes that they had left over from breakfast. As the Natives were getting ready to leave, someone asked them what they were doing in this neck of the snow banks.

The older one said they were following a big polar bear. The bear was tracking someone who had been out walking early this morning. Bear came right through the camp. They both looked at Birch and said, "Whoever was walking was wearing boots just like yours and were the same size."

* * * * *

Birch drew his .44 Magnum and double checked that it was fully loaded, six shots, before he started out.

Wonder where that lazy bird is? She should be out scouting the area.

Birch took another look around, dropped a rope ladder over the side, and climbed down and headed for the ship, because that seemed to be the only thing on the island that looked interesting. Since he had left what he was to call "the graveyard," he had made up his mind, or come to grips with the thought, that if he came across anything in the future, he would investigate and see if there was anything that would be worthwhile salvaging if he had room to carry it. Or at least get a GPS location for future reference, if needed. He better think about stockpiling anything and everything that would help him survive. He wouldn't be getting resupplied anytime soon.

The ship was about six hundred yards away and was beached high and dry but was not really listing to one side, as you would expect. The ship had two front anchors. That made no sense whatsoever. It looked like it was anchored in between two islets before the land rose. Probably never know if the ship had drifted there or was intentionally anchored there before the geology changed, leaving the ship high and dry.

As Birch approached the ship, he dreaded what he might find aboard and was not looking forward to going inside. He made out the name *Arctic Tern*. Other than that, he couldn't determine offhand what kind of ship it was. Not a fishing trawler or whaler, that's for sure. He estimated the length at 250 feet and width at forty to fifty feet. As he made his way up the boarding stairway on the side of the ship and stepped on the deck, he would have guessed that the ship had been sandblasted on the one side. The glass of the bridge windows hadn't been knocked out, but they were also sandblasted so you could not see through them from the outside, anyway. He climbed to the bridge and entered from the opposite side from the one that was sandblasted. This side looked in the need of a paint job but was relatively untouched.

Once inside the bridge he looked around before fully entering. The inside of the bridge looked like it had been ransacked. Papers and charts were strewn all over the floor but no water damage. Strange, no polar bears either. But Birch wasn't paying too much attention to the housekeeping. In reality, he was looking for bodies, and thankfully there weren't any visible. Not yet, anyway. But he had just started his search of the ship and had a long way to go.

From the bridge he made his way through the upper deck behind the bridge area into the radio rooms. No power to the communications. Birch made a quick trip down and around to all cabins, passageways, and cargo areas, then a quick return to the upper decks. He had seen no sign of anyone or bodies. He was on a ghost ship. He found nothing in the papers on the upper decks to tell him what happened to the crew or passengers, as there were no bodies. He did find the ship's manifest and bill of laden but the ship's log was not to be found. Evidently they left the ship suddenly, somehow, and took the logbook with them. Birch did not want to admit it, but the reason he ran though, searching the ship was to make sure one way or the other of anyone alive or dead being onboard.

It was getting dark, and he had not realized how late it was getting. He wanted to make it back to *SASSY* before it got real dark, so he could watch where he was walking. Besides, that's when the polar bears come out.

Tomorrow morning, bright and early, after I eat breakfast and have my coffee and read tomorrow's paper, I will take inventory of the ship. Maybe I better skip tomorrow's paper, though.

The next morning he started his inspection and inventory on the main deck. All the lifeboats were gone. Deck was swept clean; nothing there that wasn't lashed or dogged down. Next he started going through the cargo bays, checking everything and every nook and cranny.

This had to be some type of supply ship. "What we have here is a floating, or was a floating, Lowe's shopping center and your local service station right here on *Gilligan's Island*," Birch said, as he continued through the rest of the ship, noting the inventory aboard. One hold had a nice John Deere 450 dozer with a heated cab, a steel freight sled and two brand new snow machines with trailers, and two brand new four-wheelers with trailers. There were fifteen barrels of gas, thirty barrels of #1 diesel fuel and twenty each four-foot-tall propane bottles. Supply ship for where? He wondered. Years ago there was an Ice Island that was manned year around. Was it still in operation? If he remembered right, it just traveled with the ice pack. Cargo in this ship was a mixture of all kinds of various building supplies, and no large quantities of any one thing that you would see if it was freight for the oil companies. A ship with freight for the oil fields would more than likely consist of one or two things, like cement, drilling mud, and drilling pipe. This ship had supplies more like a camp or a private individual in an arctic village would need in the way of building materials. Wherever it was going, with the exception of Ice Island, it would have to be unloaded offshore and lightered ashore in shallow draft barges, for most of the arctic coast is fairly shallow with no harbors to speak of, and the ship had a deep draft. Years ago he shipped freight from Seattle to Kotzebue on Alaska's northwest coast. The freight had to be lightered the last twelve miles to the shore. The cost of the lightering that last twelve miles was the same cost as shipping the cargo two thousand miles or more all the way from Seattle.

Birch finally noticed the shrink-wrapped pallets with Mil Barter Island spray painted on the side of the pallets, along with a bundle of 2 x 4s and 2 x 6s also spray painted with the designation Mil Barter Island. Barter Island was once part of the DEW line that was located every so often along the Alaskan and Canadian coastline and could still be there until recently, as far as he knew. Barter Island was fifty to seventy-five miles west of the Alaska and Canadian border on the north coast. He decided when he finished the last of the cargo holds that he would go back up and take a better look through the bridge and communications room to see if he could find anything to shed some light on the ship's last position before this nightmare started.

In the comm room he found radio transcripts that the *Arctic Tern* had arrived and anchored at Barter Island. He also found a chart with the ship's positions and times noted on their progress and time of arrival and anchorage at Barter. Birch wondered about what occurred from the time of the *Arctic Tern*'s arrival and the Big One (earthquake like no other). After establishing a time line, he did have a theory that the ship's crew had disembarked, and while they were ashore the Big One hit. The DEW system was next door to Kaktovik, a Native settlement of around three hundred people and about thirty-six feet above sea level.

After what Birch and *SASSY* went through in the Big One, what happened to this ship would be to him another of the world's great mysteries. Just how did the *Arctic Tern* survive and remain intact? The ship must have dragged the anchors all the way from Kaktovik to where she is sitting now.

From the communications room and bridge he started going through the cabins and found them in just the way you would leave them, say you stepped out to get a cup of coffee, with the exception that all of them looked like the rooms had been picked up and shaken. Things were spilled out of closets and cupboards. But you still could tell some individuals, like me, Birch thought, were neat as pin. And others were as sloppy as all get out, like CG. I better smile when I say things like that. Hope he didn't hear that. It's just no fun at all picking on CG when he's not around. Nope! No fun at all.

Birch sat down weakly, before his legs went out from under him. Thoughts like that hit him hard and had occurred two to three times a day for the past several days. When he thought of everyone and images of friends and other people entered his mind, like CG just did, he would almost throw up and would come close to hyperventilating.

Birch knew he had to keep his sense of humor. It would be real easy to fall into a deeper depression than he already was in, if he hadn't already started sliding that way.

When Birch got his strength and his breath back, he continued on through the cabins and became acquainted with the occupants. He found a stash of whiskey in one cabin, the letter writer in another cabin, and the librarian who had an outstanding collection of Playboy magazines in the corner of his cabin. I assume it was a he; can't tell these days. Then there was the student who was studying for his ticket in seamanship and officer advancement, according to all the nautical books scattered around the cabin. One of the nautical books looked like it was made for him.

You know, Sailing for Birch and other Dummies.

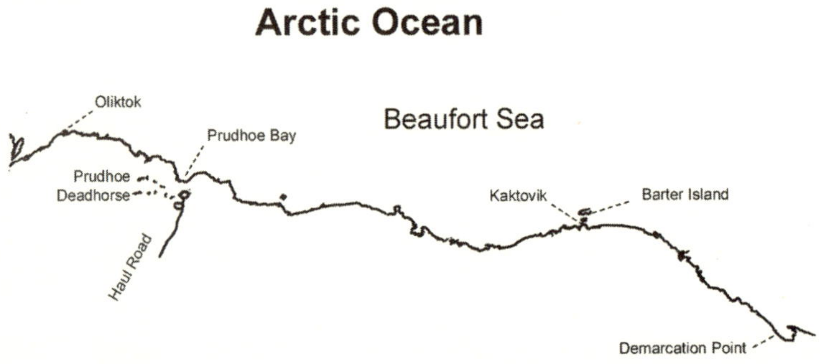

With the exception of the book and some wine, he did not disturb or take anything out of the cabins, including money or jewelry. But he knew in his heart that if he didn't liberate the cabernet sauvignon and the merlot and put it to good use, there is no doubt it would soon go poisonous. It wasn't doing a bit of good in that dark pantry next to the galley, anyway, and with the onslaught of winter coming, it would all freeze and the bottles would break. Yes, for the good of all, the wine would be better if it was liberated and protected from freezing to death.

I'll drink to that. Later.

The next morning Birch had just a minute bit of the flu. The red flu, he called it, especially when he looked at the sun low on the horizon. He checked his watch and the compass against where the sun was coming up this morning. According to his compass it rose in the northeast. Something sure took a jog. If the GPS was right, he was on the tundra just south of the Laptev Sea, or on the Laptev Sea close to the new Siberian Islands.

He looked to the south, or what he thought was south, and like yesterday and the day before, there was a low-lying layer of scud clouds. To the north he looked across the island, and he saw the same thing. But there was a difference. He went below and got the telescope and took another look. He could just make out the edge of the arctic ice pack. That could be bad news, as the pack could either push him to where he did not want to go or trap him where he did not want to be.

Birch made a snap decision and went below and slapped a sandwich together, dressed for work, and headed for the *Arctic Tern*. He had decided that he needed to head south in the very near future. Once aboard the *Arctic Tern*, he went to the bridge and made an amendment to the ship manifest consisting of the date and time, his name, and an IOU for barrels of diesel, gas, cylinders of propane, and other items. He would enter quantities after he off-loaded what he wanted. In the cargo area he found a chain hoist and other block and tackle. On the main deck he opened one side of the big hatch cargo doors to one of the cargo holds with the help of the block and tackle. Then he started rigging up the block and tackle to a spar off the near ship crane. The spar was free-turning on a bearing to the crane tower. He didn't even try or think about ship power to operate the ship crane; he would rely on Birch power. The spar was secured in the upright position to the ship crane tower. With an access ladder on the one side of the crane tower, he was able to lower the spar and hooked the block to the shackle on the spar along with a turn rope. After dropping the block into the hold, he went below and tried to start one of the Polaris four-wheelers.

It fired right up on the first pull. He took it and pulled one of the trailers over to just below the open cargo hatch. He hooked a strap around the frame of the Polaris and hooked the other end of the strap to the block. Before he hoisted it up, he went topside and rearranged the turn rope to a small block to the outside ship rail. Back below, he hoisted the Polaris above deck and pulled on the turn rope, pulling the load to the side. He let it down once the load was off to the side of the hatch.

Well, that works, but I don't know if I will survive going back and forth.

He found several small cargo nets below, along with more than enough straps to rig up several loads at a time. He could, after bending a twenty-foot piece of half-inch rebar a few inches at one end, guide a strap end onto the hook of the block from topside without going below. At least that would save him a lot of trips up and down the ladder. Now he had a plan that Leonardo Da Vinci would have been proud of, especially if he had two Polaris four-wheelers.

Birch hooked up the other four-wheeler and hoisted it up and then arranged five loads of barrels of two each in different nets. Hooked one up and from above he tied off the pull end to one of the four-wheelers, started it, and pulled ahead far enough to clear the deck and set the brake. He dismounted, grabbed the turn rope and slipped the pull rope off the hitch, and while letting the load down, turned the load to the side and set the load down. He looked over the side, and then went back and picked the four-wheeler up high enough to clear the rail and set it down over the side, picked the block up and swung it into the cargo hold and, using the rebar, guided the strap end onto the block and continued the laborious procedures throughout the morning offloading those items Birch felt he could put to good use.

One other item he offloaded was one of the new snow machines and several five-gallon cans of gas. Somewhere along the line, he figured, this would be an item that he would put to good use. The snow machine was one of the first items he put aboard. It was strapped on top of one of the four-wheeler's trailer, and he pulled it around until it was right aft of the ship. Next he dropped *SASSY*'s aft ramp and with the help of several 2 x 12-inch planks, he was able to get it off the trailer and in position to back it up the ramp.

After loading the snow machine, Birch threw a rope that was tied off at the one end that was out in the water and pulled it, using the four-wheelers until *SASSY* was parallel to the edge of the water. After hauling the fuel over to *SASSY*, he set about using the reverse procedures of loading the items to the topside of the *SASSY*, using the mast and spar and securing the loads down.

The next day back aboard the *Arctic Tern*, he made a sweep through the galley and discovered the freezer and refrigeration was still holding. He loaded up with some of the frozen meats and other items that he had room for in his freezer, which was fairly substantial, and did the same for the refrigerator items and loaded *SASSY*, and then put everything away accordingly. Made a trip through the pantry and took two loads off. In the captain's quarters he found cartons of double ought shotgun shells and a shotgun. He took two of the cartons of shells and left the shotgun, since he had his own. After lowering one of the four-wheelers below that he was not taking and putting the four-wheeler, the nets, and tackle away like he found it, he secured the cargo hatch.

The last thing he did aboard the *Arctic Tern* was enter all the quantities and other items on the manifest as amendment number two. He then dated and put down the time and signed off. He went through the bridge and found all the coastal charts from California up to Alaska and past the Alaskan and Canadian Boarder. A few were scattered around on the bridge floor. He gathered them all up and rolled the charts into a big bundle, tied a rope sling to them, and slung them over his shoulder and secured all the hatches behind him as he left.

Birch was tired, and it was early afternoon. He looked out to the north and he could see the ice pack now without the telescope or binoculars. The ice pack was closer, a lot closer. He fired up *SASSY* and cast off. Naptime will have to wait. *SASSY* was definitely heavier and a little bit more top-heavy. He had to use the bow thrusters at first in order to get away, as she had settled a little more on the beach. First he engaged the front thrusters and then the back thrusters a couple of times before she was free of the beach sand.

Coming out from the protected waters behind the island into the open sea, Birch set a course WSW right to the middle of the low-scudded skies where he guessed that he would find the mainline coast. He set the sail, and then he set the alarm guards he had established earlier, adjusting the depth warning for shallower waters at seventy-five feet. Once he had the course set, he watched the radar for a while until the radar started picking up the coastline. He looked behind and could no longer see the ice pack but knew it was there and could close in on him if the winds picked up and shifted in his direction. He decided not to dally around.

He put on his parka and harness and went topside. He needed to let the sail out and check the tie downs on the fuel that was lashed to the top deck. The boom of the mast just cleared the propane bottles as he let it out. Birch could feel the difference when the sail filled and *SASSY* set back on her heels and scooted forward, even with the extra load toward the bow. In order to get from one end to the other, he would have to either crawl over the deck cargo or go below and crawl over the new snow machine and four-wheeler, which he had stowed below to protect them. It was easier to go below to get to the other end, and that is what he did, but before he went down he took a quick 360-degree look around the horizon and sky.

From the bow turret/bridge he could control letting the sail in or out and dropping it to some extent but not completely. To completely drop the sail, he would have to watch the weather and winds and do it from topside. But now he wanted to watch the approaching coastline, maintain at least a certain depth, not getting too close or into unexpected shallow water or hit any reefs. If he remembered correctly, most of the Alaskan north coast was fairly free of rocks, but small isles were not that uncommon.

As he approached the coast he started to bear to the right, or what used to be the west, staying between five hundred and one thousand yards offshore, far away from any surf. The depth was averaging right at ninety feet. The closer to shore he went the waters were getting murky, and the water close to shore was downright muddy. He made a sketch of the coastline and entered a GPS position in his logbook. In looking onshore he saw what used to be the flat tundra as far as you could see. Part of the Arctic Slope was dotted with thousands of small ponds and lakes. That was before the winds had peeled the tundra back and rolled it up in cornrows here and there. From what he could see at a distance and through the binoculars, there were areas that had been swept clean of tundra from the flooding and receding waters. Surprisingly, there were miles and miles of the coastline that looked completely untouched. It made him wonder if some areas were affected by huge eddies and other areas that might have been in something like the eye of a hurricane and were consequently untouched by water flooding or tidal waves. Everything was damaged but not to the same extent as others.

He saw no gulls or birds of any kind, nor any other wildlife. At this time of year, this area would normally be teeming with birds of all kinds that had migrated from all the Americas: North America, Central America, South America, and Mexico. And you didn't have to go very far before you saw caribou grazing here and there. Even with the impact to certain areas, though, Birch thought that there were still plenty of nesting areas that appeared untouched, and the birds would come back in time. That is, those that had survived.

He continued parallel to the coast for another hour or so, taking in the landscape. After a while he made notes on the sketch of his current GPS position, and he headed out to sea away from the coastline. He set about doing his chores and updating the logbook and diary. When he was about five miles offshore, he changed course to follow the coastline and set a GPS waypoint fifty miles out and reset the depth gauge warning for two hundred feet. He also set the radar contact buzzer for ten miles. After doing a sweep of the horizon with the telescope, he made a nest close to the warning bells and whistles, set the alarm for four hours and started to lie down, thinking he would try to get some much-needed sleep, although he didn't like his chances. He fell asleep half way down in the process of lying down.

The waypoint buzzer woke Birch up, and it was dark, so he couldn't see anything. He checked the depth and monitored the radar for a few minutes. He was barely picking up the coastline now, and he figured out he was almost thirty-five miles out, which was about the extent of the radar from the top of the mast. After checking everything again and setting a new waypoint, he crawled back into his nest for another four hours.

The radar contact buzzer made Birch jump out of the sack. He did not know why or what the buzzer meant, but he knew enough to know he should be scared, and he should do something—what that was, he had no idea. After he stood up and recognized where he was, he took stock and started checking things out. It finally dawned on him it was the radar. He opened the turret hatch and started scoping the horizon ahead. He could just make out what could be coastline dead ahead and to his port side. He figured he was about twelve miles out. He started to close the hatch when he noticed something lying on the deck by the rear turret. He would check it out later; coffee first. *Let's get our priorities right*, he thought.

After he finished dressing and got his coffee, he went topside to the rear and found a lump of fur lying just outside the hatch door to the turret, where the canvas hooch was. "What the—" Birch started to say when he was rudely interrupted.

Screech! Screech!

He looked up, and there was *Goldielocks* sitting on her perch, crapping all over the radar atop the mast. "Welcome back, 'barbeque chicken.' Where have you been?" Birch bent over and looked, and then picked up the ball of fur. "Well, I'll be. You brought me some road kill. I can't believe it. You brought me a widdle bitty wabbit for the stew pot. Or do you want to trade for something? I'll be right back." He went down below and to the front helm and changed the course forty-five degrees to port from his present heading. Then he got out a piece of fresh fish he had in the fridge and went back topside, grabbing the telescope on the way up. He laid the fish on one of the barrels and went about checking the coastline with the telescope. He spotted something man-made sticking up in the air and headed for it. While they approached the coast, Birch picked up the rabbit and started skinning it on the next barrel. When he had the skin off, he quartered the rabbit and put the pieces alongside the fish and started scraping the hide, getting rid of any meat or fat. He didn't notice until he was finished scraping the hide that the eagle had come down from the mast and had started eating the fish and pieces of the rabbit.

"Are you really going to leave me half of the rabbit? You are such a good little bird. I see your table manners have greatly improved. I'm really impressed." He looked at the rabbit hide and folded it over and around his left hand. "Next time around, bring me one for my right hand, will you? This will make a fine glove. Yes, a very fine glove." There just might be enough for both hands, he thought.

"Nosey bird" was watching Birch work the rabbit skin on the barrel, next to the one he was using as a bench top. Nosey bird was actually getting in the way and didn't pay any attention to Birch as he was scolding her. As he handed her another piece, which she gladly accepted right out of his hand, he thought, If I quit feeding her, maybe she will get out of the way. He checked to make sure he still had all his fingers.

Birch watched the feather ball for a few minutes and thought to himself that this eagle was a very young bird and probably had not been out of the nest but a very short time and hadn't been flying very long at all.

Birch approached the shore and beached *SASSY* as close to what turned out to be the bottom third of a DEW line tower. He put his hip boots on and started slogging through the mud toward the tower. From what he could determine, the beach had subsided somewhat, and the only thing left that was visible was the tower itself. Everything else was either buried or washed away. He wanted to check the tower for any kind of identification that would tell him the location. Nada, nothing from what he could see from below, and he was not going to climb on the tower, as it looked somewhat rickety now, and he didn't see anything up there to pique his interest. The only thing up there was a big sack of feathers perched on top of the tower, looking back down at him. Just as he started climbing back aboard *SASSY*, Big Bird swooped so close to him she would have knocked his hat off if he had been wearing one. He watched her as she started flying just inland from the coast until she found an uplift in the air and then just soared up and up to the west until she disappeared. Birch opened the solar panel covers on both sides to charge the batteries for the day.

After leaving the area and setting a new course, Birch spent about an hour redrawing his map and updating the logbook and diary. He was now following the coastline as it was turning to the northeast. After he had the *SASSY* shipshape and on course, he started making one of his world-class breakfasts. While the bacon was cooking, he broke the eggs into a small bowl. They looked all right, but he thought that this was probably the last of the eggs before they go bad. At least until that feather mop starts laying eggs, anyway, and that didn't look like that was going to happen anytime soon. He wondered if he would develop a taste for rabbit, as he stirred his famous Snoqualmi Falls pancake mix recipe. No one around to argue about that anymore, it seems. He almost lost his appetite with that thought.

After he cleaned up the dishes and did other chores, Birch made a thermos of coffee and went up to the forward bridge and started to analyze the coast, comparing it to a few charts and maps he had aboard. He was getting an inkling of where he might be, well, within a continent or two, anyway. The coastline ahead appeared to come to a point. It could be a point or a cape. He thought he was in one of the coastal bays. He hoped it was one of the Alaskan bays. Birch took a sight line of the coastline he would be following when he came abreast of it and took the compass bearing. When he could sight along the coastline he would be turning away from, he took another compass reading. As he rounded what he thought must be a cape that was ninety degrees to port, he plotted his GPS position and compared the miles from the last, then scaled it on a map. Then he plotted the compass bearings and measured the angle and compared that to the shoreline of several bays. By early afternoon he might at last be able to confirm his location. He grabbed his fishing rod on his way topside to adjust the boom and sail to change the direction. *SASSY* just scooted right along after the sail was adjusted.

Now he had to focus on the important things. If he was going to have guests swoop in on him from time to time, he better get something to put on the barbie. Within a few minutes he landed a nice pan-size fish with his Top Secret lure. That same lure was probably used all over the Lower Forty-eight but was mostly unknown up here in Alaska. At least by the local fish, anyway. The fish evidently like the cover of *SASSY*. There always seem to be three or four around and under the bottom. He would try to land one more so he would have plenty on hand for Big Gulp when she came back, if she did come back.

Several hours later after a nice dinner, Birch veered closer to the shore and focused on any man-made items. He was looking for another DEW line site; following a West North West bearing, he should see a few small islands just ahead, and then the dome of the radar and radio tower should be visible, and if he was right, it should be the Lonely DEW line site. Now he was willing to bet all the Federal Reserve notes that he had. The DEW line site he just left had to be what was left of Kogru DEW station.

A little later he started edging in closer to the shoreline, which wasn't matching up with the chart he had in front of him nor was Lonely visible when it should be. The buzzer went off for the depth gauge for fifty feet. Birch turned to starboard and collapsed the sail, which he should have done earlier. He went topside to fully drop the sail. Then he started the engine and engaged the hydraulics for the bow thrusters that aided the steering, since *SASSY* did not have much in the way of a rudder system, especially against strong currents. She was designed that way to avoid having the ice tear the rudder off, the same with the keel. The keel could be dropped or raised from inside and dropped when at sea and not at anchor.

The water was clear along this section of the coast for at least three hundred yards or more out, probably cleared by the strong current. He had to throttle forward in order to barely move along the coast. That was all right. He just wanted to creep along now. He couldn't see bottom, but the depth gauge was giving readings between twenty- and fifty- feet deep. He started to turn back seaward when he spotted what looked like a reef a few feet ahead. Inching ahead and alongside, he thought it might be man-made. Going a little farther and getting closer told him it was what was left of a concrete structure. This also told him the whole area had substantially subsided, and that explained why he couldn't see the radar dome. Not seeing anything when he surveyed the area, he began a two-mile circle of the GPS waypoint position, hoping to find other items. He was near his starting point when he found what was left of the radio tower. He guessed it failed and broke in the same place where the one at Kogru failed.

I guess I should write a letter and let the design engineers know that their tower failed in measly three hundred-plus mph winds. Shame, shame. He smiled, Not saying much for the concrete either, or the compacting under the concrete. It must have been tough getting competent help in those days. You have to protect structures from those three hundred-plus mile an hour breezes and tsunamis that might happen every couple of thousand years. Just don't know about some peoples' work ethics. He looked ashore with the telescope and saw that the tundra had been swept clean by the tidal waves. He was looking at newly formed mud flats. It would be a while before the tundra came back.

He swung the ship out to sea, put the sail up, and set the course and waypoint for Cape Simpson about forty miles as the eagle flies. Birch wondered where that feather dust mop was.

He was headed for firewood. Not even a twig to build a good fire with. This was the last place he wanted to be without a good supply of firewood while being trapped by the ice pack.

After a light dinner, he checked the radar and manned the radios a while, calling out in between listing through the frequencies of the SSB and different channels on the CB. Nada, zip, nothing was coming from the radios but static. He was tired and getting sleepy, so he set the alarm and got in his bunk and thought he would get a few hours of sleep. But he couldn't sleep when he started thinking of all the coastal towns, villages, cities, and coastal areas that were lost and swept out to sea and buried like these DEW line sites. After tossing and turning awhile, he got up, made coffee, and went to the bridge. It was a good thing he didn't fall asleep, as he found out he was sailing into or very near the ice pack. The farther north he went, the closer the pack was getting to shore. It wasn't long before he had to turn south to avoid the ice.

I need to close the covers over the solar panel. The winds were picking up. He turned the deck lights on and put his parka and harness on and went topside and started closing the hatches over the panels. No easy thing having to climb over the cargo that was lashed down on the deck. To be safe, it was best to get it covered during stormy weather. During high winds and rough water, the waves could wash completely over the deck, and probably would if this weather got worse.

While he was topside he stowed the sail and started the diesel, then he went below to the helm. Birch spent the rest of the night watching the radar and maneuvering between the coastline and the ice. Toward dawn he was still following the coastline, but now he was heading southeast. This was not right. He might not be where he thought he was.

According to the chart, he was beyond the most southern part of Smith Bay and into the northern part of Teshekpuk Lake, which meant that Smith Bay was now Smith Inlet and Teshekpuk Lake was no longer a lake but had become a much larger bay. The lake was one, if not the largest, on the North Slope: over thirty miles wide prior to the Shift or Big One. Evidently, he thought, the Big One has taken out the land bridge between the lake and Smith Bay.

He ducked into a little cove that was protected from the crashing waves that had been rolling *SASSY* from side to side. The cargo on top didn't help, being top-heavy and something the waves could push against, rolling her over more than they should. He dropped anchor and decided to hole up here until the weather eased. Until? That might be until spring when the ice moved north enough to let him continue his odyssey for firewood.

* * * * *

Three days later.

Birch woke when the weather quit trying to buck him out of his bunk, but he rolled over and went back to sleep. He wasn't going anywhere in the dark, even if he could. He would see what the situation was during daylight.

After breakfast he cleaned up and washed the dishes and pans. He got a cup of coffee and went topside. He had slept longer than he thought, since it was mid-morning already. But he needed his rest because he wanted to be alert and able to give his full attention to navigating between the ice pack and the shore. It would be difficult, if not impossible to get through if the ice pack closed in anymore or the winds and current pushed the ice ashore.

As soon as he stepped out on deck, this god-awful noise busted his eardrums: Screech! Screech!

He was glad he wasn't hung over. The eagle was perched on the turret right above Birch's head when he stepped out on deck. "She could have just 'reached out and touched somebody,' or sunk a claw in my tiny little brain," he muttered.

"Where in the heck have you been? Did you bring me any eggs? Listen up, "chicken fricassee," if you got no eggs, then I might as well put you in the frying pan and make a feather duster out of your hide. You're not even a good guide. You're just a no-good-for-nuthin' bird. I can't think of anything, nope, not one little thing. Well, maybe for one little bitty rabbit hide. Never mind, I swore I wouldn't cuss on Mondays, anymore."

Birch went below and got a little bit of Spam and a fillet of fish and put it in a bowl. The eagle never backed up or moved out of the way as Birch climbed up and set the bowl in front of her on top of the turret. Big Gulp ripped into the fish and Spam without waiting for Birch to get out of the way. "Hey you, mind your manners. What's the matter, rabbits getting scarce?"

Birch sat on the other side of the turret while Big Bird ate for a little while longer, and then said, "Well, I don't have all day, you know. I can't hang around here waiting on you hand and foot. I got to get a move on. So, if you will excuse me, I will get under way."

Screech! I'm starting to understand Eagle talk. Eagle want more, Birch thought as he climbed down and went to the bridge and started the diesel.

He then uncovered the solar panels and pulled the anchor and headed out, going back up what was now the inlet. The eagle took off from the turret, circled the ship before landing on top of the mast, and pointed the way.

The inlet was free of ice, and the bay was mostly free. Beyond the bay the ice was solid, but there was open water between the ice pack and shore. He hoped it would stay open and not close in, trapping him for the winter.

Almost four hours later he found part of a radio tower just sticking out of the water about five hundred yards offshore. Nothing else left of Cape Simpson. And the ice pack would take care of that. Then there would be nothing left of Cape Simpson. He took and plotted the GPS position and compass bearing on the tower. Right where the chart said it was, according to the compass readings. The GPS readings were way off. But Birch thought that he could interpolate the distances from known GPS positions and compass bearings, and between the readings he was now getting, he would be able to tell where his next waypoint would be. Birch, being the mathematical genius that he was, and if he could remember any of his third-grade math, hoped he wouldn't end up in the Mohave Desert.

Now that he had some data, he could change mode on the GPS controller and recalibrate with the points he collected.

Once he was beyond the tangent point, he set a new bearing and GPS waypoint using the new information he had been gathering for just offshore of Point Barrow. It looked like the ice pack would accommodate him for the time being, anyway, or until the wind shifted. He had hoisted the sail and opened the covers on the solar panels and shut down the diesel engine. It was going to be a nice day. Big Bird looked happy as a clam sitting up there on top of the mast pointing the way. He even thought he heard her chirp once or twice.

Late in the day he arrived way south of the waypoint just offshore from where Point Barrow was suppose to be, he discovered a large portion of the point missing. He had to veer way south of the waypoint because the ice pack completely covered the area, and the coastline was so far south. Birch thought he had either made a big mistake or the land all the way from Admiralty Bay

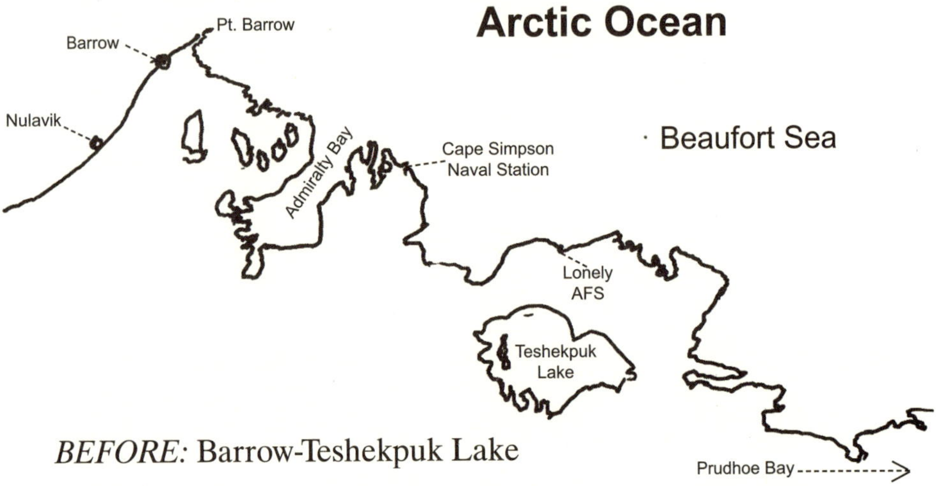

BEFORE: Barrow-Teshekpuk Lake

across to Nulavik (and maybe beyond Nulavik) was underwater.

He went below and made a pot of coffee and grabbed some fish for him and Big Bird. Birch poured a cup of coffee, fed the eagle, and started grilling his fish. While sipping his coffee, he came to the conclusion that he hadn't made a mistake, not by that many miles anyway. He figured the village of Barrow had also subsided or was washed away.

He had adjusted the sail and was now heading southwest. The ice pack had also rounded the corner of Point Barrow and was following the coast as he was, but he had plenty of room and was gaining more room the farther south he went for the time being, anyway.

Birch felt and heard a swoosh as the eagle went by and started climbing toward land until it disappeared. Birch went to the bridge and set the bearing for the compass and waypoint on the autopilot for a point off the coast by Point Franklin. Then he set the warning bells and whistles for the radar before he went below and crawled in the sack. He would clean up in the morning.

It was a long time getting to sleep, because Birch thought about the loss of several friends he had lost in Barrow, along with rest of the population of the largest Eskimo village. He had just turned eighteen and was working on one of the military sites nearby. One of the crew members was lost during a storm. He

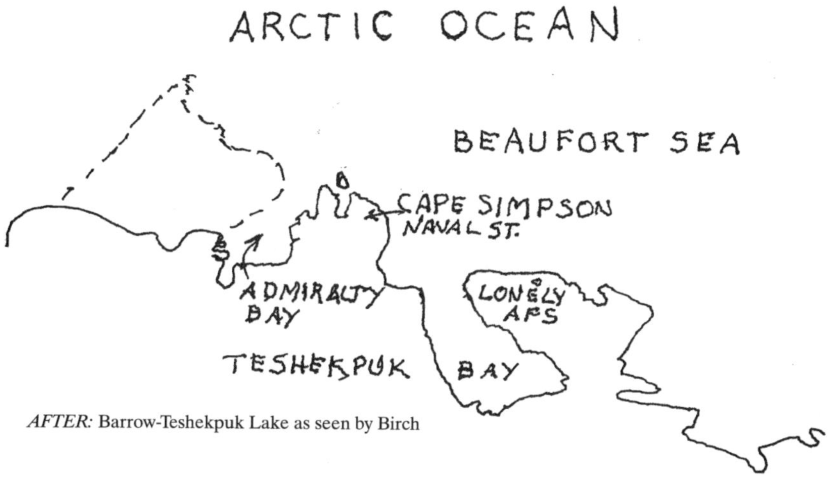

AFTER: Barrow-Teshekpuk Lake as seen by Birch

didn't know the fellow or see him, but others found him the next morning between two of the Quonset huts that the crews slept in.

When the weather started getting bad, they strung strong ropes between the huts and across the wide street to the mess hall. If you were holding your arm out in front of yourself, you could not see beyond your glove during the really bad blows. Snow could drift over one side of the Quonset hut in a matter of minutes and then drift to the other side if the wind changed.

Nothing to play around with.

Evidently, the fellow let go of the rope or lost his grip and got turned around.

Quonset huts look like a barrel sliced in half length wise and laid down along the street.

They probably slept twenty men at a time. They were heated with an oil heater in one end and a gas heater in the other. When the oil heater acted up, Birch would go down and kick the heater. One of the guys there was afraid of oil and would leave the hut. When the gas heater acted up, that same guy would go down and kick the gas heater, and Birch would leave the hut. Birch didn't like the gas.

Two days later.

He woke up feeling good. He had slept well the night before, and felt good too, as he'd had no nightmares. Feeling as good as could be expected without any coffee. Who could really feel good without coffee? Only babies and those who were unenlightened.

Oatmeal, that sounds good. I'll make some of my gourmet oatmeal and toast for breakfast. He thought of his mom and girlfriend who would both remind him from time to time, "Gourmet food doesn't come out of a can or box."

He had wondered when he invited other friends over for one of his gourmet creations when they told him they wouldn't miss it for the world, but unfortunately they had been planning this day for months in advance . . . to clean their toilets. What are the odds of that happening? That both couples he invited would pick the very same day to clean their toilets. What are the odds of that? Really strange!

Chapter Six
A Whale of a Good Day

After cleaning up the breakfast dishes and the dishes from the night before, Birch put on a few CDs over *SASSY*'s stereo system and grabbed a thermos of coffee and went topside. Once he got there he was glad he had his parka on. The wind was nippy, about ten knots coming off the ice and blowing toward shore, but with the sun shining like it was it was still comfortable. He might need a warm windbreaker rather than his heavy parka. He flipped on the speakers on the turret and turned the speakers up a little bit. A few years ago he was walking through the living room and heard this young girl about fifteen years old singing. She was incredible. Birch hardly ever listened to music, but when he did it was usually classical or along the lines of this young girl, Charlotte Church. When in his car or truck he always dialed in the news or talk radio. He liked all kinds of music. Music like Charlotte's, some country, and most classical. He liked both singers and instrumental, with some limitations.

Singers have to have talent.
Those with talent sing.
Those with lesser talent yell and scream a lot.
Most of those with no talent rap.

G. Chandler

As much as he enjoyed music, he always thought he didn't learn a lot from music. That's why he always turned to the news. Birch always felt like he had too much to do to really listen and concentrate and to enjoy good music. But that was what he was going to do now, since there wasn't any news.

He thought about getting his fishing gear, but instead he leaned back and just enjoyed the music of Charlotte and other classical music.

All of a sudden he realized he wasn't alone.

He about jumped out of his pants when he suddenly got splashed. At first he thought a nuclear sub had surfaced right alongside *SASSY* until he realized the sub was swimming.

Swimming right alongside was a whale nearly as long as *SASSY*. It had just surfaced and spouted. A lot of which bathed Birch.

"Hey, watch it, buddy."

The whale watched Birch when he stood up and poured out his coffee and refilled his cup from the thermos. "No more belching, if you please." Birch and the whale watched each other for not more than a minute, then Birch turned away to see the surroundings and if there were any other whales around.

Birch was silently grateful that at least some of the sea life survived. He also was momentarily disappointed that the whale wasn't a sub with human life aboard.

"Do you like Spam? You're lucky I didn't bring my fishing rod up from below." As he stood there talking to the whale, he wondered if his leader and tiny little hook would hold a billion-pound whale. "It's a good thing I wasn't fishing. I always eat what I hook, you know. I don't believe in that catch and release crap. And you are extremely lucky my freezer is full."

Birch turned the volume up. It wasn't long before he noticed he wasn't the only one enjoying Charlotte's singing. The whale seemed to be taken with Charlotte too.

Charlotte finished and the classical music started, and the whale almost drowned Birch as he dove and swam away. About fifteen minutes later the whale returned and edged right up like he did before.

"Hey buddy, for a minute there I thought you didn't like classical music." Birch said to the whale, and all of a sudden, very quietly, another much smaller whale surfaced alongside the much bigger whale. Birch continued talking softly to the big whale. "Well, I see you brought a buddy along for the concert.

Wait a minute; your pal there seems awfully small. Small like a baby! That wouldn't be your baby would it? That's it. That's your baby. You're a mom. You're not a he after all." Birch poured another cup, and all three listened to the music and watched the horizon. It seemed they were headed the same direction.

Birch had a strange sense of wonderment; it seemed that the animal life seemed to be drawn closer together now. Any life form whatever, whoever, or wherever was company to be desired.

The flotilla was still together when they rounded Point Franklin and were passing the Wainwright DEW line site. Birch was next to the shoreline, as the water was deep enough to allow him that close. He didn't need the binoculars to see the bottom portion of the radar dome and part of the radio tower that was still standing. He also didn't need the binoculars to see that everything else was gone. There was no reason to stop or land. He plotted the GPS position and compass bearings on the chart and set the next waypoint for Icy Cape.

"Well, I guess I won't have to learn Russian to speak to you. For a while there as far as I knew, we could have been off the coast of Russia. You could have been Russian. But I'm pretty sure I know where we are." Mama seemed to be paying attention to everything he was saying.

Birch leaned out to the side of the turret and said to the whales, "Hey, Mom, would you and Baby like to stop or maybe need a rest stop?" Mom had been watching the horizon in front of them, but now she focused on him. She didn't give any other response. It didn't appear that Mom and the baby whale wanted to stop either. "I'll take that as a no."

"Ah, some new visitors." A pair of gulls circled the ship and the whales. How did you guys survive? Birch wondered. They look healthy enough, but I'm sure not going to feed them. The next thing you know, they'll have all their friends and neighbors over for cocktails.

Was it Birch's imagination that all animal life seemed to be a little closer, or interconnected somewhat or somehow, after whatever had happened recently?

When the CDs quit playing, the whales swam off ahead. They swam right along as *SASSY* had been doing, five knots as long as Birch kept the sails trimmed. He went below and made a sandwich and followed up with a short nap.

Later that evening Birch was watching a few walrus on both the ice pack and on the barrier islands near shore. How did they survive? Usually there would be upwards of a hundred or more when you saw walrus.

He dropped the sail, raised the keels, and started the diesel before entering the lagoon at Icy Cape near the point where a part of the tower remained. Icy Cape runway was listed at forty-eight-feet-above sea level. The radar dome panels were gone, but some of the framework remained. The concrete station remained but looked to be half buried in beach gravel. Birch sounded the foghorn. From the looks of things, he would be amazed to see or hear any response. Just as every other place he had seen, Icy Cape looked to have been swept clean by the waters and wind. He dropped the anchor and called it a day. He would go exploring in the morning.

The next morning he was awakened by a loud thump and rocking of the ship. "What now?"

He opened the hatch topside and looked out to see a huge walrus trying to make it up onto the deck. *SASSY* wasn't having any part of this with her sloping sides, and every time the walrus tried to leap up, *SASSY* would just roll out from under the walrus. Birch ran to the bridge turret and gave three long blasts of the foghorn. That stopped the walrus's amorous attacks. Either that or the walrus thought *SASSY* was a big red walrus cot, and he was ready for a nap. Birch was worried that the big bull would crush the solar panels mounted on the sides of the ship.

Birch pulled up the anchor and nosed up to the beach. He tied off to a partially buried timber and proceeded over to the concrete structure. He knelt down and looked in the top where one of the windows used to be; the sand, gravel, and mud were all level inside with the outside. He walked around to the back where the shop was. The overhead doors were gone, and the top of the loader and grader were sticking out of the gravel. He went inside and, where he had to, he crawled around just to make sure every room was empty. No indication that anyone made it through the Big One.

He left right away. He told himself he did not want to be caught by the tide inside the lagoon. He was relieved when he was at sea, and that place was behind him.

Spooky.

Next stop was Cape Lisburne, an air force long-range radar station, about 143 miles as the raven flies. He would be hugging the coastline when the storm came up. He wasn't hugging the coast *in case* a storm came up. It was a matter of when. Today was bright and sunny, though, once he was a couple of miles offshore. He made a thermos of coffee, put the music on, and went up to the forward deck He set the coffee down and turned up the volume on the same music as yesterday. After opening the solar hatches, he went up front and unfolded the turret seat and was enjoying the view when out of the blue Big Bird landed on the mast after announcing her arrival.

"You have been traveling a long way haven't you?" The bird looked healthy and strong. Evidently she was eating well, but he went below and dished up some Spam and brought it back up and placed it on the other lip of the turret a few feet away. He waited and watched to see what Big Gulp would do. It didn't take long before the eagle swooped down and took care of the Spam and cleaned her plate.

Soon after that the eagle crapped her pants and did a back flip when Mom surfaced and spouted and sprayed slobber all over Birch and Big Bird. After a few minutes of carrying on and ruining Charlotte's songs, the eagle was back on her perch, looking down on that big fish. Mom dove but was back after a few minutes with Baby.

Birch couldn't quit laughing. "Boy! You should have seen your face when Mom surfaced. That was hysterical. I should have had the video camera rolling. I'm sorry, but that was one of the funniest things I have ever seen. You know, if I had a video of your somersault, we would win the grand prize. You should come down from there, these ocean swells wouldn't toss you around so much. Well, suit yourself."

"How about you, Mom? Where did you go? I thought you were way ahead of us when you swam off yesterday.*" Do you guy's sleep?* he wondered. *And if you do sleep, do you just stop where you are, or do you have to keep swimming.*

"Well, we got ourselves a convoy," Captain Ahab (Birch) said, to no one in particular, "a big fish, a bird, a machine, and a humanoid marching, swimming, flying, and steering off into the wild blue yonder."

The whales and *SASSY* kept up with each other for the next couple of hours before the whales swam off ahead, and that's when Birch spotted the polar bear sniffing the air on the ice pack. He veered over closer to the ice pack to get a better look at the bear. *How did he possibly survive?* The bear looked good and healthy. When the bear stood on his hind legs, sniffing the air and eye-balling them, Big Bird took off for parts unknown, and Birch turned back on course.

Birch figured he would be more than half way to Cape Lisburne by nightfall and would hole up in the lagoon somewhere past Point Lay. And that's what he did when he passed Point Lay. He found a gap in the barrier islands and anchored close to the mouth of one of two rivers in the area. He didn't know for sure which one, but he was going to find out if there were any grayling in the river. He was glad he had his hip boots on, because he was sinking up to his ankles as he hiked over to a likely spot near the mouth of the river. He caught three large grayling in about three minutes with his Top Secret lure, the one he got out of a catalog. *You don't see any grayling of this size around Fairbanks anymore.* He hadn't seen any this big since he was a kid. Most of the area is catch and release. *He wasn't going to fish for something he couldn't eat.*

Three were more than enough for him; he wanted them fresh, as he didn't care for them once they were frozen. A grayling is one of the best white fish around, and his absolute favorite fish. He hurried back to the boat and got the grill out. He did notice they were a little on the slim side, but looked good and gave a strong fight. He thought by the looks of them that they had been eating, but whatever they were eating might be a little on the scarce side.

Some fine, fine grayling, baked potato, and a little red vino. Where did I put those cigars?

Birch decided to hole up where he was for a while. He was in a protected lagoon, unless the seas really turned bad and came across the barrier islands. That was the problem; not knowing what the weather was going to do. It didn't look like it was going to be a good day to go sailing. He felt it was going to get stormy and rough. A good day to catch up on his reading. He had found a good book: *Sailing for Birch and Dummies*.

Four days later and early in the morning before six, Birch was underway, heading straight for Cape Lisburne. From the charts it didn't look like there were many, if any, good places to duck into if the weather turned bad again. So he took the direct route as much as the ice would allow. He was roughly eighty-eight miles away. He should make Cape Lisburne, according to his navigational skills and Viking background, roughly by nightfall. Where did he put that sailing book? He needed to review that section on "roughly" (the stab-in-the-dark-and-rough-guess section). He also wondered if passing through Norway once constituted a Viking background.

Birch found out where the polar bear was heading when he had seen the bear a few days ago sniffing the air. There was a small herd of seals sunning themselves on the edge of the ice pack. Birch veered over closer to the seals but not so close to scare the seals, although he did scare them, as most dove into the water, but not all of them. A half dozen raised their heads and watched him as he sailed by.

When he passed Cape Lisburne he plotted his positions and made circles just offshore and sounded his foghorn every few minutes. While he was circling, he kept his telescope on the 2,034-foot-high mountain, looking and watching for any signs of life. Since Cape Lisburne was about sixteen feet above sea level and looked to be in the same condition as all the other DEW sites he had stopped at, he did not go ashore. As he continued to circle, he set his next waypoint for five miles offshore of Point Hope. He sounded a long blast on the horn and circled twice more, taking a last look through the telescope. Then he headed out on his new bearing, watching the mountain and hoping beyond hope to see a sign of anything, possibly smoke, until the mountain disappeared.

Birch spotted a couple of large whales in the distance, and he turned the music and volume up, but the whales didn't seem to notice. He was sure they were not Mom and Baby. He thought about why the whales and the eagle had kept him company for so long. And he was glad for the company. They might have been as lonely as he was. The eagle he could understand. She was a pushover for an easy handout.

Birch cleaned up and got everything ready for the night. He had decided to keep sailing while he grabbed a few hours of sleep since the ice pack was farther to the west as he went south. He set all of the bells and whistles and called out over the radio and listened for a while before he hit the sack.

Birch was in a funk, dreading what he would find at Point Hope, fourteen feet above sea level. It had been years since he had been there, but he still had friends there. Friends that he had gone to school with. He had become friends with one of the kids when they were both in the eighth grade. He eventually became one of whaling captains of Point. Hope, and Birch would see him and his wife every few years when they came to Fairbanks for a few days. Finally he fell asleep but seemed to toss and turn most of the night.

When the waypoint let him know he had arrived, it was still dark and foggy. He let down the sail and let *SASSY* drift with the current, then he would motor back to the waypoint until sunup and the fog lifted. When the sun came up and the fog finally lifted, he found that the village of Point Hope was gone. The sharp point was no longer there. The coastline that he followed south to Point Hope had been rounded off by close to ten miles as it continued south and southeast.

Birch was losing hope of finding any survivors in these low-lying coastal areas. He set a course to head for Kotzebue and then go inland. He sat sail and set a new waypoint by the village of Kivalina, a strip of land between the ocean and a lake that was about as wide as Band-Aid. Kivalina was a small village, he remembered, and when he was a youngster, it had maybe about one hundred people, like Point Hope, mostly made up of hunters and their families. Birch, on one of his trips flying around to all the different villages surrounding the Kotzebue area, did land there when he was a teenager and riding with one of the brothers. The two older brothers were bush pilots who flew out of Kotzebue, their home base. Birch was always skipping school to fly with one or the other of the boys. They landed at Kivalina on the gravel strip between the beach and the graveyard. If he hadn't had so much trust in both of the brother pilots, he would have sworn they were going to crash in the graveyard, as they had to keep one wing up higher than the other because the beach strip sloped sideways. That was a tricky landing. Nothing is ever easy. We were there to pick up a couple of passengers who wanted passage to Kotzebue. That was a long time ago, and the Kivalina population had probably

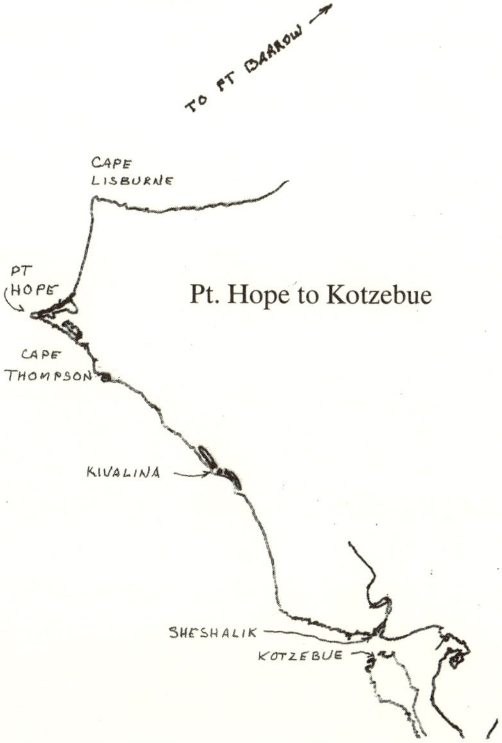

Pt. Hope to Kotzebue

doubled. Point Hope would have grown quite a bit, affected by both village and regional Native corporations that came out of the Alaska Native Land Claims Act. Plus being infected with borough, state, and, federal bureaucracies would have really inflated the populations, probably more so at Point Hope.

That ended one way of life: The traditional Native way of life by being contaminated with borough, state, and federal bureaucracies.

On the way to the village site, Birch swung close to shore where they used to go duck hunting. He remembered years ago the thousands of ducks, geese, and swans in the area along the coast. He did see a few birds now; hoping it was because it was so late in the season and year. Most would have already headed south in their migration. He wouldn't mind a roasted duck, but there weren't that many, so he passed them by and continued on his way. As soon as he decided to continue, the ducks and geese honked and hooted and took to the air. One of the ducks was dive-bombed, and feather shrapnel littered the air.

About an hour later the guilty party screeched and landed atop of the mast.

"I saw that, 'chicken wings.' You should hang your head. Bad bird. Bad bird. You could have brought me a leg or a thigh. Bad bird. Bad bird. And you probably won't leave any eggs will you? Bad, bad bird."

Screech!

Chapter Seven
The Search

Birch and crew had turned into Kotzebue Sound and had been holed up for going on three days now behind a spit of land called Sheshalik across from Kotzebue, waiting for the seas to calm down. At one time, in years past, Kotzebue was the largest Eskimo village in Alaska.

"Feathers" evidently had been tracking him and keeping him company as they camped out.

Birch remembered a time when he was a boy and he was with several of the hunters in their boat duck hunting. One of the bush-pilot brothers spotted the ducks and dropped down and made a wide circle over them and began herding the birds toward the hunters. The sky turned dark when all the ducks and geese took flight, blocking out the sun, thousands and thousands of them.

Upon entering Kotzebue Sound, he remembered watching the Native people walking back and forth on the sandbar just offshore from Sheshalik, trying to find the unmarked channel.

Water covered the sandbar by just a few inches and was murky enough you couldn't see the channel. If you missed it, you had to find it by feel, walking back and forth. Today, even with the depth gauge, he almost beached on the sandbar, though he was creeping along, looking for the channel through the sandbar. He couldn't back off without using the rear thrusters, turning the *SASSY*'s hind end back and forth. Going parallel to the bar, he found the channel by using the depth gauge. He hadn't missed it by more than two hundred feet. Not too shabby after all these years. They tried to try and stay within two points to locate the channel in the sandbar: one of the points was a hill behind Kotzebue and the other point was a hill north of Sheshalik. That worked when the weather didn't obscure the hills as it did now.

Crossing the fourteen miles from Sheshalik to Kotzebue, he would have to find the channel again. At a crawl, he kept close watch on the depth gauge until he found the channel and was through, then he poured the coals to *SASSY.*

The only thing he could see, of what used to be Kotzebue, was a large fuel oil tank, and he headed for the tank on the dock, or at least where the dock was supposed to be. The fuel tank was the only thing left of the village. Kotzebue was only about nine feet above sea level to begin with. The dock was gone, but the tank remained on what was now a gravel pad. He turned *SASSY* to the south and followed the beach for a ways and surveyed the damage. All of the houses were gone, and only parts of a couple of concrete foundations remained. There was no debris or trash. A couple pieces of equipment, a heavy dozer and a grader, were rolled over and partially sunk in the muddy gravel. The local gravel had always been poor and made crappy concrete. If you wanted good gravel to make concrete, they always hauled it in from other places.

When he returned north back up to the beach, he tied off to the large tank. He found it full to the top, which meant the tug pulling the fuel barge made its way up the coast from Seattle and topped this tank off with No. 1 Diesel oil. The only thing that could have saved it was its own weight and being round, allowing the surging waters go around it, not offering any resistance. He thought if the Big One happened before being topped-off, it would have been washed away.

So far Birch hadn't used much diesel fuel, since he had been able to use the sail and had made just as good time as if he had used the diesel engine. But he was going to top off his tank because he knew this tank was full of the winter's supply of No. 1 heating fuel. He just had to figure out how to rig some hoses and not create a spill. He was amazed that the big tank was not leaking. He could tell from the paint on the tank that the tank was almost new.

He did rig up a rubber hose by reducing down the drainpipe and running the hose to one of the barrels. He had a funnel and filter that he put on the barrel, and by just cracking a small valve he could filter and fill the barrel. That was the good news. The bad news was that he would have to hand pump the barrel into *SASSY*'s tank or drink a gallon or two of diesel before he could get the fuel to siphon into the tank. That's the way it always worked in the past, anyway. When they were kids he made sure he never belched near an open flame for a few days after stealing gas for the car. He always swallowed more gas than he syphoned.

He left Kotzebue feeling really down with the loss of adopted family and all the good friends and good memories. He was underway on his quest, still heading for the nearest good quantity of firewood that he knew of. That was on the Kobuk River, or close to it. He headed inland east, across Kobuk Lake toward the mouth of the Kobuk River delta. The closer he got to the delta, he realized the delta was gone, rearranged or submerged. Hotham Inlet was more like Hotham Sound. The inlet was much wider now, and the mouths of the main channels leading to the Kobuk were not visible and not where they should be. Kobuk Lake, Hotham Inlet, and Selawik Lake now appeared to be one big Sound. He would follow it around to the east looking for the mouth of the river.

Captain Ahab lost track of the whales during the rough trip along the coast. He hoped they wouldn't come this way and get beached on the Kobuk River delta. Some of the channels were too shallow for them.

While he was under sail, he got out his Top Secret lure and trolled in the lake for a minute or two and landed a small twenty-six-inch sheefish, which he shared with Big Bird, who attacked her portion like she hadn't eaten in days. Birch found it fascinating that the eagle had been staying close as they made their way south. It was cooling off, and he wouldn't be surprised if they didn't get some snow before very long. Looking at the eagle, he wondered how long before it headed for parts unknown to the south. The eagle could stay ahead of the weather, but Birch wouldn't be able to. He had to hole up for the winter someplace. Someplace where there is firewood.

Three days later Birch was sailing east along a rift that had formed a gash, cutting through the thirty-mile-long Selawik Lake and the wetland complexes beyond. He remembered the alpine

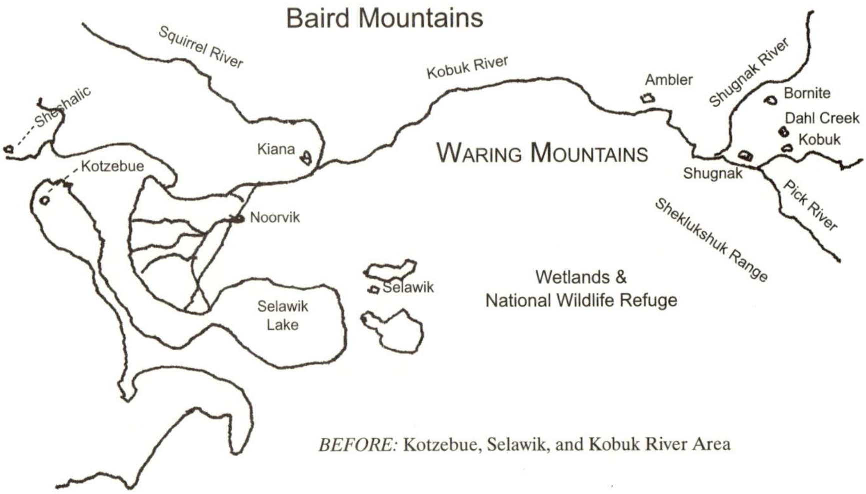

BEFORE: Kotzebue, Selawik, and Kobuk River Area

tundra, arctic tundra, taiga, open grass, sedge meadows, and low-lying muskeg ponds and twenty thousand lakes running west to east. From Kobuk Lake past Selawik almost to the Pick River and up to the villages of Shungnak and Kobuk, it was a distance of almost 150 miles. In some places he now found the rift to be over thirty miles across. And in other places the rift was over three hundred feet deep, and in one part deeper than his depth gauge would indicate. The rift appeared to be two hundred feet deep as he passed over the village of Selawik.

Looking off in the distance to the east, he was seeing indications of volcanic activity. Looking both to port and starboard, the weather was turning stormy, wet and cold. The rain was almost freezing as it came down.

Later, after the deck was washed clean by the heavy rain, he opened the rain scuttles for a while and filled the water tank, which didn't take long. This was probably the last time this winter. Next time would be in the spring of next year unless he found an open spring running somewhere. He would keep watch for such a spring when he got closer to the mountains where he was headed. A good, clean, and clear stream or river water would do nicely too.

Every once in awhile since entering the Kotzebue Sound, he had tried the CB channels. With the flat terrain and open

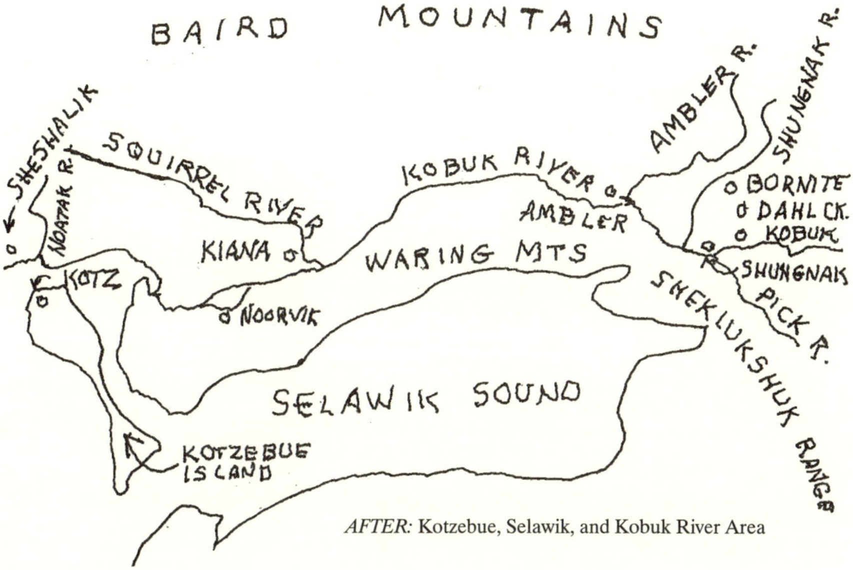

AFTER: Kotzebue, Selawik, and Kobuk River Area

waters, the line of site of the CB radio waves would travel a long ways. So he kept trying and even telling jokes over the radio to keep his spirits up. He knew he was still fighting depression. Talking to Big Bird and threatening to throw her into the stew pot probably helped Birch keep his sanity. Feathers was shrill, but he was glad for the company.

Birch brought down a couple of ducks with the shotgun and tried his hand at roasting one with some wild rice. *Should have videoed Big Bird's acrobatics and her fowl language when the shotgun went off.*

When he offered Big Bird some of the wild rice and roasted duck leftovers, she sniffed the plate and voiced her opinion of his gourmet meal.

Screech! She waddled off a ways and then took off.

She seemed to like the fish, though. "Persnickety!" Oops! He tried to cut back on his trash mouth when the youngster was around.

A few hours later when he went back topside, Birch found a big feather ball perched on top of one of the rear turret antennas preening herself. There was a pile of feathers, blood, and guts all around the bottom of the antenna.

"So you didn't care for the meal I cooked for you. After I slaved over a hot stove for hours, you went to your local market and cooked your own. A little rare, don't you think?" You had better have this mess cleaned up before you go to bed, or you are going to end up on the barbie. You got that 'chicken roast'?"

Screech.

The weather cleared, and the eagle stayed close during the day but took to the hills for the night. Maybe looking for friends, or maybe she was just tired of Spam.

He kept close to the northern shoreline and tied off whenever the fog rolled in, not wanting to miss the mouth of the Kobuk River or any other rivers. He was under sail, taking it real slow, keeping watch on the coastline with his binoculars and looking for any signs of activity. As the days went on, he did pass many streams and small rivers but nothing the size of the Kobuk. Birch thought the Kobuk could have been dammed up or redirected.

He should have found the mouth by now.

At the very east end of this big new gash in the earth, what was once a valley pass between the mountains was now similar to one of the fjords found in the southcentral part of the state.

This area somehow looked to be spared of the destruction he had witnessed so far on his journey. Now he was at the edge of the mountains and forest. He would have thought the water that rolled into this new rift would have rolled up the mountainside. But evidently there had been no tidal wave. The rift must have filled somewhat slower than a massive inrush of water. The only noticeable thing in this immediate area was all the wind-blown trees knocked down. Not all, by any means, but still quite a few.

"Firewood at last. Firewood at last." *Shut up, Birch, that sounds familiar.*

He sailed east as far as he could go with the boat by feeling his way and watching the depth gauge. He decided to tie up at the mouth of a fairly good-size stream but still shallow enough to wade across. Actually, this was a very pretty spot; the stream was bordered by tall white spruce and birch trees—couldn't find a better camping spot.

The sun was out, and he had repositioned *SASSY* parallel to shore to take full advantage of the sun on the solar panels. He turned the valve to fill the heat panel collectors to heat up the water tank while he went exploring. Nothing like a hot shower after exploring, he always said.

Birch went over the side and walked to the stream, took one look, and turned around and climbed back aboard *SASSY*. He decided he needed his fishing rod, as the stream was teeming with a late run of salmon. He also decided he needed his "BB" gun, as he had spotted grizzly tracks on the stream bank. The track was real fresh. The tracks were real big, too.

Birch didn't know what kind of salmon these were. He didn't know one from the other, a chum from a dog, a chinook from a pink or a sockeye from a coho, except for the kings. You can always tell the king salmon from the others, though, by their size because they are much larger. He wasn't sure, but he did think kings were called Chinooks. He just never paid that much attention to the different kinds of salmon. *Details, Details*, he thought. *Things like that gave me headaches.*

However, he could sure tell the difference between the salmon and a grizzly. So he strapped his .44 magnum on and threw his carbine rifle over his shoulder. If those wouldn't keep a bear away, he'd just whip him with his fishing rod. Stings, yeah, that can really sting. He had found out from first-hand experience when he laughed at a tiny little fish that his girlfriend had hooked. He tried to tell her he wasn't laughing—he was just having a coughing fit.

On the first cast with his Top Secret lure, the one sold in all the catalogs, it barely got wet before what he assumed was an arctic char took it. The char was following the salmon and taking the salmon eggs where the salmon were spawning. He cut off a willow fork and strung the char and a salmon through the gills and put them back in the water to keep them fresh while he decided to go exploring.

He left the rod by the boat and headed off to climb a nearby small mountain, or a big hill, to see what he could see. On his way up he wished he had brought a pail or bag. There must be a thousand cranberries to the square foot. Well, maybe he was stretching it a bit, but the side of this small mountain (or high hill) was covered with the berries. Still some blueberries here and there, but not enough to make it worthwhile, as it was too late in the season for blueberries, but just the right time for the cranberries. Just before the frost, tomorrow he would spend a good part of the day picking his vitamin pills and finding a way to dry the berries. He might be able to freeze some if he got enough. Birch did not have anything with him like cranberries, naturally rich in vitamins. Since he hadn't passed any drug stores or pharmacies lately, these cranberries could help, he hoped, in preventing scurvy and protecting his longevity, as he didn't have a garden for vegetables.

Continuing up the hill, he could see what he thought should be the Pick River valley. Shungnak should be about fifteen miles northeast and five more miles upriver to Kobuk from where he stood, if he was right. He looked around where he was standing: flat enough on top and large enough to make camp for several families. He suspected that people of the area had used this point for hundreds of years and maybe longer, as a lookout point to see the caribou when they migrated from place to place. This area to the west no longer looked the same now. More than once, before the valley was rearranged and it was still a wide valley, he remembered flying back and forth from Kotzebue to Fairbanks throughout the years. During the winter you could see caribou tracks from one side to the other. They had to be in the thousands. Birch had seen many caribou when they were moving but nothing like the herds that had moved through this valley. Like a monstrous cattle drive thirty miles wide. He would have liked to have seen that. Standing there, he could imagine the Natives watching for the caribou to arrive and getting ready for the hunt. Caribou was a big part of these inland Eskimo people's diet. They used the hides for their winter clothing, and the elders still do to some extent. If he recalled correctly, the fur of the caribou hair was hollow, and clothing or anything made of caribou hide was extremely warm.

Birch also had to remind himself that from now on he would have to watch his every step. The ground near the bottom of the hill and the muskeg ahead back to the stream was made up of hummocks that grew closely together, and when you step on top of one hummock it could roll to one side, or if you miss your step and step in between, your leg could sink down to about knee high. This tundra was extremely tough walking, and it would be very easy to break an ankle or twist a knee. What if he did break an ankle? He would have no help if he were injured. You didn't walk very far on this type of ground; besides, most of the time it was cold and wet. *I hate cold and wet! What was that 911 number again?*

Returning back to the mouth of the stream, he was careful like he had been when going up the hill, so that when nearing the brush and willows he wouldn't disturb Big Bear, taking a catnap with a belly full of salmon.

He got back to the mouth of the stream in the nick of time. "Hey, chicken gizzard, get your own fish." Big Bird was creeping up to the edge of the stream where Birch had put his fish in the water. The eagle fluttered down the bank a few feet. "Don't want to get your feet wet getting your own, huh?"

Birch looked around for some firewood, something dry. He was going to cook this fish over a wood fire. He gathered up some sticks and twigs. The eagle had flown up to the top of one of the taller spruce trees and watched the human idiot who was going to ruin a delicious piece of fish by throwing it on a fire. "Hey, girl, you got any matches?"

He went to the boat and put some cornmeal and flour into a big baggie. Got some foil, a plate, a potato, salt and pepper, and some matches and returned to the stream. He finally got a small fire going, and after letting some bigger stuff turn to embers he left a potato in foil to bake while he cleaned the fish and filleted them. Birch took a small piece from each of the fish, the salmon and char, and dipped them into the baggie of batter and rolled them around real good so they were both covered well with the batter. He threaded two pieces onto a willow branch and supported them over the small fire and let them cook. Birch was interested to see if he had any preference for the char or the salmon. While the fish were cooking, he got up and retrieved the rifle he'd leaned against a tree and moved it closer. He still had the .44 strapped on, just in case.

Birch had already given Big Bird a cooked piece of both fish and a piece of both sashimi-style. He didn't watch the eagle eat, as he was watching the fire, but later he noticed it was all gone. That was really good, and he hadn't made up his mind which was better, the salmon or the char. He wished he had brought a lemon with the rest of the stuff from the boat. Onions would have been nice too. Earlier he had spotted what he thought were wild onions, and he would have to check that out. *Heck, I might get the hang of this survival thing yet.*

He packed a lunch and thermos of coffee, put it into a five-gallon pail, and strapped it to his backpack along with a couple large baggies and set off to the berry patch. Actually, there were berries everywhere. It was drier on the hill, though, where he could sit down. Picking berries was hard work, very strenuous, he thought. If he was going to do such physically hard work, he deserved to do it where he could sit down. And of course if he overdid it, he could lean back and rest his eyes in the sun for a few minutes. *After all that work it would only be fair,* he thought. *After all that hard physical work.*

Three gallons later, shortly after lunch and a short siesta, he headed back to the ship, washed the berries, and put two gallons in the freezer. He grabbed a large towel and laid it out on the deck and spread the remaining berries out to dry. A few berries would be good on his cereal. He would have to learn how to make cranberry muffins to go with the salmon this winter that he had yet to catch. Still room in the freezer for a few more salmon.

The salmon right at the mouth of the stream were still solid, firm, and overall in very good shape, but after going upstream to their spawning grounds they would spawn, die and decompose and give nutrients to other life. When they were decomposing and washed up on the bank, you hoped the wind was blowing away from you, or that the rivers would freeze over, one or the other you didn't care which. Stinky!

Three days later he finally filled the freezer with a good supply of salmon for the winter, more than enough, really. Taking stock of things aboard *SASSY*, Birch thought, *I've been on a fish diet since leaving Fairbanks and haven't made a dent in all the steaks I have aboard. Lots of canned vegetables and fruit. No fresh salad material or fruit besides the berries.*

SASSY has the latest in technology when it comes to insulation and consequently has used very little propane. The main tank is still practically full, plus I haven't touched the propane bottles topside, so that takes care of the primary heating and refrigeration. Diesel tank is full, as we, me and Big Bird, were under sail for the most part, except for the tricky unknown docking and beaching. Plus we topped off the tank in Kotzebue with the No. 1 diesel fuel and sailed from there to here.

Yes, he thought, this is as good as any place to anchor up for the winter.

Birch temporarily tied *SASSY* off with bow to shore. Then he tied off with a hawser rope, high on the largest tree he could reach and still have plenty of slack in the heavy rope. He set an aft anchor out a ways and left slack to a Japanese float, large enough to handle the anchor. The float should stay on top of the ice. The anchor set was placed directly below the buoy, with the idea that if something drastic were to occur before breakup and the ice going out, he could raise the anchor through a hole chopped in the ice, disconnecting the rope from the anchor chain and pull the rope under the ice back to the boat.

He didn't think there was much of a tide here, but he left slack in the ropes for a fairly large wave caused by earthquakes.

Such was his plan for something drastic happening. Like has *drastic*" happened anytime lately?

Birch still had a little prepping before freeze up and winter setting in. He set about washing *SASSY* down with clean, fresh water from the stream. He especially wanted to wash the salt off the solar panels and the rest of the boat while he was at it, along with the "feather duster's" poop. He looked up and the feather duster was sitting high on the spruce tree, looking down at him.

"Hey, "chicken thighs," you're definitely going in the soup pot if you don't stop messing up my deck."

Screech. Screech. Screech!

Birch thought that must mean nag, nag, nag in eagle talk.

He pulled *SASSY*'s hind end a little more to the north, into an indentation in the bank where he could let the ramp down with a little brush cutting, if needed, for access to the four-wheelers or snow machine. Where she was now allowed *SASSY* to take full advantage of the solar panels, which supplemented the heating, refrigeration, and charging the batteries. *Solar panels also heat the water for my seasonal showers*, Birch thought. He also sprayed the solar panels' cam locks with WD-40 for the winter.

Pantry is stocked up for several people for long durations, but there is only me. Cranberries galore, what more could a guy ask for? All and all, I'm in good shape—at least for the winter.

* * * * *

Birch always enjoyed this time of year in the late fall, like here and now. The birch trees were turning colorful and mostly golden. It was chilly and sunny, not a cloud in the sky. Neither were there any vapor trails in the sky.

Birch and Big Bird were on deck enjoying the sun, and he was having his morning coffee. He asked Big Bird, "What do you think happened? What caused all this damage?"

Birch had noticed the coastal area had, for the most part, been swept clean while a few areas had not suffered damage from the tsunami waves. It gave the appearance of giant eddies sweeping along the coast, though the winds seemed to have touched everywhere. There was damage everywhere but not to the extreme here in this valley, very little damage in fact. Maybe the continental divide and the Brooks Range had provided some protection from the tsunami waves. Then what caused the violent shaking and the upheaval to the surface to the planet? What caused the new volcanos appearing where there had never been before? Whatever it was, it sure wobbled the earth for a few days.

He gradually came to suspect that it was not caused by any meteor or comet's impact to the planet. If there had been, he suspected he would have seen more sky blocked out by dust and less damage the world over by tsunami waves. He had already ruled out nuclear warfare. The only other thing he could think of would be the eruption from a super volcano or mega volcano the likes of Yellowstone Park or Toba in Sumatra, Indonesia. He also had read about one located in the Atlantic; he couldn't remember exactly where, though. He also remembered that more recent eruptions of Mount Pinatubo and Krakatoa; as large as they were, they were nowhere near the scale of the super volcanos.

During the next two weeks Birch and his hunting partner did a good bit of exploring the neighborhood. Together they found and shared a few willow grouse, or spruce hens. Birch didn't know one bird from the other, like the salmon. *I should have paid more attention when I was out hunting, fishing, and camping with friends when I was a kid.*

He had only shot one moose right after he got out of the army and found out right away he didn't know the first thing about cleaning animals. It took hours to get it quartered and loaded up; it turned out to be a really good moose, though. It was a big moose with a small rack, young, he guessed. He fished for grayling on occasion and enjoyed camping, canoeing, and panning for gold but never really hunted again.

Big Bird and Birch enjoyed their fishing time everyday up and down the stream. Birch fished only for one or two grayling—just enough for dinner. Big Bird, on the other hand, didn't care what kind of fish she went after. Nope! Not choosy at all, and her table manners sucked, but he wouldn't tell anyone.

They had a good time.

It was definitely cooling off. Fall was here.

It's a good thing his food stores were in good shape, as the next morning ice was forming on the edges of the fjord and stream. He didn't need to feed the eagle; she had taken a liking to the salmon farther upstream in the shallow water. Easy pickin's for her, but they were now thinning out. Birch guessed the run was almost over. He went over to the side of the boat deck and looked down into the water at the mouth of the stream, and for the first time in the last couple of weeks, he did not see any salmon, not one.

He gave a slice of bacon to Big Bird, her daily treat, which she seemed to really enjoy. This morning, though, she just seemed to just play with it.

In fact, Big Bird appeared nervous or restless. She was moving all over the place, up to the mast, back to the turret, up to the top of a nearby spruce tree, and all the while she was fluttering around, making tiny screeches, like she was whimpering. Birch looked all around and up the stream. Did she smell or see a bear? He couldn't see or hear anything out of the ordinary. Suddenly she dropped down from the spruce tree and landed right next to him. He knelt down and scratched her head and neck, looked her in the eye, and asked, "What's wrong girl? Are you feeling sick or something?"

With a small whimper she took off over the side of the ship, climbing and circling overhead until she was at least two thousand feet high before she rolled on her back and dove toward him. Just like a fighter plane. She continued down, doing acrobatics that he had never seen her do before. She was swooping down and dive bombing so close to him he felt the air moving from her flight. From there she screeched as she climbed until she found the winds high above, circled, and disappeared to the south.

"She was saying good-bye."

Birch went below to lie down in his bunk. He didn't stir or get out of bed for two days.

Chapter Eight
Freezeup

Two weeks later he got up early and went topside to find six more inches of fresh snow on the deck, and it was still coming down hard. The temperature had really fallen, and the ice had enclosed *SASSY*. She wasn't going anywhere until next spring. Birch wasn't concerned about the possibility of the ice crushing the bottom of the ship. He had specifically designed the sloping hull and had his team confirm the design of the slope to avoid crushing. The more the ice expanded and froze around *SASSY*, the higher she would rise above the ice. In other words, the ice would expand, lift, and slide under, keeping *SASSY* sitting on top of the ice.

It continued to snow with the winds growing stronger, and all the while the ice covered more and more of the fjord and completely iced over the stream. When this storm blew over, he was going exploring; he planned to follow the stream for a ways and then turn northeast to where he thought he could intercept and follow the Pick River to the Kobuk River.

Waiting for the weather to improve, Birch had plenty of time to think about what had happened in the last several months. One of the things, he realized, was how much he missed the eagle. At least he had someone to talk to while she was around. He had always thought he was more of a loner type. He found out he was wrong, and it surprised him how alone he felt.

Birch decided to keep busy so he wouldn't dwell on the fact that Big Bird wasn't around to pester him.

He made a list and revised it ten times, trying to make his pack lighter by deciding which things he thought would be needed and other things that he would like to have "just in case." There wasn't any way he could put everything in a pack and carry it. He would have to use the toboggan. The one Birch had put aboard *SASSY* to tote groceries and supplies back and forth during the winter months between the drilling camp and where the survival ship was staged. The ship wouldn't have been staged too far away but far enough to avoid fires or dangerous sulfide gases if a blowout ever occurred. Now he would put the sled to good use for a different purpose.

He spent a week packing, unpacking, and reloading his supplies on the polyurethane toboggan. He put a few extra items in the pack, so that if he had to he could get to it quickly without having to unlash the cover and unload the sled, in case something happened to the toboggan or it got wet. The pack would be tied on top of the sled. From now on he would be wearing his "bunny boots" when outside during the winter months. Especially when leaving or getting away from *SASSY* for any distance or length of time. He knew that feet do not last very long in leather or light-weight rubber boots when the temperature drops below zero. The air-insulated bunny boots had kept his feet warm at sixty-degrees below all day long when he was on his knees, bolting up split culvert on one of his previous jobs early on in Tok, two hundred miles south of Fairbanks.

Originally, bunny boots were big, bulky, white felt boots with ankle straps developed by the army. Later they adopted big white rubber boots with an air pocket and air valve for use when flying. At high altitudes the air pocket expands in unpressurized airplanes, and air is released. The air pocket acts like a thermos bottle, keeping your feet warm. The air pocket can also do just the opposite: keep your feet freezing for a very long time if you put them on at forty degrees below zero; Birch knew this from firsthand experience.

The windblown snow was usually hard enough to walk on along the arctic coast, but occasionally skis were helpful if you were going any distance. The skis that he had brought along were a military cross country-type that fit the bunny boots. It was still too early for the snow machine. The ice wasn't yet thick enough to support the weight of the snow machine. It would need another two weeks of below-zero temps for the ice to get thick enough over the streams and rivers. It was also doubtful that there was a trail from where he was to where he wanted to go; at least until he was on the Pick, then he would follow the river. Been a long time, but once he was on the Kobuk he knew, in general, where to find the trails. In order to get back and forth between the Pick River and the stream, he might have to cut and brush out a trail from the stream up and over to the next drainage and the Pick River, taking advantage, where he could, of game trails in the area. If it was a mile or two, he probably could handle that. Anything longer than a mile or two might be too much. For the most part it is too tough to try and take off through the scrub forest of spruce trees. It is usually too thick to get through, especially pulling a sled. It was doubtful that he would be lucky enough to find any dogsled trail in this area, as it was so remote and far between any of the villages. But again, he might luck out and find trap-line trails from Kobuk or Shungnak. Until he found out, he would be better off with the skis.

While he waited for the weather to let up, he went through everything he had laid out for the fifth or sixth time. He started with his winter clothing: first his parka, insulated pants, wool shirt, long johns, and down vest. He was glad he decided to take the sled. Now he could take his own big sleeping bag, his preference over one of the many lighter mummy-type survival bags aboard the ship. If the temperature really dived, the big bag would be better but too heavy to carry comfortably.

Birch had thrown the canvas tent inside *SASSY* at the last minute before leaving Fairbanks. It wouldn't really have served any purpose on the ice or water offshore the north coast where they were initially headed, but it might have come in handy on the haul road, in case they broke down or encountered trouble along the way. Since the circumstances had dramatically changed, he was glad he had brought the tent and also the camp stove. He also had a thick foam ground pad. You had to have something in between you and the frozen ground or (1) you could get the sleeping bag wet or (2) you would wake up in agony and arthritic from the cold or (3) you might not survive by freezing to death.

What he would like to have is some camp cooking pots and pans, but he didn't. All he had available was what he stocked the galley with. He found a little tie wire in the tool box and fashioned a wire handle on two large cans. One can was slightly smaller that would nestle within the larger coffee can. Inside these he put some silverware and salt and pepper. He also packed a small wire-frame grill that he could use over a fire, a bowl, and a couple of plates.

Birch kept going over what food to take with him for what he would guess to be anywhere from three days to a week. He hadn't stocked *SASSY* with camp-type food or dry food for the trial and training period. "Never anticipated anything like this, you know! Survival situations," he laughed. *I do have cups of noodles,* he thought, *but as I'm still a growing boy, I can't live on snacks. Have to take a few salmon fillets and pilot bread. What can I take other than bubble gum that won't be ruined or spoiled if it freezes?* Of course! Why hadn't he thought of it before? He threw in three cans each of Nalley's Jalapeno Hot Chili and Stagg Dynamite Hot Chili into a canvas bag.

Birch found the axe in one of the storage spaces under one of the bunks. That wasn't too smart. What if he needed it right away? When he got back he would leave it in a more readily available place. He put a baggie filled with half a can of coffee and some tea bags in one of the pockets of the pack, along with the thermos. The only small compass he had was a key chain type. It was accurate as long as he kept it away from other iron. Birch attached it to his parka zipper and put the hand-held portable GPS in the inside pocket, along with a usable map that he printed out on the computer.

What else would he need? Toilet paper. He could use bear fur, but the bear might not like it, so better off to take a roll or two with him. Anything else? Nothing came to mind, but he knew with every other step he would think of something. All he needed now would be a D8 dozer to pull the sled. Nah, it wasn't that bad. Now he just needed good weather.

After he got a cup of coffee, he looked out the turret porthole. Still dark out, but he could tell the wind had quit blowing. Warming up a little, the temperature was ten degrees below. It was a little colder when he went to bed. It might be a nice day for a walk, after all.

As soon as he cleaned up from one of his better breakfasts, he took another look outside. It was clear and sunny. He hauled everything up the stairs onto the main deck, including the sled. Went back below and set all the controls where he wanted them to be until he got back. He put on his parka and pulled the sled down over the side, putting it on the snow, and repacked everything and lashed it down. Birch had already filled the cartridge belt and reloaded the rifle. He strapped the pistol belt on under his parka and put his skis on, then his pack, and slung the rifle over his shoulder. Birch didn't lock up, in case the neighbors stopped by for coffee and wanted to warm up.

Grabbing the toboggan harness, he started off. The sled pulled easy, at least on level ground. Actually, it pulled along very easily. The snow on the ground next to the bank or in among the trees was too soft where it had been protected from the wind. Where the snow was not protected from the wind, it was packed enough to walk on. He was glad he brought the skis along now, as he almost didn't; where he was originally going, Prudhoe Bay, the skis were not really needed on the wind-swept and hard-packed snow.

As he started following the stream to the northeast, he stayed to the inside edge of the stream where there would be less current and the ice would be thicker. He avoided the opposite cut banks on the other side of the stream, mainly because the stronger current caused the ice to take longer to freeze thick enough to get on. Also, the snow would be drifted higher and softer along the higher banks, which would make for tough going even with skis. He wasn't too concerned now; that was just good practice this early in the winter. Also, the ice would be somewhat thinner over fast-moving water or rapids. He was not worried that much here on this stream. The Pick River was another story. He remembered flying up the Kobuk and seeing where the Pick entered into the Kobuk. There was fast moving water and a lot of rapids there at the mouth of the river. It was doubtful that you could get a normal river boat up into the Pick from the Kobuk. He might be wrong on that; it was such a long time ago. The main thing he remembered was how pretty the river and the whole area was. All along the Kobuk was magnificent to see from the air, and it was beautiful farther on downstream by Ambler and Kiana, with the crystal clear river waters and the tall timber. When he got to the Pick, he would look it over very carefully before getting out on the ice. And he would only travel on the ice during the daylight hours for the time being, so he would be able to see any open water or steam rising from the snow, indicating thin ice.

Trying not to overdo it the first couple of days, Birch started off slow and easy. He knew he could pull or strain a muscle very easily, if not careful. Not that he was out of shape, but this would be strenuous, if you weren't used to pulling a sled day in and day out. He was making good time and thankful that he did a little hiking from time to time and had built up some endurance.

As soon as he got through congratulating himself on being in not too bad a shape, he started getting woozy or having a feeling of getting woozy. Birch remembered when he had that feeling before, where the ground rolled for a few minutes before it ripped apart in front of him. He started to sit down on the sled when the quake knocked his skis out from beneath him. The ground shook enough to whip the trees back and forth and violently enough to snap off a couple of the taller trees along the bank of the stream. "Oh, no, not again!"

After a minute or two when the ground stopped shaking, he got up and sat on the sled. Fifteen or twenty minutes later, when he finally stopped shaking and felt no more tremors, he took off the pack and hung it up high on a nearby tree branch. Since he had not gone more than two or three miles, he turned and backtracked to make sure *SASSY* was still tied off and had suffered no damage. He thought if *SASSY* didn't suffer any damage from what they had already been through, then this little flicker didn't concern him in the least. But he had to go back anyway, as he had forgotten his toothpaste. And while he was there, it wouldn't hurt to check on his pride and joy, he laughed. He needed some kind of excuse to go back. He also knew what came after the first quake on the haul road. He would never survive out in the open with winds like he had encountered before.

When he got to the ship, he didn't even stop. He walked around the ship and checked the hull and heavy rope tied to the tree and made sure the hawser was suspended in the air and wasn't hanging down and frozen in the ice. He decided to spend the night, just to make sure nothing else was headed his way. When he made sure everything was okay the next morning, he headed back to the sled.

After picking up the sled and getting the pack off the tree, he continued on his hike along the stream for a few miles until it took a southeast turn, not in the direction he was headed. He backtracked about a quarter of a mile to an open area that led in the direction he wanted to go, toward the Pick River. You more than likely could not have walked in this area two weeks ago or even gotten a canoe through it. It was probably a watery bog that was so prevalent in this area and other places in Alaska and Canada. Now that it was frozen over it made for good traveling, especially when pulling a sled.

Soon he was at the edge of the tree line bordering the bog. Birch followed the tree line, looking for an opening, a gap, or a game trail that he could get through without having to brush or chop his way. After dropping the sled and his pack, he explored several until he found one game trail that looked promising. Retrieving the pack and sled, he paced his way up and over the higher ground and to the valley below. He could see a ribbon of tall trees a mile or two ahead that he hoped was the Pick River, where he would camp at a suitable campsite for the night. The animal trail must be very old and well-traveled by many animals, as most of it was as wide as a country road, or wider, through the forest. Could be where the caribou migrated from one area to another. The trail did lead right to a wide spot on the Pick River that probably served as a shallow crossing for the caribou during the summer months.

When he arrived at the river he looked it over carefully, like he promised himself, for any indication of thin ice or overflow water on top of the ice. Not seeing any evidence of any danger on the ice, he started downstream to the mouth of the river where it entered the Kobuk.

Birch was seeing more and more animal tracks the closer he got to the Kobuk, which was a good sign. That was until he saw the fresh grizzly tracks. He would have thought the bears would have denned up by now, but again, it hadn't been that long since freezeup.

Birch slung his rifle over his shoulder, and from now on he would be more alert and listen carefully to what was going on around him.

He was seeing rabbit, mink or marten, and wolf tracks along the banks of the river. The wolf tracks were of several wolves; he was sure there were four at least, if not more, in the pack. Hard to tell exactly how many from the prints in the snow.

Birch was looking for any place that would make a good spot to camp for the night. A camping spot out of the wind that would provide protection for his back, so nothing could sneak up on him would be nice. *I just hate it when you're just getting to sleep and some cold and hungry bear wants to share your tent. That really ticks me off.*

A spot also has to have plenty of easy-to-get firewood. He also wanted to be able to hoist his pack and sled up off the ground, where animals and bears couldn't get to them. Remembering the bear tracks, he wondered how he could hoist himself up for the night.

Soon he found what appeared to be a good spot on a ledge of a bluff, looking over the river with lots of downed timber and driftwood on the opposite bank for firewood. With the sled he soon had enough firewood for a couple of days. He also made one more trip across the river to gather up a sled load of spruce tree branches. Before very long he had a good little fire going up next to the rock bluff, radiating back on him while he made camp and pitched his tent. When he had the tent up, he layered in the spruce tree branches and made a soft and bouncy insulated bed to roll out his sleeping pad and sleeping bag on. Serta mattresses should take note.

Birch woke up fairly early and stirred the embers and stoked the fire. He had slept really well and only woke up once. That must have been right after he fell asleep, when he heard the wolves howl. He stretched and felt refreshed. *Must be this country living,* he thought. The oatmeal he made for breakfast hit the spot, and he couldn't taste the difference between the powdered milk he used with a little brown sugar and that of fresh milk.

Chapter Nine
Friends or Foes

Birch hadn't gone very far after packing everything up on the sled when he paused and took in the scenery. That's when he noticed shadows moving on the next bend of the river. The shadows were milling around a cut bank under a rocky bluff, similar to where he had camped last night. He dug his binoculars from his pack and focused in on the shadows. The shadows turned out to be a pack of wolves, five or six of them pawing at a pile of rocks at the bottom of the bluff. Birch unlashed the rifle from the sled and pulled his parka up over the .44 on his hip. When he looked back downriver at the bluff, the wolves were gone. They must have either heard him, smelled, or seen him, none of which seemed to be very likely since he was partially hidden by the trees he was looking through on the river bend, and the distance too far to be heard. He was sure he had not made any noise. It was eerie the way the pack vanished.

He continued to move downriver. Not about to let a few fur balls scare him off. He unslung the rifle and made sure it was loaded and had a cartridge in the chamber, same with the pistol. Moving slowly, he continued to look at everything in front of him and also to his backside. When he got to the pile of rocks on the ledge above the river, he stopped and dropped the sled harness he had made and did a slow 360-degree sweep or the area. His curiosity was up on what or why the wolves were digging. He went down the bank a ways where he could climb up on the ledge to take a closer look. What he found was a rockslide, just as he thought. Taking another look around the area and seeing nothing, he started to drop over the side of the ledge to the riverbank when he heard a soft yipping.

Birch went up to the edge of the pile of rocks and dropped down on his knees and listened. Nothing. It must have been his imagination. Starting to get up, he heard the yipping again; it was not his imagination. He started throwing the rocks he could toss to the side and rolling the bigger ones out of the way. He worked for a while, then paused to catch his breath and listened but heard nothing. Then he had this disturbing thought and said "Birch, where did you leave the rifle? You idiot!" He knew exactly where the rifle was: leaning up against the sled at the bottom of the ledge. He looked down over the ledge, and yes, the idiot had left the rifle leaning up against the sled and pack. He looked up and could just make out three of the wolves one hundred yards away, across the river just inside the tree line. Looking to his left, he could see a gray wolf behind some driftwood, and to his right he had to watch for a minute or so before he spotted a black wolf about the same distance away. He couldn't see the other one or two, but he knew they were there. He called to the wolves "Well, come on over here and lend a hand. It would go a lot faster if I could get a little help, you know?"

What the …., he thought, and went back to attacking the rock-slide when he heard the yipping. Before long he had cleared the rocks away from an opening in the rock face, and out fell a little ball of fur that would just fit in the palm of his hand. It must be a den.

The little ball of fur was trying to nurse on his fingers, squinting its eyes in the bright sunlight. Probably hadn't had the eyes opened very long, and then this was the first time the pup had seen daylight due to the slide. It had warmed up enough that he took off his parka and laid it down and started to wrap the pup up, but before he did, he asked, "And just what are you anyway, a bull or heifer? Well, now we know, Joe, don't we?" Putting the pup in the parka, he went over the side of the ledge and got his thermos bottle and went back up the ledge and finally got some water into the pup. He needed to make something that would work like a nipple for the time being. When he was thinking about constructing something, he heard a growl under the rock by the mouth of the den or cave. Back over the ledge and up again with a small flashlight, he took a look inside the opening. He could see and hear the mom trying to move around, but she was trapped and held down by the rocks. She was probably crushed by the weight of rocks falling on her during the quake a few days ago, but she was definitely alive. With nothing else on his immediate schedule, he attacked the pile of rocks holding the she wolf down. As he removed the rocks, he began to talk to her. It looked like she was in a lot of pain and exhausted from trying to free herself. Birch could now see that her hindquarters were completely buried and her head was free but her upper body was incased by loose rocks, and the wolf was now watching him intently as he continued to move the rocks.

He had to be careful to move the rocks from the top so he wouldn't pull one out from under the others, causing the rest to slide down and over her. Now he was getting exhausted and had to pause. While he was resting, he looked closely at the momma wolf, and for a minute he thought she died. He checked, and she was still breathing okay. But evidently she was slipping in and out of consciousness. Birch was digging her out when he felt the wolf's jaws around his wrist. The wolf wasn't putting any pressure on his wrist to cause him pain, but he knew she could snap his wrist.

Birch didn't stop moving the rocks from around her head and off the back of her neck. He didn't try to pull his wrist away but continued to softly talk to her and rub her neck and shoulder when he had dug them out. After a few minutes, she opened her jaws and watched him as he continued removing the rocks. He had to rest a few minutes more, and they watched each other for a little while until Birch caught his breath.

He grabbed the thermos and took a swig, then filled the palm of his hand and slid it under her mouth while he held her head up with the other hand, as she was too weak to hold her own head up. At first she tried to move her head away until she smelled the water, then she tried to lap it up. Out of the four handfuls he tried to give her, most went on the ground. But she got some in her, and that seemed to help her breathing some. He continued throwing the rocks to the side and noticed one of the wolves lying on the ledge not too far away and another one not too far away from the sled, lying in the snow just watching. *I hope neither one of these two fur balls yelps in pain, or I will be tonight's dinner.*

Soon he had her free. She was not moving, but she was still alert, even though she couldn't hold her head up. He petted and rubbed her head and neck. She made a halfhearted growl and then lay quiet. He gave what was left of the water in the thermos to her, and then brought the pup up where mom tried to lick the pup's face. It was then that he shined the light around inside the den and could see three other pups that hadn't made it, off to the side and partially under the rocks. He left the two together and climbed down with the thermos, heading to the sled. As he approached the sled, the one close wolf moved back off a ways but did not leave, nor did it growl or threaten in any way.

Thankfully, it had warmed up to what he would guess to be about twenty degrees above. Birch grabbed the ax and moved out about twenty feet from the sled and the edge of the riverbank and started chopping a hole in the ice. When he had a good-size hole about two feet across, he filled up the thermos and grabbed one of the small bowls, went back up to the den, and watered the mother and pup until they didn't want anymore. Momma wolf was out of it or asleep again. Hopefully she was out of it, as Birch was going to try to move her onto the sleeping pad and sleeping bag and then onto the sled to find a suitable campsite for tonight, which would be where he camped last night.

He started to go back to the sled when he stopped and watched the pack, one at a time, approach the water hole and drink their fill, then move back a ways. He didn't like doing it, but he unpacked the sled and took it and the sleeping gear down the bank where he could pull the sled up and over the ledge. He folded and laid the bag on the sled and then took the pad over to where the she wolf was lying. This was going to be the tricky part: getting the pad under her without hurting her anymore than she already was. Right now she was still unconscious, and now was the time to do it. She was no lightweight, either; he would guess her around 150 to 160 pounds. While he was moving her onto the pad, he was also checking to feel for any broken bones and was glad, or hopeful, in not finding any, at least not obviously broken, anyway. Once he had her on the pad, he easily pulled her up onto the sleeping bag in the sled. She never woke up, but she was breathing okay. Next he got the pup and held it for a minute and then tucked it alongside Mom. He covered all but the head of her with his parka, and he lashed the parka down loosely and headed for last night's campsite. The big gray wolf nervously followed him at a distance, not really comprehending what was going on. The others were out of sight, but Birch knew they were close and watching. At the campsite he made a bed for Mom like he had made last night. He pulled the she wolf and the pup off the sled and laid her on the spruce needle branches and went across the river to the other side and gathered up another load of the branches for his own bed. The pup was trying to nurse, but he was sure the pup wasn't getting anything. At least they were comfortable. He took the sled and went back to the rockslide and retrieved what he had unloaded.

Birch noticed all the wolf tracks around the little pups that didn't survive. It looked like they all came around and paid their respects. While he was there, he moved the little wolf pups that had died down a ways along the bluff and placed them together between two pieces of driftwood logs and bridged them with shorter pieces across the top of the logs and covered all with rocks until he had a good mound where nothing could get at them other than the grizzly. He didn't know if it would do any good, but he peed around the edge of the rocks, hoping his scent would keep the bear away.

Returning to where he left the gear, he could see the snow had been packed down all around the stuff he taken off the sled. It would appear that the pack had inspected all the goods but did not touch or ruin anything there. The rifle was still leaning against one of the bags.

Back at camp, he pitched the tent around and over the beds where the wolf was lying and made a nice little fire out in front of the tent so the smoke wouldn't bother the houseguests.

Okay! He needed to get some nourishment into the fur balls or they wouldn't make it. Now what would that be? Let's try some warm powdered milk for babysan. He would need some meat for mommasan. Chili wouldn't cut it for Mom just yet, especially in a closed-off area, like a tent. He would go out after while and see if he could locate some birds for stew. First he made the warm powdered milk slightly on the thick side for the pup that lavishly lapped it up out of the palm of his hand and off his fingertips as Mom looked on until the pup went back to sleep, and then Birch laid it alongside her. Mom still hadn't changed her position from where he had originally put her.

Birch wasn't a hunter anymore, but he liked to be out camping, prospecting, and panning along a river or stream, and maybe fishing for a grayling or two. The present circumstances have dramatically changed his thoughts on hunting. Always before when he was out in the woods or country, he looked like Poncho Villa, at least he did until he shaved his mustache. He was always armed just like he was today. He had the Marlin lever action brush rifle and the big pistol and lots of cartridges. He also had a large bowie knife on his pistol belt that was made by a family in Montana. Everyone always made fun of the knife and asked him why he needed such a large one. Within an hour they usually asked if they could borrow it to cut some kindling or open a can or for some other reason. Birch would always tease them telling them to use their own little pocket knife, before he handed it to them, telling them not to cut themselves as he usually only let adults use his knife. The knife was extremely sharp, and when he first got it he was afraid to try and sharpen it, as he thought he might ruin the edge.

He always carried some birdshot with him, which worked just fine on spruce hens or ptarmigan. Most of the time he kept one or two shells of the birdshot in the first couple of chambers ahead of the slugs. He did not want to shoot a Bear. He would rather just scare it away by firing one or two shots first. But if he saw fresh signs or lots of bear sign, he would change out the ammo. Every now and then he wouldn't mind getting a bird or two, and that was what he needed now. He double checked to see that he did have the bird shot up front in the chambers.

He took off upstream and didn't start looking for birds until he thought he was at least a mile away from camp. When he was far enough away, he began looking for openings in the trees, either trails or drainages where he might spot spruce hens and in swampy areas where ptarmigans might be among the willows. Before long he fluffed up several spruce hens, which flew to the tops of the short trees nearby about thirty feet away and just sat there. He dropped two of them, and that would be enough for tonight. On the way back he would walk into a swampy area that he passed and look for the ptarmigan. He lucked out and got two. That would work for breakfast.

He made a hole in the ice and got water for the stew. "Since I don't really have anything in mind, or with me, to add to the birds I should just call it soup." He hung the coffee can over the embers of the fire and cut up the birds and placed the pieces in the can to simmer. While the birds simmered away, he gathered up some more of the spruce limbs and covered the hole in the ice, hopefully to delay it from freezing closed. He shredded the meat, put a little salt in it, and let it boil some more to make a thick broth. He would mash up the meat and bones every so often as it simmered. He considered it to be one of his finest gourmet creations, and he let it cool by setting the can in the snow. When it cooled enough, he woke up Mom by scratching her ears, and when she was awake he put some soup in the bowl and held up her head so she could see and smell it. Then she tried to raise her head so she could lick up some of the soup. Not quite strong enough, but she tried. He got a spoon and dribbled some of the liquid in the side of her mouth. *This is working,* he thought. After taking about a cup, Mom laid her head down and watched while Birch fed a little bit to the pup off his fingers. After a couple of tablespoons he figured that was enough for his little belly. The pup didn't think so, but didn't squirm when he put him up with Mom for the night.

Early the next morning before sunrise, Birch heated up the bird soup for the mom, thawed out some powdered milk, and fed the little fur ball some of the oatmeal he had made for himself. He was surprised when Mom had some too. Both Mom and Pup had seemed to enjoy the oatmeal, or they had a secret sweet tooth. The reason he was up so early was to get the sno-go and transport the wolves to *SASSY* where he could better take care of them and where he had more of an assortment of food on hand.

Or, he could let nature take its course.

NAH! Go get the snow machine.

As he strapped his skis on, he looked for the signs of the relatives in the forest across the river and in the brush and trees up and down the river. He knew they were close, but couldn't see hide nor hair of them, but he sure noticed all the tracks in back and in front of the tent. Before he left, he raked the snow in front of the tent with his skis, erasing some of the tracks. It shouldn't take but a few hours to reach *SASSY*, and all he would be carrying would be a light pack and the thermos. It was still dark, but he had enough moonlight to see his ski tracks. The previous ski tracks that he had packed down frosted in and set up enough to keep his skis in the tracks. Birch would make good time, as long as he stayed in the tracks rather than break new trail.

When Birch got to the ship, he walked completely around it following the bear tracks. The bear never figured out how to get inside. Like most doors, *SASSY* had exterior and interior openers for the doors and hatches. If you did not know where the exterior handles were you wouldn't get inside, as they were less than obvious. Just in case, he would remember to wear gloves and not use his bare hands when closing doors and hatches. That way he could avoid leaving his scent on any handles that would interest some snoopy bear that would not mind his own business. No harm done, but the bruin did try to get on top of the deck, but kept sliding off until it gave up.

"It's about time for that bear to den up. And he is not going to use *SASSY* for a cave," Birch muttered. Now he wished he had brought along that rifle, but he had left it with Mom in case she saw any wild animals. "Sometimes you just aren't too smart there, city kid," he said to no one in particular.

The sno-go trailer was partially on top of the sno-go to make room for other stuff. After he rearranged things and checked the gas and grabbed a couple of extra blankets, he dropped the ramp and fired up the sno-go and drove it outside, closing the ramp behind him. *Electric starts sure are nice.*

With about sixteen inches of snow, he worried about a rough ride for the she wolf while transporting her back to the ship. Going out wasn't bad at all, though, and he was moving right along. In less than an hour he was back at the tent. The sound of the snow machine arriving probably upset the neighborhood. He gave the wolves water and made a fire and heated up the soup. The pup took some of the soup, but he couldn't get Mom awake, which was just as well for the trip.

After he struck down the camp, he made a nice springy bed with a bunch of smaller spruce limbs on top of everything to absorb shocks and bumps, and he covered those with a blanket for the she wolf and the pup, and then he tied the little sled with some of the rest of the gear to the rear of the sno-go sled. A couple of the wolves didn't quite know about all that was going on and were mostly out of sight, but he could see them nervously moving back and forth in the tree line. *What are they going to think about all this?* he wondered, as he took off

The ride was smooth and easy on the river. After a few minutes of following in the same track coming over the rough frozen swamp, which wasn't that bad, he veered off the packed-down trail and started making a new track in the soft snow. *This will be a lot better ride for Mom till I get back on the stream ice. At least that is mostly smooth with very little drifting.* Half way into the return trip Mom woke up and realized what was happening and became aware of the noise from the sno-go. Birch had been looking over his shoulder, and he saw Mom trying to lift her head. If there was anyway she could, she would have been out of that sled in a minute. But she didn't have the strength.

Birch stopped and calmed her down with some water and by scratching her ears and putting the pup up where she could see him. From there on Birch idled along for a while, gradually picking up some of the lost speed but not going too fast. It looked like the shock had worn off some from when she first woke up, but the she wolf remained conscious but incapacitated for most of the remainder of the trip.

When they got back to the ship, Birch put Mom on the little sled and untied it from the other trailer and pulled it up and in through the bow ramp. After he made a nest for the wolves, he brought the rest of the camp stuff inside, leaving the sno-go outside. This concerned him, knowing that bears sometimes had an affinity for four-wheelers and sno-go seats. After everyone was settled in, he turned on the deck lights and grabbed the axe on his way outside. With the axe he soon had a tripod alongside the ship and over the sno-go. With the tripod and the side of *SASSY*, he rigged up a trip wire that would swing a heavy log over the top of the seat of the sno-go. Some vandal trying to tear up the seat would more than likely get a good poke in the ribs.

Mom seemed to survive the trip all right, breathing easy and full but asleep. Birch hung a flap of the wall tent overhead, thinking it would seem more like a den when the she woke up. He thought he would find something to feed her, and if he could, something to feed her with. Something for needle teeth—he was tired of getting his finger shredded. *What's the best thing in the world for down and out animals?*

"Spam," Birch barks, a little too loudly. "Tonight's main entrée is going to be Spam. Spam on whole wheat, if that's your preference."

The pup was stirring around, Birch tousled his ears, and the pup attacked his hand. He picked up the pup and tucked him into his shirt like a baby kangaroo. He went to the galley and opened a can of Spam, sliced it up, chopped up a couple slices, fried two slices, and mashed up part of a slice. He also warmed up the bird soup and found the eagle baster he had used with Big Bird. Warmed up some powered milk, pulled the pup out and held him like you would a baby, and used the baster to feed him. After the milk, he let him nibble at a plate of the mashed spam.

"Let's go see Mom." He went forward, taking a tray of food for Mom to see what, if anything, she would take. The pup mewed when Birch put him down at Mom's neck. The she wolf opened her eyes and tried to reach the pup to nuzzle her but couldn't. Her eyes were clear, so Birch started feeding her and wondering at the same time what was keeping her down. The rockslide could have put too much pressure on some of her internal organs so they were not functioning as they should. If that is the case, then she would continue to shut down, or she would continue to heal. Same thing with her blood flow; if it was cut off completely she could lose limbs. If she did lose limbs she would die, as she couldn't hunt. If there was no permanent damage, she would heal. After she was done feeding, he checked her all over, looking for any sores, loss of fur and any breaks or painful areas on her body. Finding none, he gave the she wolf a quick massage and then gently turned her over and massaged that side, and she did not yelp. He covered her up for the night.

By the next morning Mom could just lift her head up high enough to eat breakfast and groom the pup. Birch noticed the she wolf intensely watching every move he made, and all the while he brushed the pup and then her with his hairbrush. Her stare followed him around wherever he moved, and it was like the first time she realized his presence. But the more he thought about this, he knew she had been aware of him before, or she would now be all upset and trying to attack him. It was more likely a sense of wonderment. Who is this animal, brushing my pup and me? He chuckled and said to Mom, "I can only guess what I would be thinking if I came out of a coma or woke up and here you were, a she wolf brushing my hair and trying to shove a vole down my throat. I guess I would be saying something to the effect of, 'What the . . . oh, forget it.' "

Birch felt something tugging at a button of his shirt and look down to see the pup trying to get inside his wool shirt. "You ready for a nap now that you just woke up? Well, I can't blame you. I'm always ready for a nap after I eat, too." He tucked the pup inside his shirt and continued to brush, easy like, the side Mom had been lying on for the last few days or since the earthquake had pinned her down.

While Mom slept, he went topside and checked around the sno-go. Lots of tracks but no bear tracks. He looked all around and saw no sign of the pack. He figured they were near and watching him. He put the pup down on the snow and watched as it waddled over to one of the pole legs on the tripod over the sno-go and tried to lift his leg and peed on the pole and fell over on his side.

"Good job, 'Wolf,'" he laughed. "Good job."

He let Wolf play while he took the battery out of the sno-go. He would take it inside and keep it warm until he needed it again. Birch watched Wolf play in the snow for a while until he tried to climb up his pant leg.

Over the next two weeks his new friends kept him more than busy. Mom was gaining strength day by day and seemed to be enjoying her daily scalp massage and neck rubs. She could now sit up and stand up for a few minutes at a time if Birch lifted her hind end. Wolf pup wanted food every few hours and was trying to nurse on Mom. He couldn't tell how much, but the pup was getting some quantity of milk now but not enough, according to his yipping.

"You are eating me out of house and Spam, you know. We are going to find something else in the pantry for you, now that you are getting your appetite back. Likewise for you too, little one"

Birch gathered up firewood nearby on the edge of the stream where driftwood and trees had fallen down from the undercuts of high water and the stream currents. He gathered both spruce and birch, chopping the trees into pieces that he could carry on his shoulder. While sitting down to catch his breath, he absently swung his axe against one of the birch pieces and split off a small piece with no intended purpose in mind. But after looking at it, he began shaping it with his axe and knife.

After stacking all the wood near the boat on the stream bed, he made a cup of tea and located his drill motor and drill bits. On the top side he drilled tiny holes into the hardwood spatula he had shaped out of the piece of birch. Then came the hard part: the time-consuming job of whittling enough small pegs that he could pound into the piece of birch. Small but not so small that they would snap off. After he had cut enough to the same length, he took his hammer and gently tapped then into the spatula. When he was finished inserting the pegs, he held the peg ends over the fire long enough to harden the ends. Then he took his knife and scraped the ends of the pegs.

With his newly fabricated tool of pure torture, he snuck up on the fur balls and started brushing them with his newly made fur brush. Both wolves, in turn, had to sniff and check out this new thing, all the while trying to keep Birch busy brushing the one but not the other. *Oh, oh, what have I started.* The lady wolf told Birch telepathically he needed to patent that thing.

* * * * *

One morning Birch got up all nervous like, edgy and pacing around, not knowing what to do with himself. He quickly fed the fur balls and grabbed the battery to the sno-go and filled it up with gas from one of the five-gallon cans. He had to get some fresh air. He made a couple of sandwiches and a thermos of coffee. *Enough for a day trip*, he thought.

He took off full speed ahead. He needed to see the Kobuk River. He needed to see if anyone survived at Shungnak or if Shungnak was even there. He needed to see if anyone survived at Kobuk, five miles upstream, or if Kobuk was even there. Even with the fresh snow, he could still see the tracks that he had made before going to and from the Pick River. Once he passed the rockslide, he slowed down and started taking in the scenery and watching for tracks.

When he turned upriver at the mouth of where the Pick emptied into the Kobuk, the first thing he noticed was the fallen timber. Some were felled toward downriver and some had fallen toward upriver. He guessed more than half of the timber was down, and what was left standing had been stripped of most of its bark and branches. One hundred yards of timber on each side of the river was affected. With the snow cover, it was hard to determine what would cause that kind of damage. At the mouth he turned upriver to find one of two channels leading back downstream to Shungnak, if he remembered correctly. It should be close.

When he found the channel, he turned back downstream and found the same damage to the town site. He also found the landing strip that, even with the snow cover, he could tell was awash with gullies across and down the gravel surface. It looked like a large slug of water went up the river and then another slug of water went downstream. *A very large slug of water ran through here, washing away everything in its path,* he thought. *The river sloshing back and forth caused massive damage.*

The buildings of the village were gone, but there were pilings left sticking out of the ground. He found the village of Kobuk, ten miles upstream the same way. He had slowly circled both villages looking for tracks and sadly found nothing but animal tracks.

Slowly he turned around, heading back to *SASSY* and not remembering any part of the return trip. He was in a daze. All he could think about was that if some of the animals survived in this area, then surely some humans could and would have survived.

The next morning back at the maternity and recovery room, he took the five-gallon can of gas and poured the last of it in the sno-go. He took it outside and cut the top out of the can and stuffed a few sheets from a roll of paper towels into the can and set them on fire to burn the gas out. Next he filled it with water and hung it over his fire pit outside that he had rocked up. He had cut up a couple of blankets into Pup-size squares and Mom-size squares to keep under them. The one thing he had plenty of was blankets. After the water came to a boil, he set about doing diaper duty.

He seemed to have a recollection of one of his high school teachers telling him that when he grew up he would probably be a low-paid dog crap collector or something to that effect. Who would ever have guessed she was clairvoyant.

"Good morning, folks. And look who is standing up. What a difference two weeks made." Mom was standing up on her own four paws. The rear-end section seemed a little wobbly. "Yeah, I see you too, Pup. You can let go of my pant leg." His cuff would be shredded if he didn't find a way to break him of that. Besides, the pup was getting too heavy to drag around while clamped to his pant leg. "Come on, everybody, outside. Grab your coats; it's cold out," he said, as he put his parka on.

* * * * *

It was ten- to fifteen-degrees-below zero. He let the ramp down and raised it as soon as the wolves were out. The ramp was the easiest way for the wolves to get in and out, but it let more cold air in through the larger opening than one of the hatch doors. It took longer for *SASSY* to warm up inside with the settings he had set for the heat and ventilation system. Both Mom and Pup went around taking care of first things first, while sniffing every single thing in sight. When Birch got chilled, he went back inside and left them to wander around. The cold didn't seem to bother Pup one bit, but he would keep close watch and bring him inside at the first sign of a shiver.

He put a couple of packages of creamed chipped beef on the stove to cook. While it was cooking, he cut off a hunk of salmon that he had put out to thaw the night before. *Let's see what Mom thinks about this.*

"Dinner time." While Mom devoured the salmon, he sliced a taste off for the pup. "Well, I see that went down big." And, of course, everyone liked the creamed chipped beef since he didn't have a real large supply. Not to say he didn't have some, but how long would a couple of cases last when he was feeding three instead of just him, as he had originally planned.

A few days later while he was outside, he noticed from all the tracks around the fire pit and front of the ship that the pack had made their nightly visit. Looks like Mom noticed the presence too, as she let out a scary howl. Immediately, Birch heard movement in the tree line. Birch was just about to start a fire but changed his mind when he heard the "something" in the trees. He went inside and got a cup of coffee and went back to the bow turret and watched through the porthole. He felt it wouldn't be long before his wolves had visitors.

And it wasn't. Everyone was excited, milling around, carrying on nuzzling each other, and nuzzling the pup over and over.

Mom must be like a queen or a leader, as the rest of the pack all had their tails down and paid deference when they were near her, even the two he thought were males.

Birch ran and got the small video camera and filmed the wolves as they played. He didn't know for sure, but the wolves might be able to see movement through the porthole when the sun changed position. Right now, though, they evidently couldn't with the present glare on the outside of the window.

He didn't tire of watching the wolves, even when they were all lying down and looked to be napping. Birch knew they were ready alert to the slightest movement or noise, even when they were resting or asleep. Mom was dark but not a true black. Of the other six there where three black, two grays, and one white. Who knows what color the little one would end up, but it would be dark.

While the wolves were resting, Birch went to get another cup of coffee and returned to the porthole and found they had disappeared from sight. Since the wolves had left, he went outside and asked Mom if she was ready to go inside, and she understood and herded the pup to the ramp door. He had never run across any dog that came anywhere close to being as smart as this she wolf appeared to be, not even close to being in her class.

One afternoon he put Pup in his lap and took him for a short ride on the snow machine around the ship, making circles and each time making the circle larger. All the while Mom watched anxiously. After a time Pup seemed to be comfortable riding on the sno-go with him. Next, Birch somehow convinced Mom to get on the sled. He pulled her by hand all the way, for nearly two feet. With a couple of slices of salmon, Birch got her to ride ten feet. What other bribes did he have? The next day he got Mom in the sled again after a lot of persuasion and bribes. Then he put Pup in the sled with her and she stayed as long as Pup did. In the next few days he had them riding up and down the stream behind the sno-go.

Chapter Ten

The Leader of the Pack

A couple of weeks later Birch yelled to the wolves, "Come on, get your coats, and let's go for a walk." Outside he strapped his skis on and took off to get some exercise and explore some of the nearby country. Fifty feet out, he turned around and saw Mom and Pup just sitting there. "Are you guys coming?" Mom started off following him, staying in his ski tracks. Pup launched into the soft snow and came up sputtering. The pup hadn't learned to use other tracks or packed-down areas. What do you know. All of a sudden they were all in step. Mom was moving right along with Birch, with Pup doing double and triple time trying to make up time after falling off to one side of the tracks or the other.

After they made about half a mile, he turned around and headed home. After everyone made yellow holes in the snow and watered the weeds, they all went inside for a nap. The pup barely made it to the edge of his pad before he was asleep. Every day for the next two weeks they took different routes, exploring the area and going a little farther and faster. Every once in awhile Mom would show and teach the pup how to find voles and other critters. She wasn't fast enough yet to get the rabbits. Pup made magnificent attempts going after the ptarmigan and rabbits. It was fun to watch.

Midwinter, on one of the warmer days during one of their afternoon jaunts, Birch was resting on a downed tree, and the pup was chasing a rabbit in what would be an open marshy area during the summer. Pup was not making any headway when the gray came out from the trees and started running alongside the pup, startling Birch. He jumped up, then sat back down when it was obvious the gray was trying to help the pup and do him no harm. It was a teachable moment. When they would lose ground, the gray would run ahead and drive the rabbit back toward the pup. With Pup tiring, another wolf, a black, joined in, and between the two big wolves, they drove the rabbit and brought it down at the pup's feet and then disappeared into the woods. Pup sat there looking at the dead rabbit, probably thinking, Well, now that we caught it, what do we do with it? The she wolf came up and butchered it for the pup and had a leg or two for herself. Eventually, the pup caught on and enjoyed lunch. Birch was somewhat amazed that the relatives would come out to play with Pup when Birch was in such close proximity. Birch never saw the other wolves until they came out of the woods to help the pup with the rabbit. Evidently they had been keeping pace with them all the time, unseen.

No more diaper duty. The wolves, even the pup would let Birch know when it was time to go outside. They did their duty out and away from the living and working areas in front of the ship, which was good. Birch didn't have to worry about watching his step. Mom and Pup would sometimes stay outside for hours, and it didn't seem to matter how cold it was. One evening at thirty-five below, he called to them twice to come in, but they just rolled around and stretched in the snow awhile longer, just like they were lying on a beach in the Caribbean. He watched from the porthole in the forward turret until they were ready to come in.

Birch started thinking about making another trip. He wanted to check out Bornite and Dahl Creek, north of Kobuk. Supposedly Bornite was a huge sulfide copper deposit with no way to get the minerals to a deep water port for shipping. Native Alaskans have known about bornite for years, and Birch remembered the brothers telling him what the local Natives said to the early prospectors, when they found out some of the newcomers had been looking for copper. "Why didn't you tell us you were looking for purple rocks?"

While Birch was going through his pack and taking inventory, he looked over at the two wolves who were sitting there watching him, he said, "What, you guys got something you want to pack too?"

He was looking forward to making a short trip to Dahl Creek and maybe to Bornite. He also knew he was getting antsy. "Okay, what do we need for you two? No hotels where we are going, you know. Take notes now. We'll need the canvas tent and an extra can of gas. Just for the heck of it, let's take some fishing line and a couple of lures, and when we get to the Kobuk we try our hand at jigging. How about a couple of extra blankets, in case it turns cold on us?" Birch continued to jabber away, thinking out loud and talking to the wolves.

The wolves were looking back at him and looking as if they understood every word. *Who knows, maybe they do,* he thought. He continued putting everything in a pile along with food that wouldn't hurt to freeze that would go on the sled. Then he started making a list of food that he would pull out of the freezer. He needed something for the wolves. "How about us taking some frozen salmon for your breakfast, and then for dinner you could have some thawed salmon? There are always lots of voles out there, too."

After a week and a half of very cold weather, they were on their way with Birch leading on the sno-go pulling the sled, and the wolves trotting behind or alongside him. The temperature had dipped down to fifty-six below last week, and now had warmed up to around zero. He hoped it would stay in this range for a few days. Birch was pacing the wolves and watching. He was surprised at both. Mom had gained a lot of strength back. To what extent he didn't know, but she seemed to be cruising along just fine. At this pace the little one was doing fine and had time to check out other interesting stuff along the way. *Their endurance is amazing,* he thought. They ran this way for almost an hour. He stopped and piled them on the sled and started moving ahead at a faster pace when Pup jumped off. After Birch stopped, Pup came around and jumped up on the sno-go in his lap. "So you like the front seat, do you?"

It was good going as they followed his previous tracks with a light covering of snow, but the tracks were still visible, not yet drifted over from the wind. So far they hadn't had any real blows for several weeks now. It was just a matter of time.

They passed the place where the village of Kobuk used to be, and now Birch had to find the Dahl Creek landing strip. He had heard that BLM had a small camp facility there now. He knew about where that should be and continued on north where he found the runway and what remained of the buildings. One of them looked to be intact. The runway, like the others, had gully washes from the flood and would take a lot of work before a plane of any size could use it. When he slowed down, the wolves jumped off. Not stopping, he continued on to the building. The doors and window were gone, but the walls were standing. After taking his pack off, he climbed up to get inside, since the stairs were gone. The wolves were content to sit outside and had no desire to enter the building. Once inside, he could see the heavy file cabinets and furniture turned over. He walked through that room to an adjoining area and into what could have been an office and was taken aback when he spotted what was left of two skeletons. There wasn't much left, as the rodents and ravens had gotten to them and cleaned them to the bone. He couldn't tell if they were both male or male and female. They had been dressed in jeans, heavy shirts, and work boots. He would guess the smaller of the two with the ponytail was probably female. He didn't touch them or check to see if they had IDs in their wallets. He left them as they were. And unknown.

Walking through the rest of the building, he found some usable things but nothing that he didn't already have or didn't need, at least right then. He climbed down and headed for what could be a garage or shop. He found it to be in the same shape: windows and doors knocked off their hinges, along with part of the back wall missing. The concrete floor was undermined and all askew. A tool room or cage with heavy chain-link walls was off to one side. The chain-link never slowed the water down. Lots of good tools were lying on the floor, knocked off the shelves. He wondered if any of them would work after being in the water. The water that came through must have been fairly clean, as he didn't see any muck around like you would normally see after a flood. He saw a gas-powered drill with several auger bits. One that would be just right for ice fishing. With the concrete floor like it was, he had no difficulty in reaching the auger drill and a tool box lying on its side. All the water must have drained out, as there was no ice inside. It had all the wrenches, sockets, and screw drivers that you would normally need. With the exception of a handsaw, he would leave them for now. Out back he found a 4 x 4 pickup wedged up against some bigger trees.

After he had gone through everything else, the wolves and he had water and tea and a couple of crackers each. Birch, while sitting on a log staring off at nothing, was soon in deep thought, thinking about what he had found inside the building or what was left of it.

Birch could not get the image out of his mind, wondering who they were. He would guess that they were young doing research or surveys for the department they worked for since they were in a government building. He hated the thought of the two whose lives were cut so short. He hated the thought of losing everyone else in the area along the Kobuk and the coast of Alaska. He hated the thought of the worldwide catastrophe, of losing his family and friends. With his head in his hands and weeping, he was brought out of his despair when he felt the soft warmth and gentle pressure on his knee and next to his ear. The she wolf had laid her head on his shoulder next to his head. Opening his eyes, he saw the pup with his head on his knee. Birch put his arms around the she wolf and pup and thought, *I have to quit thinking like this, or I will lose it altogether.*

Giving the wolves a vigorous hug, he asked. "You guys want to ride or trot? We will be going uphill." The wolves sprang up and leaped in front of the sno-go, heading out before turning around, waiting impatiently for him. "Trotting, it is." Birch started the sno-go, started up the valley, and found the creek leading up the mountain. Three or four miles later he came to a familiar place.

One summer some years ago, Birch and his friends (the bush pilot brothers and their kids) spent a week prospecting and camping on Dahl creek. One drizzly, cold day they explored the Dahl Creek, following it up the mountain, and they came to a place in the creek where some miners had spent what looked like years stacking rocks into fences. The claims could have belonged to the brothers' dad and grandfather, who had claims in the area during the Gold Rush days or shortly afterwards. Then again, they could have belonged to one of the many in the area at the time. The miner had more than likely stacked the rocks up out of his way so he could get the sand and gravel through his sluice box. There were the remains of a cabin that long ago had collapsed and rotted into the ground. They also found an old Blazo can full of black sand. Birch never did find out how much gold they got out of the black sands. There could have been more than a few ounces. *Sure could see the gold in the black sand when we put some of the sand in a quart jar,* thought Birch. *It might have been worth some money at today's prices. And then again, what would today's prices be? Somewhere between zip and zero.*

Never did see any bears that day, but all the way up the creek and on the return we had to watch where we stepped, he remembered. There were blueberry pies all over the trail from where the bear or bears had crapped. You sure could tell what they were eating. A couple of the pies were still steaming.

Everyone was wet when they got back to camp on the landing strip at Dahl Creek. The boys and their families decided to spend the night with relatives in Kobuk about five miles away, where they could take a shower and get dry. After they piled onto the little Pug, an articulated miniature truck that could go anywhere, they left. Meanwhile Birch stayed in his ten by twelve white canvas wall tent and fired up the woodstove, cleaned and oiled his rifle, pistol, and sharpened the axe. The kids had been chopping up small stuff for firewood on the rocks with it the last few days. He really needed a grinder, but he would do what he could with what he had.

After he cleaned up and put everything away, he was lying on his cot in his sleeping bag and heard something running around the tent skirt or trying to get in. The wind was gusting up and making loud noises, blowing the tent flaps around and brushing up against the tent, making it sort of spooky. He was having a hard time getting to sleep, so he got up and went outside the tent a ways and was taking a leak when he heard a loud growl. Scared the blazes out of him, momentarily, and then it dawned on him it was his stomach growling and not a grizzly. But the rest of the night he lay on his back holding on to his .44 magnum. *I was probably lucky I didn't blow my head or jewels off in my sleep.*

The rock fences that were once standing now looked like snow berms from the after-effects of the quake. The only other time he was here was in the summer, and he and his friends never went to the top of the mountain, but they were in the high country. He called to the wolves, "You guys want to ride? Maybe you would like to wait here? I'm going to the top or as far as I can get on the machine." Starting off real slow, he watched to see what the wolves would do. They started to lope behind him as he maneuvered his way up the dry creek bed. The last three hundred yards they climbed by foot and paws to the top. Standing on top of the 3,400-foot-high mountain, he and the wolves, one on each side of him and up tight against his legs, had a good view of the valley and the big mountains on ahead to the north. He'd never been to Bornite before, but he knew where it was, and he also knew there had been no volcanic activity there before. From the top of the mountain he could see Bornite and the nearby creek and steam rising from the water where there shouldn't be any steam. It would seem there was some new geothermal activity going on the area.

To get to Bornite he would have to go back down the mountain and take the next valley over, which was west of here, and then follow the Shungnak River to the valley on the back side of the mountain.

They had just started down when the wolves stirred up a flock of ptarmigan. Everyone got a couple or more. Both wolves turned somersaults when he shot two of the birds. They didn't know what to make of the big booming noise. Both were flat on the ground spread-eagle looking at him, wondering what in the blazes was that? Birch was already laughing when they got over this new thing. Then the pup rose up with a questionable look on his face and a bird in his mouth saying, look what I got. Now that I got it what do I do with it? Mom sure was a good teacher. Pup tried his best to follow her lead and was sputtering feathers everywhere when he wasn't gagging.

"Well, you guys have fun. I'm going down and make camp. I'm going to grill mine."

Finding four small trees, he stripped the branches off and used the poles to pitch his tent. He spread the spruce needle branches out on the floor of the tent for insulation and soft beds for the night. He grilled the birds, wishing he had something like a good green Caesar salad to go with them. The wolves showed up just as it was getting dark and just in time to enjoy the bones from his grilled birds. The next morning, after a breakfast of salmon and crackers, they broke camp and started north up the valley, following the stream on a narrow road. Nobody wanted to ride, so Birch took off and stopped up ahead where they couldn't see him beyond a couple of bends of the road. When they caught up they still didn't see the need to ride with him on that noisy thing. They had a good pace going and arrived at Bornite just before noon. What they found, with the exception of what they saw yesterday from the top of the mountain, was entirely unexpected for this area. A geothermal event was occurring at the copper deposit of Bornite. Bornite now had its own hot springs.

"Well, the way I see it, we can put the greenhouse right by that little knoll. What do you guys think? Then we can have vegetables this fall and winter. Wouldn't that be wonderful? What do you mean as long as they are good and bloody? Yuk! How gross. You two act just like a couple of animals at times," Birch mumbled to the wolves by his side.

As Birch walked up to the edge of the stream, he was checking the air to see if he could smell any sulfur. If he did, it was so faint it wasn't noticeable. Bornite being a sulfide copper deposit, he was surprised that the smell of sulfur wasn't more pronounced. In the mist he found the source of the hot springs. He could wash dishes in the hot water a short distance downstream, but it was too hot to swim in. Going downstream farther, checking every so often, he found where the bath water would be just right. If he needed it a little warmer, he could swim upstream. If he needed it a little cooler, he could float downstream. How neat!

Looking around, he couldn't see any trace of any type of a facility anymore. It was his understanding that at one time there were one or more shafts sunk to test the ore. Supposedly ore was good enough to make a mine, but there was no way to ship the ore out to a deepwater port. The river was too shallow for any barges of any size, as was the Kotzebue Sound. There was even talk of designing a plane like the 747 to fly the cargo out. Evidently it wasn't feasible. The only way would have been by building a road. No way had they ever gotten the permits for the road or, for that matter, the mine with the former administration. All the mineralized areas had been locked up.

Since Birch appeared to be the sole-surviving permitting agency, he then declared, "Let this yellow X in the snow be the necessary signature and environmental impact statement and authorized permit required for both the road and mine. Hearing no other objections, so be it! I now do declare." For further clarification for the wolves, he said, "Quit looking at me like that. It's a human thing, a bureaucracy thing; you wouldn't understand. It would give you a headache," petting them all the while he talked and took in the area.

Gathering up some firewood, he wondered what happened here. More than likely a landslide rearranged the landscape. He suspected it would be barren for the most part this year, but next summer would see new growth. A year from now you wouldn't be able to tell that there was any recent disturbance to the area.

When he had a good bed of coals going real close to the edge of the stream, he heated up a can of chili and some salmon for Mom and Pup. After they ate, Birch stripped and tested the water with his toe, and then jumped in. After washing up, he called to the wolves, "Come on in, stinky and stinky, you both could use a bath." The wolves, testing the water with their toes, decided they would wait until the water cooled off. They wouldn't even drink the water, preferring to eat the snow when they were thirsty. Before they left, Birch began filling up his thermos with hot water for tea and coffee and noticed the temperature was starting to warm up. He made the wolves ride most of the way back to Shungnak, as the trail was starting to get mushy.

They crossed the Kobuk River and found a good campsite among the tall timber on the high south cut bank that had firewood close by and a good view up and down the river. Rather than pitch the tent, he hung it up between two trees like a tarp and spread some spruce branches underneath for bedding.

While sitting around the fire with a cup of tea, Birch looked at the wolves and thought he should give them names. He also thought that one of these days they will need to go their own way. Who was he to give them names. They did not belong to him. They were not pets. They were animals of the wild. But he would defend them to the death just the same.

Consequently, they would just have to live with being called Lady, Mom, Pup and Fur Balls or whatever came to mind at the time. He almost forgot about Feathers. Momentary lapse on his part.

Chapter Eleven
Exiled

The next morning it was still warm from the Chinook winds that blew in the warm weather, and the trails were still too mushy for any strenuous travel. So everyone enjoyed a lazy morning with naps after breakfast, until Birch's boredom set in once again. "Let's go ice fishing," he said, out of the blue, and both animals jumped—startled by his rude disturbance of peace and quiet. Grabbing his pack and axe, he skied across the river where he hoped a deep hole would be by the far side of the north rock-faced bank, next to the mouth of the Shungnak River. The river narrowed down for a short distance, and he would try there first. Should be narrow and deep, and it could have some deep pools before the narrow part and beyond where the Shungnak River entered the Kobuk River. He cut a couple of willow sticks while going down the bank. Finding a likely spot, he chopped his first hole and dug out some line and fastened it and the lure to one of the willows and fixed it to the ice, so he could watch it if he got a bite. He was on his third set when the wolves started acting up.

"What's wrong with you two? All up in arms, or in your case, paws, like two nervous Nellies."

Then he felt the tremor and then another. He grabbed his pack and skis and started up the near bank, calling to the wolves to follow him. He needn't bother; they did not have to be told. He wanted to get off the ice during an earthquake. No sooner had they reached the top of the rocky bank than a massive quake hit, shattering the river ice and snapping trees here and there. Mom was right up against Birch, and the pup was right up against both of them. Birch had ahold of their neck fur to keep them from running off to hide and getting hurt.

"We are better off right where we are on this high bank with nothing near to fall on us."

He thought the quaking would never stop. He got a first-hand view of what might have happened earlier to some of the areas of the river. The ice in the rivers now was nothing more than giant ice cubes and slush. With every new tremor, the water and ice were sloshing over the lower banks of both the Kobuk and Shungnak

When the quakes quieted down, Birch had a growing feeling of abandonment, a feeling like that of a castaway or of being marooned. "This is not good!" he said, as he petted the wolves. He knelt down and put an arm around each of the wolves. "This is not good at all."

Both Mom and Pup were still shaking, Mom more so that the pup, who was trying to crawl up on his lap. They sat there and watched the river ice as it was now flowing downstream.

After a while Birch got up, found a spot, and kicked what snow he could to one side and gathered some small firewood to build a fire. Then he discovered he didn't have any matches. He spread his parka out on the snow and dumped everything out on it from his pack and pockets. He had a big coffee can, and he took the top off and dumped the contents onto the parka. He hadn't looked inside this can in years but knew it contained a few items that he might be glad to have in circumstances like now. No matches, but he had a gift from one of his Native friends and schoolmate. It had a bone handle with a rod of flint. He had about six wire rabbit snares, fishing line, and flies. A few corroded .44 cartridges, a couple of candles, salt and pepper, some string, and a small length of rope and some wire. The coffee can already had a wire handle. He had a few other odds and ends in the pack he hadn't seen in years. Things he hoped he wouldn't need. Thankfully he had his .44 pistol

"Let's see if I can get a fire going. Going to need one tonight, 'cause it will cool down when the sun goes down," he told the wolves. He was really worried about the temperature taking a big drop when these Chinook winds died down. How many days ago was it down in the minus fifties? Not too many. "No, this is not good."

From what he could see on the other side of the river, the camp might have taken some snow that fell off the trees above, but otherwise it appeared, from what he could see, to be okay. Everything they needed was now across the river at their camp. Until the temperature dropped below zero for a few days, the river would be unsafe to cross. And while he was waiting for the river to freeze back, those same temperatures could do him in. The kids would be fine, though. If only he had fur and liked voles and other critters.

From a downed birch tree, he cut off a square of bark and spread it out flat. Next he took his knife and held the blade straight up over the birch and started scraping very fine tender. When he had more than enough, he put some on the square of birch. He did the same with a dried piece of spruce, and then he gathered dried cotton-like grass from under the snow below one of the bigger spruce trees. Last, he gathered up a couple of handfuls of very small, dead, dried spruce limbs that he set aside close by, along with a small handful of very fine thin strips of the birch bark. He ran the back edge of the knife down the flint and created a nice spark. A couple of sparks on the shavings and cotton and he had smoldering that he blew on till he had a small flame. He added the twigs and strips, and soon had a nice blaze to build on. "This is good, very good. Just wish we had something to put on the fire, you know, like nourishment. Like food."

"You know, it's going to be a while before we can cross back to the other side of the river. It will freeze back but not at these temperatures. I don't know about you guys, but I need to build a shelter." He was cut off from Shungnak and Kobuk villages and what was left of the Dahl Creek BLM facilities. He also would be cut off from Ambler by a river coming down from the north.

Birch set about building a snow shelter large enough for the three of them by trimming a tall spruce tree for a pole. He put the butt of the big end on the ground against another tree and poked the other end onto a branch of another nearby tree. He started laying the branches that he gathered up from the tree and several others against the pole, starting at the bottom, layering one on top of another up the pole. *This might have to last for a few days or longer,* he thought, so he put a second layer of branches over the first in a way that melted snow would shed from one branch to another and not drop underneath. The double layer of spruce branches not only made additional insulation but also provided an additional barrier, keeping the snow that Birch began scooping up and covering the shelter with, from filtering down through the branches. The snow would act as another layer of insulation. It wouldn't be all that warm, but it would keep him from freezing to death. It can be thirty degrees below or colder outside, but under a good cover of snow, voles and mice scurry around thirty or forty degrees warmer than the air temperature, and with moss and leaves it might not be too many degrees below the freezing point of thirty-two. He finished up by making his spruce branch mattress for the wolves and him, and tying up a branch door he could swing to the side.

He was so busy he didn't even notice the wolves were nowhere around and didn't answer when he called out to them. He had worked up a sweat earlier, but now he was cooling off, because he was finished working hard and the temperature was dropping. He put on his thick wool shirt for now; that was enough.

Blowing on the embers brought the fire back to life. When the snow melted in his coffee can, he gathered up a few clean spruce needles and threw them in to make tea. While the tea brewed, he took a look at the snares. He thought they would have to do for now, unless a moose wandered through the camp.

After he drank some tea, he strapped on his skis and began stringing his snares. He strung three snares off to the side of the animal trail along the Kobuk River and the remaining three along the Shungnak River. Just to the side of game trail were rabbit runs among the brush. There seemed to be lots of rabbits this year. He could tell not only from the tracks but the little pellets they left behind. They might be near or at the top of what was considered their seven-year cycle. His only worry was that the wolves would step in one of the snares. He would have liked to have had them with him when he was setting the snares. He might have been able to teach them not to disturb them. They were so smart, ten times smarter than a smart dog.

When he got back to their new camp, the wolves were back with two voles and two rabbits lying in front of them. "You guys are so good," he laughed, as he playfully tousled their fur. "Did you two already eat? You can keep the hors d'oeuvres for yourselves. I'll take the rabbits medium, if you don't mind."

He stoked the fire, skinned the rabbits, stringing the pieces of one on a wire between two long willows over the fire. While the rabbit cooked, he reheated and added some needles to the weak tea and got the salt and pepper out. He cut the uncooked rabbit into pieces and offered one leg cooked and one uncooked to Pup to see which he would choose. "I should have known," he said, when the Pup took both. "How about you, Mom, any preference for you?" She took the uncooked first, then sniffed the roasted one for a while, then started nibbling on it. Birch ate most of the roasted one and laid out what he didn't eat with the rest of the uncooked one. Picking up one of the rabbit skins, Birch started scraping the fat off. "I got a skin for my left hand; this should do for the right hand. I could make you some booties if you want. What's that? You say booties are for wusses? I need some stitching, though."

The two wolves, sitting side by side, watched him with both of their heads cocked a little to the left. *"Little wolf" is growing like a weed*, Birch thought. He also realized that he had to be careful when playing with him and pull his hand away before it was shredded by the little sucker's razor-sharp teeth.

He set the snares out a ways but still close enough to hear if either one of the wolves stepped in one and howled. Birch hadn't seen the relatives in a while, and he hoped they were on the other side of the Kobuk where they would be fine. If they're on this side, they could also step in one of the snares.

"I wonder how that would work out. I can just see me trying to get that big black or gray's paw free of a snare. It shouldn't be a problem, well, not a big one, anyways. One big hundred-fifty-pound pissed-off, long-fanged, carnivorous canine." Both Mom and Pup looked up at him, and he could swear that they were both grinning at him.

Over the next week Little Wolf continued to grow and gain the weight that Birch continued to lose. He was starving to death on the rabbit diet. Wolves were doing well enough, though.

They kept bringing him voles with the rabbits. Maybe the vole hors d'oeuvres were the answer. *I might have to try them! Nah! Not just yet.*

One night Birch woke up with the wolves next to him, thinking that if all these animals survived, then there *had* to be some humans who also survived. If not, what gave the animals the edge? Speed, endurance, and the ability to live off the land?

Temperatures were all over the place but mostly in the upper teens during the day but dropped down in the minus forties one night. On that night Birch was glad for the wolves; they kept him from freezing, one on each side of him. He kept trying to pull the wolves up around him like blankets. Birch was shivering uncontrollably, and the wolves sensed he was in trouble, and they kept as close to him as they could. Without the sleeping bag or his insulated pants, it was a very uncomfortable night. The rivers were completely iced over, but it hadn't stayed cold long enough to make ice thick enough for crossing safely.

When the ice stabilized enough on the river, Birch cut a couple of spruce trees and trimmed them on one side and slid them out on the ice, leaving the big end on the edge. He used these two trees like planks to spread his weight on the ice as an added precaution. Only then did he chop a hole and start fishing with what he could find and devise for bait or a lure. He wasn't having a lot of luck with the flies right now. Using bait, he finally pulled in a very ugly but very tasty burbot, what many call a poor man's lobster. He tied the hook and line to a willow stick and wedged it in upright between the trees he was standing on and secured it. Two hours later he saw the willow whipping back and forth. Trying to keep his balance, he walked out on the log and pulled in another bigger burbot. Taking a very narrow strip of the skin off the fish about one half inch long, he threaded it on a hook behind his mosquito fishing fly, much like a tail, and dropped it into the waters and quickly caught a grayling. His favorite. He had picked a good spot for his fishing hole, in the eddy at the edge where the two rivers, the Shungnak and Kobuk, joined.

More warm weather and some fresh snow made it easier to tell by the lack of tracks in the area that they needed to range out a lot farther when setting rabbit snares. The next morning they set out, following the Kobuk downstream in the direction of Ambler. Watching for tracks, they found signs of rabbit, martin or mink, and birds. Birch was surprised when they found recent moose tracks following the river for a ways. The wolves didn't get too excited by the tracks after sniffing them out. "Well, I don't think they are that fresh, either, maybe a day or two old."

Traveling west along the river trail, they came to a juncture where the game trail branched off to the north away from the river and headed for some higher country. The wolves decided they were going to follow this game trail for a while and left Birch to tag along behind them as they raced ahead. Continuing on the trail, they were steadily climbing and turning back east in the direction of the Shungnak River. Having gained altitude, they were soon above the tree line, and he could see that they were looking at the Shungnak River Valley by the ribbon of big trees growing along the river.

Mom came running back and almost knocked him down. "What is it? What has got you all excited?" He looked ahead and then spotted a couple of caribou stragglers. "Okay, I see them too, but I will never be able to catch up to them. They are heading in the same direction as we are."

Mom looked at him for a moment then took off heading back into the tree line and toward the caribou. Birch continued in the same direction for fifteen to twenty minutes until he heard the wolves. They had stayed in the trees until they had circled around in front of the caribou and now started chasing them back toward him. When he saw what they, or what Mom was doing with Pup tagging along, he found a hole to hide in, dropped his pack, and watched. He unzipped his parka and pulled out his pistol, removed the bird loads, replaced them with standard slugs, and kept watching. They were driving the caribou right at him. Caribou can flat-out move when they have to. The she wolf could keep up, but the pup was slightly losing ground. Every time the caribou started to veer off, the she wolf was right there, making them turn back in his direction. Birch, kneeling in a hole behind some brush, took aim and shot when the caribou were abreast of him. One caribou dropped and the other continued in flight down and into the trees. He had hit the caribou high in the shoulder, bringing him down but not finishing him off. Birch went over and shot the caribou in the head. It was a good shot, not amazing, but still a good shot with a pistol and not a gut shot. He hit a few inches above where he aimed.

Right away he set about skinning and butchering the caribou. The wolves jumped right in and wanted to help, but he was able to convince them to wait a few minutes until he had the animal gutted. He cut off a couple of slices of the liver and gave a slice to each one. Once he pulled the caribou away from the gut pile, he didn't watch when they tore into it, eating heaven only knows what. Meanwhile, he continued skinning and then quartering the caribou. Birch had never been a big hunter, but he had learned enough over the years to make quick work of it.

While Birch was working on the caribou, his attention kept going back to something in the tall trees at the base of the mountains to the north. It just didn't seem like a natural setting. But whatever it was, it was too far away and the snow was too deep to travel by foot or ski with what daylight that was left. If he had the sno-go, he was just curious enough he would check it out.

From where they were, he figured they were not all that far away from the lean-to, as they had been circling back in that general direction. Thankfully, it was mostly downhill until they hit the river. All he could carry at one time would be a quarter of the caribou, and he strapped one on to the pack and started skiing back to camp, figuring the wolves would follow in good time. Since they made this happen, he left them to eat in peace to do what wolves do. He would come back and salvage what he could. It would be too late to make another trip today, so he would get an early start in the morning. He especially wanted to save the skin. About forty minutes later the wolves showed up, dragging their bellies in the snow. From what he knew, like any wild animal, they would gorge themselves or feast until there wasn't anything left, whichever came first. Up till now he had been pretty good about rationing the food.

The next day he made three trips until he wore himself out. He did save the skin, a side and another quarter. The rest was fairly well chewed up, not only by Mom and Pup but by other animals as well. He would decide later if he would have any need for the antlers. He didn't think so right now, but he would see later on. Then he thought he would bring them back when he had the sno-go.

The following day he built a nice fire and set about scraping the caribou skin. Later in the afternoon he checked the fish line. Nothing on the line, but something took the bait. He didn't bother putting it back out but did try for a grayling. While he was jigging for the fish, he looked at the ice, checking the thickness. He also noticed what he thought might be some movement in the tree line across the river by the tent. *Bet the pack is keeping watch on us.*

The next morning he cut and fashioned a long pole from a skinny spruce tree and, not carrying anything except the pole and axe, he started across the river. He thought if he did fall through the ice, the pole would give him something to hang onto and keep him from going under. He chopped three holes going cross to the other side to see how thick the ice was to answer the question: Will it support the sno-go? *It shouldn't be a problem as long as I keep it above a hundred and don't slow down."*

On the other, side Birch made sure the sno-go would start, and then he cleaned up around the tent. He decided to leave the tent up for now, and after shaking the snow off, he packed the rest of the gear on the sled and crossed back to the other side. At the shelter he dropped the sled and told the wolves to stay and that he wouldn't be gone long. Birch left to pick up the antlers; he had a use for them after all.

After picking up the antlers, he looked off in the distance to see if he could see anything. Maybe it was just his imagination. *Nope, something was there in the trees, alright.* He would just have to check it out. He wouldn't be satisfied until he did.

When he got close enough, he could determine it was a cabin, a really nice log cabin. No smoke coming out of the chimney, and the door was drifted in. In fact the whole cabin was drifted in without a sign of tracks anywhere. He knew he shouldn't have gotten his hopes up, but he did.

Birch called out, "Anybody home? Hello!" He just couldn't help himself. Knowing it was unoccupied, he still felt like he was imposing.

He checked the inside of the cabin by looking in the window. Seeing nothing and no movement, he kicked some snow away from the doorway; he was about to give up because there was too much snow when he found a broom and a shovel. With the shovel, he made short work of clearing the doorway and entered and took in what appeared to be a well-stocked cabin that someone had just stepped out of for a while. Clean and neat with plenty of split firewood with kindling nearby.

There was no sign of any damage to the inside or the exterior of the cabin. Even with all the snow, he could tell the roof was made from sod, and it didn't look like there was any damage from the winds. No water damage, as the cabin was in the high country just barely below the tree line. *Must be a creek out front, since the trees are so tall here.*

So where were the occupants? The cabin was unharmed. If the occupants were here when the earth was deconstructing, then they would have been unharmed.

He noticed how well everything was crafted in the cabin: table, chairs, and bed frame. Birch sat down on the bed in more or less a state of confusion. How could this cabin and this small part of the world be totally untouched and still have no survivors?

Birch had no idea how long he sat there, but it was long enough that he was freezing cold, shivering uncontrollably, and in deep depression.

It was late and dark, and he did not feel like traveling, so he lit a fire in the fireplace. While the cabin was warming up, he split some firewood near the front porch. More than enough to replace what he would burn through the night. He wanted the owners, in case they came back, to find the cabin just like they left it with everything they needed to build a fire.

After he finished stacking the wood inside, he looked through the shelves to find something to eat. Something within his capabilities to cook, preferably.

“What have we here? Chili and crackers and . . . company at the door.” He got up and opened the door and was attacked as the animals rushed in and jumped all over him.

“What are you two doing here? Think I wasn’t coming home?”

With his spirits raised by the appearance of the wolves, and after snacks all around, Birch found a good book on one of the shelves. He started reading to the fur balls, and they had an enjoyable evening.

“Nothing like a good warm cabin,” Birch commented to the animals, the next morning. “Okay, let’s cleanup after ourselves and get moving.”

Back at the shelter he reloaded the sled, putting the heavy meat on the bottom and the lighter stuff on top, and then he lashed the antlers over it all. Crossing to the south bank, he stopped and called to the wolves. The she wolf walked out on the ice a ways but kept the pup from getting on the ice until she was half way across, then she woofed to the pup, who gingerly stepped out on the ice. After taking a few cautionary steps, the pup took off at a full run to the other side. *They are so smart*, Birch thought to himself.

Once everybody was safe, Birch headed out at an easy pace so the wolves could keep up. Then he saw them disappear into the forest. Knowing they were visiting with the pack, Birch continued on the trail to *SASSY*. The wolves would follow in their own good time. It was slow going, as the ice was all jumbled up on the Pick and the stream, and Birch had to pick his way around the chunks.

Birch was feeling a lot better now in the company of the fur balls. All Birch could think about was a good shower and a good meal and a good wine and a good, warm bed.

"*SASSY*! You're looking good. Can't say much about the ice, though." Even with the snow cover, he could see the fractured ice. The waves from the quake had washed up thick chunks of ice from the fjord into and on the mouth of the stream, almost blocking it off. Just to be sure, he walked around the hull to check it and to open up the solar panels. No damage that he could see from the quake.

First things first, though. He unpacked and hung up some things to air out, secured the meat, and put everything else away. After he scalded himself in the shower, he started digging around in the fridge and pantry. He had this hunger for greens and possibly some fruit. He wouldn't be surprised if he were coming down with scurvy. If it were not for the spruce needle tea, he probably would have. Yes, first things first. He dug some of the berries out of the freezer for dessert. Finding some frozen turnip greens, he put them on the stove to thaw out and cook. He also pulled three big rib steaks out to grill over the fire when the wolves came back. In the meantime he would get a fire going and a good bed of coals to grill over. *I wonder how the wolves like their steaks*? he wondered. *They had better not destroy a good rib steak with A1 sauce, like some of my friends are prone to do.*

Going back aboard to check the stove, he turned on the radios, both the CB and short wave. While he was waiting for the greens to boil and the wolves to get back, he set about searching the radio waves. He called some of the more common and emergency frequencies, and was only answered by silence.

It was getting dark out, so he grabbed a platter with steaks and turned the deck lights on and went over the side to his fire pit. He put the steaks on the grill and was wondering where the devil dogs were. He gave a whistle and started to call out to them when two beasts suddenly attacked him, a big one and a small one. They knocked him down on the soft side of a snowdrift where he was just floundering and couldn't get back up. They were all over him, and he didn't know if he would survive. He knew for sure he would drown in all the slobber from the two fur balls.

"I hope your steaks burn."

"No dessert, unless you eat your vegetables," Birch told the wolves. He actually dished out a small spoonful of the greens for each. They sniffed and played with it and then ate it. He wondered if it was the vinegar that swung the deal. He was surprised the fur balls took their time and seemed to really enjoy the steaks, which were seasoned with lots of salt and pepper just the way he liked his. When they were through eating, he sat back on the stump by the fire and looked up at the sky, as did the wolves. The stars were out and the aurora borealis was kicking up back and forth across the sky. The temperature seemed to be dropping, and dropping fast.

"I don't know about you guys, but I'm going inside." It was too cold away from the fire. Surprising him, not so much the pup, but the she wolf was right behind him going inside.

Three weeks of forty below or colder was driving Birch bonkers. He knew he had a box of books stored away someplace, but hadn't found them yet. Having read everything else, and the wolves not being able to read, he had to read to them. But they just put their paws down, when he tried to read the same book to them twice. The wolves seemed to be content with a couple of quick trips outside each day, and they lay nearby while he read. He was down to the last few books he hadn't yet read and kept putting those off till later, as they didn't really seem to be that interesting. But you never know, sometimes a book will surprise you, and in the end you can't seem to put it down. By the time he got through these last few, and if it didn't warm up, it would be Easter. Having stocked up on books at a used bookstore, he remembered seeing the cardboard box loaded onto the ship somewhere. He was going to have an Easter book hunt soon.

When he wasn't reading or keeping busy, he would start going into a slump thinking of everybody who was lost. The she wolf seemed to know when he was depressed, as she would come over and grab his arm in her teeth and pull him to his feet. She wasn't satisfied in getting her ears rubbed; she wanted him up and moving around. He could never tell exactly what she wanted or wanted to do, but she would ease off if he were moving around doing something. When Birch thought about it, the pup sometimes would come to him when he sat in one place staring off into space. The pup would grab his pant leg and start shaking it until he got him playing. Birch had always thought the pup was just getting bored; maybe that wasn't it after all.

The caribou was long gone, but he still had lots of the salmon left that he had put up from that last late run up the stream. The wolves never seemed to tire of the fish. As soon as it got up to twenty below or warmer they would go hunting. He hoped they could get a moose. If they did, he would make some mittens, among some other things they needed. When it turned real cold, he brought the battery in from the sno-go after checking everything over. Having put hardly any miles on the brand new machine, it wouldn't do to break down somewhere. He didn't remember seeing any Honda, Polaris, or Yamaha sales and service centers in his journeys lately.

The temperature gods must have been listening to him moan, because it warmed up enough to go hunting. The wolves started getting all excited when he threw a bunch of stuff in his pack and other camp stuff in bags. The next morning after they ate, they headed west on the ice out a ways from shore where it seemed to be smoother. Every once in a while Birch would stop and glass over the shoreline ahead. He was looking for a way farther west that would lead north to the Kobuk near Ambler and game. Caribou or moose, either one would be fine with him and the wolves.

Although Birch was pulling the sled with the toboggan attached in case the wolves wanted to ride, they had decided to run, and run they did. The wolves were loping along at a brisk pace out ahead of the sno-go, and Birch gave them plenty of room but still kept up with them. The She Wolf pulled up short and hunkered down, the pup following her lead. Birch pulled to a stop behind them and took the binoculars out and looked over the terrain ahead of them. Not seeing anything at first, he started to question the She Wolf when he saw a shadow far ahead move in the tree line. He should have known better than to second guess the She Wolf, the huntress.

Birch quietly put on his skis, slung the pack, then his rifle over his shoulder and headed for the tree line. Once there he started following it, looking for tracks. The wolves flanked him and were sniffing out every twig and tree and, occasionally with their heads up, sniffing the air. The stubby spruce tree forest was too thick with growth to walk in without a game trail, so they quietly continued on the ice until they found fresh moose tracks. Evidently the moose had come out of the forest finding the wide fjord and, not wanting to cross the ice, was also following the shoreline looking for a game trail in another direction. The three of them pressed on, in and out of the tree line without a sound, pausing once in a while, listening to hear and determine where the moose was. Still following the track, they found where the moose turned to the north on a narrow game trail, more like a rabbit run. How a moose, as big as they are, could move through the spruce trees and not make a sound amazed Birch. Coming to the edge of a burned-out area, they stopped to listen, look, and sniff the air to spot or position the moose. The tracks turned again to the west and then to the southwest, still in the burned area. The moose wanted to go south, but this direction would lead back here to fjord. Birch said to himself, "I guess they haven't got On Star in this area yet." A few minutes later they dropped down in the snow when they heard ice crack. More than likely, a skim of ice in the tundra gave way under the weight of the moose returning back to the burn area. When the moose appeared and paused at the edge of the burn, Birch dropped him with his rifle. The wolves took off on a dead run toward the moose, just in case they were needed, he guessed.

The wolves wanted to start butchering right away. Birch had other ideas, so he told Pup, "You start a fire. Mom, you go get the sno-go." The wolves sat on their hind quarters looking at him like he was out of his mind. "What's this? Do I have a mutiny on my hands? Okay! You two stand guard then."

He tousled each of the wolves' heads as he started gathering firewood. When he had a good fire going, he started skinning the moose. The pup couldn't stand it, wanting to help so badly. When he had enough of the skin pulled back, he cut off a couple of slices of the rump and bribed each of them to be still. He finally got the skin loose and set it aside where it wouldn't get bloody when he gutted the moose. Having gutted the moose and sliced a couple of pieces from the liver for the wolves, he put a piece on a stick over the fire for himself. While the liver cooked, he cleaned the blood off with some dry grass he had dug out from under the snow, and then warmed his hands.

They followed the burned area to the fjord where the moose had gone and turned around. Not trusting the wolves, he made them go with him to get the sno-go. When they got back, he put the moose skin in the sled and quartered the moose with the axe and bowie knife, then loaded it up. By the time they got back to the ship, it would be close to getting dark, and with the load he was pulling and the rough ice, it would be slow going. But they had accomplished both things they set out to do: They got food and found a way farther west to possibly get over to the Kobuk River and Ambler.

Later that night after three huge grilled moose steaks, they sat around the campfire telling tall tales and lies to each other and just enjoying each other's company. Birch was enjoying the merlot quite a bit, too.

Birch checked the moose hide to make sure no flames were rising out of the fire and that the coals were only smoking. Over the last several days he had set about tanning the hide as best as he could under these temperatures and conditions. Keeping a fire going under the big washtub to soak and rinse the hide was a lot of work, along with keeping the stove stoked in the big tent, to make it easier to scrape and work the hide. The hide was too heavy to handle alone when dry, much less when wet, so he had cut it to the size of a blanket. It was still too heavy. When he asked the fur balls to pitch in, they just looked at him as if to say: If you need a blanket, you furless human, you handle it, wuss. We are much too busy lying here by the fire daydreaming; besides it should be obvious to you that we can barely hold our heads up.

Part of the hide was for a blanket, and the rest he had plans to make moose mittens from the leather, for one thing. When he was marooned across the river, he had almost frozen his fingers more than once. He also would like to have some lightweight mukluks. If he fell through the ice or ran into some overflow on the rivers, it could be serious. The bunny boots he wore were like thermoses; they kept his feet warm, but if he had to put them on outside and they were cold to begin with, it took a long time before they warmed up. He had been there and done that, and got the sock or tee shirt, as the saying goes.

A very painful memory.

After a couple of days of airing out the moose blanket, he rolled it up and was surprised that it wasn't nearly as stiff as he thought it would be. Nor was it quite as soft as some of the Natives' moose hides. *I still have a couple at home that were given to me, and then again . . . maybe not. Had at home*! That was a thought he didn't relish thinking about.

Property values were probably way down, he thought. "Birch, you got big, big sick sense of humor."

He must continue on his search. If so much of this wildlife survived, there must be others that also survived. The question was even if they did survive the initial devastation, could they then live off the land? Birch knew he wouldn't have lasted if it wasn't for his floating kitchen and pantry. He needed to continue the search.

Chapter Twelve
Downriver

Birch read the maintenance section of the owner's manual under the seat of the sno-go, where he also found the tool bag. When he and the wolf pup finished reading, he spread out a tarp on the floor and dumped the contents out of the bag. It took a long time to read through the service section of the manual. Do you know how hard it is to read around the side of a wolf's head if it is stuck in the manual, sniffing each page? Along with a few wrenches, the kit also had a small grease gun inside. Both of the wolves had to sniff and check out each item.

Birch checked every nut and bolt he found, and they were all still tight. He greased the fittings as described in the manual and took up some of the slack in the drive belt. It was to be expected that the new belt would loosen up a bit after a few miles were put on it. With very few miles on the machine, he determined it did not need an oil change yet. He put another can of gas in the sled, just in case, with the other one that hadn't been used and added a couple of oil cans also, just in case. Throwing a tarp over the fuel and oil to protect everything else from a leak and throwing a wolf pup out of the sled, he continued packing until he wore himself out by throwing the pup out of the way.

He chased the beast off to play for a while so he could look around and see what else he needed to do before they left.

When he figured he was finished with the outside chores, he dug a short ditch just deep enough to kneel in right next to the path in the snow from where the fur balls had left. Then he went and cut a bunch of spruce boughs and found some dry grass. He brought the boughs and grass over by the ditch and knelt down in the ditch, arranged the boughs around the hole and over it, and placed the dry grass on top. Then he waited. And he waited some more. His legs were going numb, and then his legs and knees were killing him.

Then he heard them coming.

The next thing he knew, his camouflaged fortress was under attack from the top down. Both beasts were on top of him, pawing through his carefully arranged camouflage so he could pull a sneak attack on the fur balls.

He thought he was going to drown. Both the fur balls were sitting on, or trying to sit on, his chest at the same time before he finally got them off.

So much for plan A

Birch immediately started plotting plan B.

Back aboard, he made out a list and started bagging what he could. He found some paper plates that he added to the camp pots and pans. He boxed up a lot of oatmeal, beans, and rice. Salt and pepper he already had. In the morning he would get a little salmon and moose meat. When they got to the general area and set up a camp, they would hunt to supplement what they had brought along. What else did he need? Ketchup! He had a cooler he could keep the ketchup and other items from freezing up or to delay freezing. He liked ketchup with the moose meat. The axe was by the sled. He had already fueled up the sno-go as soon as they arrived back from their journey. There was one thing he had yet to do. He found a hand saw and went outside to cut a fork off the caribou horns. Back inside, he cut a couple of three-quarter-inch-wide rubber strips from an emergency rubber patch for the hull. Before very long he had an ergonomic sling shot made out of the rubber strips, the caribou fork, and a two-inch-square from the moose leather. He probably couldn't hit the broadside of a barn from the inside. He would just have to practice. Using a few shotgun shells that he broke open, he poured the double ought BBs into a sturdy little cloth bag he'd found and put the little pouch into one of the outside pockets on his pack.

While the animals where outside, he oiled the pistol and rifle, and he added a couple of luxury items to the list. He honed the knife edge on the bottom of his ceramic coffee cup, washed up, let the wolves in, and settled in with a good book that he had found during his Easter book hunt.

"Up and at them, boys and girls! Oh, you are already up. Well, I guess I better get up then." After a big breakfast and setting the *SASSY*'s controls and grabbing the thermos, he shut the hatch behind him. The wolves outside were jumping up and down. "Off we go into the wild white tundra."

The wolves would run several miles, and then Birch would make them ride on the sleds he pulled behind. Then they would run some more. The pup would now and then get up on the sno-go with him, even though Birch would tell him, "You are getting too big for this; too big for me to see around. You could learn how to drive and steer, and then I could just sit back and take in the view."

Birch turned into the narrow gap leading in to the point of the burn where they got the moose. The fire must have died out when it hit the swamp or water, because whatever was there at the time didn't burn. Now the cycle had started again. The burned-out area would first be taken over by brush and willows, then next by the aspen and birch, and followed by spruce trees. The spruce forest would then grow dense, the trees drying out and vying with one another for the groundwater. Eventually, with the forest dying and some of the trees falling over here and there, on a long, hot summer, a passing thunderstorm fires lightning bolts to touch off yet another growth cycle. With the snow cover, Birch couldn't tell how well the new growth was coming back, but he could see the willows poking through the snow here and there, making a good, new moose pasture. In the spring where the willows were thick, you could tell how deep the snow had been the previous winter. The moose would eat the willows down to the top of the snow cover.

Although the burned-out area was pretty much wide open with some still-standing burned-out trees, Birch used a little caution, not wanting to hit a fallen log that was buried beneath the snow with a sno-go ski and not wanting to cause the wolves to get injured running too fast over what they couldn't see.

"Coffee break!" Birch announced, stepping off the sno-go. He dug out his thermos and a baggie containing a couple of dried salmon strips that he shared with the wolves, and he rested for a bit. The wolves sniffed his cup when he offered his coffee to them but declined. "Too late in the day for you two to have coffee?"

He was sure they were not too far from the Kobuk River by now. The north edge of the burned-out area was just ahead of where they were. From here he would start looking for a game trail or creek leading to the river. He found a way in the direction he wanted to go: a creek running north with game trails on both sides. It was too narrow for the sno-go but just right for the wolves. The wolves seemed to be enjoying the trails, and by their sense of smell they could get all the latest gossip and news of the area. Who and what had been visiting the area, and what they had been dining on—just a whole lot of new information on the community. And by what Birch had read, they could also tell when these events occurred.

By following the creek and staying on the banks or in the middle of the creek where the ice was not so broken up, Birch entered the Kobuk some five hours later. If they had gone the other way, it would have been a long day trip going all out. Now he had to determine which way to Ambler. He could see a long way in both directions of the river, which was running west and east. From what he remembered, west of Ambler there were long straight stretches, so he headed east, hoping to find some indication of the village. As he traveled he kept looking for any sign of foot tracks, dogsled, or sno-go tracks. When he came to an island, he followed the north channel until he came to what he thought was the Ambler River. At that point he turned north into the hill and followed what used to be a dirt road that led him to the runway of the landing strip. After exploring the runway and the surrounding area and finding nothing there, he followed another road leading to the streets of Ambler. Directly along the river he could see what might have been cleared areas where houses and cabins once stood. Farther away and on higher ground stood what was left of the school and clinic. They hadn't been swept clean by the water, like in the lower and closer areas to the river, but the quakes and winds had left them in a pile of tangled rubble.

Further searches would have to wait till tomorrow. "Okay, you guys, pitch the tent and build the fire, and I will go get water." As soon as Birch started to unload the sled, the wolves took off on a dead run into the trees. He decided to put up the big tent and spend a couple of days in the area. Once he had the spruce limbs spread out in the sleeping area of the tent, he set about building a nice cooking fire. He decided on some rice and grilled salmon, but he had to melt some snow for water first.

He wondered where those useless fur balls were off to. He should have known; when the salmon was grilling, here they came, bouncing out of the woods with a rabbit and a spruce hen and laid them at his feet. "Oh you are such good little wolves! All is forgiven," he told them, as he tousled their ears. They sat there looking up at him, both very proud of themselves, he could tell. He dished out some rice along with a piece of salmon on a paper plate and let them cool for a little bit, sprinkling a little soy sauce over everything, a little more on his plate. He should put a section on cooking gourmet meals over a fire in the Arctic in his new book. "Don't eat the paper plates." He grabbed the paper plates and added them to the fire. They evidently liked the salty soy sauce that had soaked into the plates.

The next morning he relit the tent stove with some kindling he'd set aside, since the tent stove didn't burn for very long. After he got the stove going, he snuggled back in his sleeping bag and slept a little longer. The tent stove had taken the chill off enough that he didn't freeze to death getting dressed. It had dropped down to twenty below when he went to bed last night. He stoked last night's embers in the fire pit outside. After getting a fire going, he put some snow on to melt for some oatmeal, and then roasted the rabbit and spruce hen that he dressed out last night. Birch found some loose gravel near the fire that wasn't frozen. While things were cooking, he raked up a pile and picked through it, gathering a couple of handfuls of quarter-inch stones. In between stirring the oatmeal and turning the meat, he got the slingshot out of his pack and started shooting at an empty chili can he had brought along for practice.

Ping!

"Hey, I am a natural at this." Or so he told himself, until he missed the next twenty shots at the can. But then he started to get the hang of it. If he didn't hit the can, at least he would come fairly close. "Ten to fifteen years more practice, and I will become a master slingshotter."

By the time he cleaned up and put things away from breakfast, it had warmed up quite a bit, and with the sun shining it was becoming comfortable for working outside. He took a hard look at what used to be a clinic in front of him.

He didn't like the idea of rummaging through things to see what he could salvage from the devastation. He felt like a dumpster diver. But now he had to think about survival in the long run. Like what might be handy or needed in the future. He climbed up on what was left of the steps and then onto a piling and onto the twisted floor, watching to make sure he didn't disturb anything that was supporting things overhead. He surveyed what he could see that wasn't covered up. He made his way to some steel cabinets off to the side that caught his attention and looked intact. With a little bit of work, he thought he could check them out and see what was inside. Most of the upper cabinets were locked, and the locks were not the flimsy kind, either. He would need a few tools. A bar, like a crowbar, a large screwdriver, and a two-pound hammer would be nice. In some of the drawers that did not have locks or that were unlocked, he found gauze and bandages. Of these he boxed up supplies he thought would supplement his first-aid kit, which was one of the best outside of having a treatment room on board. He looked for what would be a mechanical room, and seeing some chimney sticking up, he started making his way over. There should be a tool bin or tool cabinets. Crawling in and around, he found what he was looking for and made his way back and started popping off locks and doors. Disregarding one refrigerated cabinet and other fluid medicines, he concentrated on capsules and pills. Some he recognized as antibiotics, but most of the bottles were meaningless without a guidebook, which he was sure was close by. He kept searching until he found a library. After he boxed up some surgical items: needles, scalpels, and sutures, he loaded everything on the two sleds. He went back in, looking at what else he might need in the near future. What he found under the main floor in a rack fastened to the piling was a welcome surprise. Several bottle tanks of various gases. Propane, at the moment, was all he was interested in. *SASSY* was still adequately stocked with propane to last not only through the rest of winter and on into the summer, but sooner or later propane was going to be one of the most important items to have around. Propane was the mainstay of *SASSY*'S operating systems for the most part. It supplied refrigeration, hot water needs, heat, ventilation systems, and sewage disposal systems. Solar panels supplemented some of the systems and charged the batteries when the diesel engines were not running. Along with the solar panels supplementing and supplying the electricity, there were also solar panels which, when the valves were open, would supply heat to the hot water coils in the water storage tanks.

In the utility room, which was still enclosed under the main floor, he found several items more valuable than gold: cases of two-ply toilet paper. "Glory to be, God is great!" he said to himself. Also stored were several cases of paper towels and a five-gallon wet/dry vacuum. He could use the vacuum on *SASSY*, as he hadn't yet got it through the wolves' thick skulls that they were supposed to wipe their feet when coming aboard.

Lugging his requisitions out of the mess and hauling them to a better location took most of the rest of the day. The wolves were out and about most of the day, but they would check on him from time to time, not letting him get too far out of sight. Birch watched the wolves for a while as they chased voles and mice under the snow out front. The pup had learned well from Mom, as he was getting his share, and it appeared there were plenty to go around.

The next morning Birch started in on the school, and the wolves continued on the voles and mice population in the area. The architects and engineers must have been the same on the two buildings. The design and structural details seemed to be the same. From what he could gather, he would guess the teacher's quarters where on one end of the building and the one-room classroom on the other end, with bathrooms and a small kitchen and storage units off to the side. The mechanical room was suspended from the floor system, which was supported by piling. As the mechanical room was easy to get to, he checked it first and found it to be locked. Locked for the time being, anyway. Around to the side he found more propane bottles secured in a padlocked rack attached to the piling. He almost missed two Grumman aluminum canoes on a rack, attached between two of the big glu-lam beams that supported the floor system. One canoe was an eighteen-foot freighter and the other maybe sixteen feet long. Both were padlocked to the rack.

Upstairs, using the same precautions he used at the clinic yesterday, he watched where he walked, what he stepped on, and what he moved out of the way so he did not bring the jumbled roof structure down on him. Finding a set of building and master lock keys in a desk drawer, he unlocked the propane rack, the padlock on the canoe rack, and the door to the utility room. He loaded up the propane bottles in the sled and roped the canoes in behind the sled.

Upstairs in the kitchen and pantry, he discovered cases of dry packaged dinners. "The teacher evidently was a hiker, lazy, or just not in the same league as a supreme gourmet cook like me," Birch said, laughing to himself. A lot of the dinners were just the things when camping out in sub-zero temperatures in deserted villages. Yes, just the thing. He dropped the cases of dry dinners over the side into the snow along with other items he found that wouldn't hurt to freeze, like a couple of cases of breakfast cereals, dry milk, flour, spaghetti noodles, salt and pepper.

In another cabinet he found several classic books he had always wanted to read. Classics like *Ivanhoe, The Last of the Mohicans*, and others. All of these he put in a sack.

He was just thinking that this was just like being in a candy store, when he discovered the bones in the teacher's quarters. The bones of a small man, by the way he was dressed. All of a sudden, he felt like a thief and grave robber. He couldn't bury the remains since the ground was frozen, so he left the remains where they lay and departed the building as quietly as he could.

Over the next couple of days Birch and the wolves scoured the surrounding forest and the village site. "Whoa, hey guys, look what I found. We can have a lot of fun with this." He unsnapped a dog chain and harnesses from one of the trees close to where a house or cabin once stood. "Come over here, I have a surprise for you. Now you're going to earn your keep. Can you say skijoring?" The pup looked at Birch, then grabbed and started shaking the harness. Well, if it had been alive it would be dead now. "You don't even know what it is, and you don't like it?"

As Birch was finishing up the loading and packing, he said to the wolves, who were sitting on their hindquarter not helping one bit, "I need an eighteen-wheeler." Behind the sno-go he had the sno-go sled loaded with three propane bottles and camp gear. Behind the sled he had fashioned a harness and hooked it to the eighteen-foot canoe that was loaded with mostly all the light stuff he had found. There was still room for the wolves to ride in the canoe when or if they got tired.

The other canoe and propane bottles he left up the hill from the riverbank. The sno-go didn't lug down one bit going up the other side of the riverbank. The snow machine wasn't a big racing machine, but it seemed to have more than enough power to pull the loaded sled and canoe. The canoe just glided along on the packed-down snow from the sno-go and sled. The warm sunlight shining down on the snow didn't hurt either.

Birch stopped several times and made the two wolves get into the bed in the canoe and ride awhile, and they would until they came to or saw something that caught their attention. He happened to be watching closely when he first made them ride in the canoe and when the she wolf and Pup jumped off for the first time. He had to stop the sno-go, he was laughing so hard. Although he wasn't going very fast, they both tumbled into the snow when they leaped out of the canoe. They discovered it was a lot different jumping off something that wasn't moving, and especially when jumping off something that was moving fifteen miles an hour or so. The pup looked like a racing skier taking a fall going down the mountain, legs all up in the air and turning end over end. At first it scared them, but then they shook the snow off and started chasing whatever it was that caught their fancy. He couldn't help but laugh. Birch was kneeling down in the snow watching them run when they turned and made a beeline back to him. He was still laughing and called to the she wolf, "Hey, Lady, that wasn't very lady-like, going head over heals off the sled like that." Just then she hit him and knocked him over, nibbling at his ears and neck. Wolf pup had to get in on the action, growling, shaking, and just plain killing his pant cuffs.

They arrived back at the ship in time to enjoy a nice moose steak on the barbie and watch the sun go down. He grabbed a book for some nighttime reading and settled in to read how to charge and fill the propane system without blowing everybody up. Tomorrow he would transfer the propane fuel from the bottles to *SASSY*'s main tank.

Chapter Thirteen

Playing in the Snow—Surviving the Storms

"Come here, Pup, let's have some fun." He'd put the harness on the she wolf earlier and walked her around a bit. She didn't like it one bit at first, but when she discovered it wasn't going to hurt her, she settled down like she had been in training all her life. Now Pup was a whole 'nother story. Finally, after the next couple of days of very strenuous training, Birch had the pup stopping and starting whenever the damn pup felt like starting and stopping. Hooking up the she wolf and strapping on his skis was probably something Birch would like to have seen, if it was happening to someone else. When he got the first ski strapped on and bent over to strap the next ski on, the she wolf took off at full throttle in the opposite direction he was facing. No need to go into any details here. It wasn't very pretty. The pup just sat there on his hind end with what seemed to be a big grin on his face. They probably remembered Birch laughing at Pup when they jumped out of the canoe while it was still moving.

The next day they kept at it until they nearly killed him. The next day was not much better. He kept trading off one for the other, and no one would give up. Not only would Birch not give up, he couldn't get up. He lay there in the snow for the longest time until the wolves got bored and ran off to chase voles. But by the weekend, all of a sudden, they acted like they had been skijoring all their lives. Even Birch was getting the hang of it. The fur balls even started stopping when he crashed. Within a few days he had taught them to heel, lie down, and sit. Birch had said it before: They were so much smarter than dogs.

Over the next couple of days, while he was recovering from teaching the fur balls the art of skijoring, he practiced with his newfound toy. After making a few modifications and adjusting the tension as he got stronger using the slingshot, he started to get pretty damn good hitting anything the size of a paper plate within thirty feet.

"Let's go hunting." That brought them right out of a dead sleep from a mid-morning nap. Once he got his skis on, with some confusion and with Pup on the other end of the rope, they headed south, following the coastline of the fjord around to the southwest. On ahead some miles out, he saw what looked like an island. Staying on the ice and changing out the pup with the she wolf, they made good time getting to the island. Once there, he took off his skis, and they climbed to the top of the five hundred-foot-high island. From where he was standing, it was a beautiful view of the fjord. It would be a great camera shot for a photographer. There was no wind, not even a breeze, but recently the top had had strong winds, sweeping the top of the island bare of snow, making it easier to climb the steep parts near the top.

Birch thought that the island was once part of the foothills of the mountain range directly to the south. Now there was a narrow part of the fjord that separated the island and the foothills. Prior to the big quake, the spot where he was standing was for ages and ages a lookout point overlooking the surrounding valley that now was transformed into the fjord. He recognized some of the ancient signs of the nomadic peoples and of hunters past. He also recognized more recent signs and activities of hunters who more than likely had spotted game from this viewpoint. A rusty tent peg and the remains of a spoon lay near what was once a campfire pit made up of a ring of rocks.

Standing here and looking at this site, he would have liked to be with an archeologist who really knew what he or she was doing and investigate this area to see if they could put a date to the earliest artifacts. While hunting with some of the local boys when he was a teenager, he had run into other areas along the coastline north of Kotzebue that had really piqued his interest. Places along the beach that looked like foxholes that G.I.s would dig in the ground with berms around the hole. He knew these were old Native shelters and houses made of skins and tented by whatever was available in the way of whale bones or driftwood washed ashore from far, far away, because there were no trees on the arctic coast.

"Okay guys and girls, back to business. You see anything on the menu?" Birch took his binoculars out of his pack. He had learned his lesson, and now he didn't take much more than twenty paces without his pack. With his binoculars, he started glassing the area across the fjord to the north and swung around to his left, looking out across the ice to the west to see if any caribou were crossing the fjord. Seeing none, he continued turning left and glassing the countryside. Miles to the southwest he spotted what could be two moose among willows and brush, up a draw in the foothills. If they were moose, they were too far away and up too high to go after without the sno-go. They didn't seem to be moving, either. Spotting what might possibly be tracks, he glassed first one way, following the tracks, then the other, and could just make out five or six caribou traveling to the east, grazing way up high on the slope of the mountain. They must be up high where they don't have to paw through the snow as much. The wind could almost leave bare spots up higher where the winds were stronger. Likewise, the caribou were too high and far away for someone on skis and for a wuss like me. The Eskimos of old would have already started up after them by now. Tomorrow was another day. The trick, now, was to climb down and get back to the ship without the wolves seeing the caribou.

Early the next morning after the sun came up, Birch took the big telescope, and from the rear turret he scoped the slopes of the mountains across the fjord. He found the caribou still grazing, working their way to the east. After breakfast and some bribery for getting the wolves in the sled, they took off at a speed just shy of bouncing the wolves out of the sled behind the sno-go. Birch headed east of where he had spotted the caribou, aiming for a draw to his left out of the line of sight of the caribou. By mid-morning they were in position, high up the draw above where he hoped the caribou would cross. Hiding behind and poking his head over the snowdrift, he watched the caribou moving toward them. The caribou would cross the draw just below them. The wolves crouched down right at his side, not making a sound. When watching them looking at the caribou, he thought of lions crouching in the grass, waiting till the right moment to go after their prey.

"Psst! Go. Go on." The wolves watched him as he tried to motion them down the draw. "Go on," he said quietly. The wolves started down the draw, watching him over their shoulders until he motioned them to drop by dropping his palm down toward the snow several times. They dropped just behind the crest of the ridge and waited. The caribou crossed the ridge lower than Birch anticipated. But his lions drove the caribou up the draw right toward him. He was careful not to let the wolves get in his line of fire when he dropped one of the caribou, and he allowed and watched as the she wolf with the pup brought another down. While the she wolf was on one caribou, the pup started after another, but Birch interceded and got between the pup and the caribou. "That's enough for now, Pup. Let the rest of them go. Besides, you need to grow a bit yet. Good job," he said, rubbing the pup's head.

Birch gutted them and pulled the skin back on the one caribou that Mom brought down, then let her and the pup go about their natural way, with Pup learning his table manners from Mom. While they were doing their thing, Birch went up the draw and started cleaning the one he shot, loading the quarters and ribs on the sled, covering the meat with the hide.

When he was finished, he sat on the sno-go with a cup of coffee and watched the wolves feast a while longer. Caribou aren't that big, and these two won't last all that long for the three of them. He was in no hurry; no need to rush them, that is, until he noticed they were soon to have visitors. The wolf pack was about to join them. This should be interesting, he thought. The wolf pack ran right past the she wolf and Pup till they were more than half way between him and his fur balls, less than a hundred feet. They just milled around for a bit. Birch sat there finishing his coffee, then pouring another cup from the thermos as he watched the goings on. The pack watched Birch for a few minutes, then a couple of wolves howled at him. Birch stood up, calling out "Well, won't you join us at the table?" The wolves howled again and then turned around and went back to where the she wolf and Pup were. Evidently, the she wolf and Pup were full, and after exchanging greetings with the pack, they got out of their way and started preening, cleaning their paws and muzzles, while the rest of the pack began feasting on the caribou. It didn't take long for the pack to make short work of it. When they were done, they lay down in the snow around the carcass.

Birch started the sno-go, and without revving up the engine anymore than he had to in order to get the machine to move, he circled slowly around the pack and caribou, went down the draw apiece, and waited a few minutes before he headed back to the ship. He could tell the fur balls weren't ready to head back yet.

"Well, then they can just walk."

Looking back over his shoulder while taking off, he saw no movement from the fur balls, so he increased the throttle. When he arrived back at the ship, he off-loaded the four-wheelers and trailer. Then he ran the sno-go up the ramp and inside. Making a table out of the plywood bottom from the four-wheelers trailer, Birch started in butchering the caribou after rolling up the hide and putting it up out of reach of animals and birds. Having covered the meat and with the quick trip back, the meat was not frozen, and it cut up easily enough, and he put most of it in the freezer. Some he put in the fridge. Building a fire in the fire pit outside, he readied a few of the ribs. He wondered if the fur balls would like barbeque sauce on their ribs. If not, too bad.

"Oh sure, just in the nick of time for dinner."

And then the next day it to snowed, and then snowed some more. It continued for the rest of the week. He didn't think it would ever stop. When it first started, he threw tarps over the four-wheelers and firewood. He needed a snow shovel, but all he had was a square shovel made for leveling dirt and gravel, and it didn't hold much loose snow. It wore him out shoveling snow off the turrets and the ramp and making a small area for the fur balls to do their thing. He also shoveled and swept around the solar panels, not that they were any use right now, but he didn't want ice building up around them so that he couldn't open them when it cleared up. He laughed when Pup ran out and jumped up into the soft snow and got high-centered. It took the pup several minutes to get back on solid ground where he had shoveled. Birch, not having anything else on his immediate schedule, kept shoveling and cleared a loop off to one side, where the wolves would go when they felt the urge. By now he knew the wolves would go out quite a ways if they could, rather than mess up their front yard.

"You know, we are going to get some big drifts when the winds come." The larger and heavier animals were going to be in for it in this deep snow, until the winds would come and bare some ground so they could graze and feed. They would also be easy prey for wolf packs. By late evening the winds started as it continued to snow, and before daylight the winds howled. The winds were strong enough that they woke him up, not so much from the noise but from shaking the boat. He got up and watched from the turret after he turned the deck lights on. His fur balls climbed up into the turret with him and watched, with the pup trying to get up on his lap. Not that they could see anything but snow blowing sideways by the portholes.

It continued to blow with gale force winds for the next three days, lessening each day thereafter, with the temperature rising until the low pressure system passed. Because of the winds, the ramp was drifted over so much that he couldn't lower it The wolves found out they didn't have any trouble getting to or from the turret and getting outside and over the side and back up, thanks to the drifted packed snow. When the snow melted, he would have to make or find something to lean up against the ship so the wolves could get up and down. It would save on power and not let so much cold air in when he lowered and raised the ramp.

From one extreme to another, Birch thought. Snow like he had never seen before, then the winds turning into a Chinook, and then this: the bottom dropping out. It was colder than all get out, and he was trying to teach the wolves how to play the scrabble game he had just found in a drawer. It wasn't going well at all: Mom had ADD and Pup kept trying to eat the letters.

Suddenly both of the wolves' ears went up. Something besides scrabble had their attention. They both beat him to the turret, and when he got there he had to shoulder them aside as he said, "Why didn't you turn the deck lights on?"

He couldn't see a thing, but the wolves were scratching the door. He made them stop scratching up the door and told them to wait right there. He went below and put his boots and parka on. Before he went outside, he took another look but still couldn't see anything through the porthole. Birch didn't see anything when he got outside either, then the she wolf shouldered him aside just before he stepped on the big gray wolf lying on the snow. He shined his flashlight around and saw the rest of the pack lying around, not even raising their heads up as he walked by. They were exhausted from the looks of them. There was one missing. He counted and shined the light on each one again. The other big gray was missing, and the rest were in really bad shape.

Back inside he grabbed one of the wolves' bowls and a jug of water and went back outside and watered each one as long as they would drink. If they emptied the bowl, he poured some more into the bowl. That seemed to perk them up a little, but they still looked like they wouldn't make it much farther, or through the night, unless they had some nourishment. No! I don't want to start that. No way!

Back inside again, Birch grabbed a couple of salmon out of the freezer and sawed them into equal pieces and did the same with some caribou. Then he set some of it aside to thaw for in the morning if they were still alive. He also set aside a portion, just in case the missing gray showed up. When he got back outside he didn't see the she wolf or Pup. He called and called but got nothing. He dished out an equal portion of the frozen salmon to each one, and in time they all managed to gulp it down. Then he heard his fur balls howling.

Before long, they busted through the snow and nearly knocked him down. The she wolf turned and ran back in the direction she had just came from and stopped, looked at him, and ran back and forth until Birch realized that he was going with her regardless if he wanted to or not. He understood! He pulled the sled and skis out of the snow, went inside and grabbed a couple of blankets and threw them onto the toboggan, and skied behind the she wolf until they reached the other missing gray, as he knew they would. The gray was just barely alive. It was so exhausted from trying to survive the deep snow that it did not move or resist when Birch managed to put a blanket under the wolf and then slid it on to the toboggan. He doubled the other blanket and covered the gray with it. I should have brought some water with me, and I should have brought one, if not both, of the harnesses with me. Birch didn't get very far before he fell down, gasping for his breath. It was hard making it through the deep, soft snow where it had drifted. The wolves must have had to swim through some of the drifts. To make it worse, the snow had crusted over after the Chinook blew through and the temperatures dropped. The snow would barely support the skis but not the wolves' large paws. They kept breaking through the hard crust. Eventually, they made it back to the ship. Birch watered and fed the gray, as he had fed the others. When he was done, he shoveled out the fire pit and started a fire, went back aboard and grabbed some blankets and covered them all for the night. All of the pack took some more water when he poured it out for them. When the fire was going good and had burned down a bit, he put some large pieces of birch on top of the coals, hoping it would last most of the remainder of the night. He climbed aboard with Mom and Pup and turned off the deck lights and went to bed.

Early the next morning he found that all the wolves had survived the night. In fact they all appeared to have recovered, as they were all sitting up when he brought them water. When he came back outside with food, the smaller black wolf growled and started coming at him like it was going to take the big pan from him. Before Birch could react and pull back, the big gray bowled the black over and shook him by the throat until the black was whimpering and cowering on its back. The She Wolf had been behind him and off to the side, but all of a sudden she was standing over and snarling at the black. Then she nipped him in the butt and lay down alongside the smaller black, and in a minute or two licked his muzzle until he quit quivering.

They all sat there quietly while Birch dished out a portion to each one of them. Birch stoked the fire in the pit, and again put some big pieces of birch on top of the coals. Sometime during the night it had started to warm up, right after it had fallen to the lowest point in several weeks. That should at least take the chill off, if they stay close to the fire, he thought, as he went back aboard and to bed for another hour or two.

By mid-afternoon the thermometer read twenty below. It had warmed up almost forty degrees from early last night.

Birch came in from outside, having thrown a couple of logs on the fire for the wolves lying nearby. He was taking his parka off and saw through the porthole the smoke from the fire, but where were the wolves? One minute the wolves were there, and the next minute they were gone. Stepping back outside, he could see their tracks heading out in the direction they came from last night.

As the days passed, they were getting longer and warmer, warming up to zero, sometimes ten above. The fur balls were bored. He was bored. There was only one thing that would cure his boredom. He needed an immediate transfusion of grayling. The wolves would be on their own while he was fishing. He would tell them to go fish for voles or just amuse themselves.

Birch had an idea where some grayling might be holed up. Plus he had an ulterior motive, that is, another chore to do while he was on the grayling hunt.

"You guys pack your bags and get a good night's sleep. You're going to have to get up early in the morning, if you're going with me," Birch informed the fur balls. He started to layout things for the trip and listing the food items he would need from the fridge and freezer in the morning.

"And away we go," Birch commented to himself then next morning. The fur balls were already out in front of him and already out of sight. "Nice of them to wait," he muttered.

It didn't take long before he caught up to them floundering through some deep drifts. It wasn't as bad as it would have been if they had tried making this trip right after it snowed when the snow was still fresh, but it was still tough on the wolves as it was. The long-track sno-go wasn't having any trouble whatsoever going through the snow or snow drifts. He stopped about a mile ahead after he went around the wolves. A few minutes later they arrived, panting up a storm. He let them rest for a couple of minutes before he offered them a ride. It didn't take much persuasion to get them in the sled. They made quite a sight, lying side by side with their heads up and faces in the wind, like dogs hanging their heads out the window in a car.

Up stream and across to the Pick, down the Pick River to the Kobuk, across the Kobuk River to the Shungnak, up the Shungnak and on the road to Bornite, where the new hot springs had formed. Arriving in the same area they had been before, Birch unloaded the sled and went back down the road a ways and cut tent poles and picked up firewood for the night.

After setting up camp he built a fire outside and built another inside the tent stove. When the fires were going good, he stripped down and ran to the springs and waded in where he had tested the temperature. Just right. "Come on in, the water is good. I don't want to embarrass you guys or hurt your feelings, but to put it bluntly, you stink." All Birch got in reply was two bored stares before they both rolled in the snow and watched from the bank. Birch picked up a stick from the stream bank and tossed it in the middle of the stream. "Get the stick, go on get the stick." The fur balls put their heads down on their paws, sighed, and closed their eyes, and then they both rolled over on their backs at the same time, just like two synchronized swimmers. They stretched and looked at Birch upside down, and he could tell from the expression on their muzzles: You want a stick? The stick has no value. You want the stick, then you dive in.

Birch knew he should keep his sense of humor, or he would lose his sanity. But looking at the wolves grinning at him, he thought, It's too late.

After his spa, Birch dried off and got dressed inside the warm tent. "Get away from me. You will get me all contaminated," he told the wolves, when they wandered in from outside. As he was putting on his socks, the wolves knocked him over and wanted to get a massage, just like everyone else enjoying a spa. That was only to be expected wasn't it? "Gee, thanks a million. Now I need another bath."

After strapping on his skies and grabbing his fishing rod, Birch started following the stream downstream looking for cooler water and likely spots where the grayling might be lurking. He saw earlier that the stream was open all the way to the Shungnak River. Every so often he would stop and check out the stream to see if he could see any movement in the water. With the sun low on the horizon and over his left shoulder, he had a good view of the shallow waters. Not seeing anything of interest, he moved on downstream. He stopped every hundred yards or so, looking and checking the water temperature. The farther downstream, the cooler the water became. At his present location the water was cold and deeper but not frozen. Telling the wolves, "If there is anything in this stream, my special lure will seek them out." Throwing the lure out and watching it float downstream and moving closer to the bank, he thought he saw some movement near the lure. The she wolf saw it too and leaped to the edge of the bank, looking intently at the water. Birch cast again, and when the lure got close to the bank downstream, he got a bite. He almost got two bites as the she wolf jumped in the water after the grayling on the end of the line. Birch had to pull the fish back upstream away from her. "Get your own grayling," he yelled at Lady. Pup was running back and forth on the stream bank, quite confused. He didn't quite know what was going on, but he knew he was missing out on something of great importance, and he should be doing something about this situation.

"Well, if you two can control yourselves, we will have scaled, grilled grayling, using my world-famous recipe." Birch got nine nice-size grayling, with a couple being almost twenty inches long. Not record size but very nice, more than enough for dinner and breakfast.

"I know you're not going to help, so you might as well go and play somewhere out of the way." With that, the fur balls spun around and ran off downstream as Birch set about boiling some water for rice and cleaning the fish. He put the rice on and cleaned up while it cooked and put the fish on sticks to cook. "Well, guess who's coming to dinner," as the wolves bounced into camp.

After breakfast the next morning, Birch took the frozen caribou hide out of the sled, stripped down, and jumped into the hot springs with it. The fur balls watched for a few moments, and not wanting any part of work, they took off for parts unknown. After he got the hide thawed, he laid it over a boulder and started scraping and cleaning. Several hours later when he figured the skin was as clean as it was going to get, he hammered a small pole into the riverbank and strung a rope back to the tent pole and hung the skin up like a tent to dry out. He had been careful and did not cut or tear the hide.

After his nap he put some beans close to the fire to cook. Not knowing how or what to use but also not having anything else to use, he smeared some olive oil he brought with him on the inside of the skin and rubbed it in with the end of a soft, smooth stick, hoping it would help in the tanning process. When he finished oiling the hide, he hung it over the rope above the fire again to dry and to let the oil soak in. Stoking the fire with a couple of big pieces of birch and watching it for awhile, he made sure it wouldn't flame up and burn the skin. After checking the beans and adding some water, he put on his skis and pack and took off to go exploring beyond the hot springs, hoping he would see some ptarmigan or rabbits.

He hadn't been gone too long or too far when he did spot some ptarmigan perched in among some small willows in a draw on the hillside. At first glance they appeared to be clumps of snow that hadn't blown or fallen off the branches. If he hadn't seen a couple flutter to the ground, he would have missed them altogether, because they were so well camouflaged against the background. You couldn't see the white birds on the snow until they moved or they took flight, and then you could see their black beaks. Birch ducked down and backed off. He dug his slingshot and bag of BBs out of the pack. When he was ready, he crept along just below the crest of the draw to get alongside and closer to where the birds were. Peeking over the snow, he took aim at the lowest bird and let fly. The bird fluttered quietly to the snow and didn't move. The rest of the flock didn't move.

Ptarmigan and spruce hens aren't the brightest bulbs in the chandeliers. It's a wonder they didn't go out with the dodo birds.

He brought five down before the fur ball pup snuck up and brought Birch down in a ferocious attack. It was a wonder he or his pant leg survived in the attack by the pup. It was only when the birds took off because of all the noise the pup was making that the pup took notice and gave chase, to no avail. The she wolf had seen what was going on and had circled around below and grabbed a bird out of the sky as they were gliding just above the snow down the hill.

By the time they gave up the chase and came back, Birch had gathered up the birds and headed back to camp. With Pup bouncing up and down, Birch informed him, "I don't need any help in carrying the birds, and if you weren't playing all the time instead of working, I probably could have gotten you a couple of birds too, but now, you see, you will just have to go without dinner." Lady told the pup the same thing with a very mean growl when Pup offered to help her carry the bird she held in her mouth. Birch realized there was still a lot of training to be done. Pup slunk down, knowing he messed up and followed quietly behind.

While the birds were cooking, Birch got the caribou hide down and soaped it down good before he rinsed it off. After the Birds were cooked, he hung the hide back up to dry. He hoped he hadn't ruined it with the olive oil. He would know in the morning after it was dry.

"Well, it's not rancid. Actually, it smells pretty good. Sort of smells like a "Palmolive" plant, don't you think? What do you mean you have never seen a "Palmolive" plant before? You've just got to get out more. What do you think, Lady? Smell okay to you? And you, Mr. Birch, have got to quit talking gibberish to the fur balls. If someone overhears you talking like that to a pair of wolves, they will think you are crazy, isn't that right, Pup?"

Lady stood up on her hind legs, and with her front paws on his shoulders she cleaned the side of his face real good for him. Birch thought about how big and tall she was. He was having a hard time holding her up without falling over. Standing on her hind legs like that, she was way taller than he was.

Birch and crew spent the next few days fishing and hunting, plus enduring a couple of days at forty below before it warmed up. It was nice to have the new caribou skin to wrap up in when it was that cold. The hide turned out to be surprisingly soft and flexible. Birch spent three days cleaning, scraping, and tanning the hides of a couple of caribou stragglers. They were lucky enough to catch up to them after finding fresh tracks of a herd moving east farther to the north. The new meat would be needed in the near future, when travel would be difficult during breakup.

After gathering a string of twelve or fifteen grayling, Birch announced. "Okay let's break camp and head home." And with that announcement of work, the fur balls ran off somewhere to tend to other important duties, like gathering a string of voles.

Leaving the tent poles in place, Birch continued breaking down the camp while he brewed coffee over the fire for the thermos. He repacked all the heavy stuff in the bottom and the lighter things on top of the sled, so the load wouldn't be top-heavy. The fur balls were nowhere in sight, but he took off toward Shungnak. When he rounded the base of the mountain between the two villages, he swung east toward the BLM camp and picked up the power auger with the six- and eight-inch bits, plus some extensions. He put the auger, a fuel can, and some mixing oil he'd found and secured them on the sled.

The wolves caught up with him near the river where Shungnak used to be. From there they made good time, as the trail was in good condition. The heavy snows had covered and bridged the jumbled and broken ice. By the time he was half way back up the Pick River, the wolves gladly took a ride. They were almost worn out trying to keep up with Birch, the merciless.

They made their way up the Pick River and then crossed the high ground between the two watersheds where they picked up the stream and followed it downstream home to the ship.

The next day after all the chores were completed, things put away, knives sharpened, and guns oiled, everyone took a long nap. The wolves were lying in the sun by the fire pit, and Birch was inside on his bunk.

When Birch got up from his nap, he started fooling with the power auger, draining the gas and oil, rinsing it out with gas and then filling it with oil and gas mixture. He pushed the primer bulb a few times, adjusted the choke, and it started up. He let it run a few minutes before shutting it off. After making a thermos of tea, he grabbed his fishing gear and loaded the toboggan with the auger, a big pry bar, and his pack.

As he started out into the fjord toward deeper water, he told the sleeping lazy wolves not to wait up for him, he would be back later. Birch didn't take more than two steps when the wolves took off like a bullet in his general direction and disappeared. He never caught up with the wolves but when he stopped, figuring he was out far enough, about a half mile from shore and in waters deep enough to ice fish, the fur balls ambushed him. They had been creeping and hiding behind snow drifts somewhere.

The auger was actually a two-man job, but he managed with no help from those lying around watching him and his goings on. Ever the optimist, Birch drilled three holes, making a triangle. Then he busted out the ice with the big pry bar in between holes. He wanted to make sure the hole was big enough to pull up the grand champion sheefish he was about to catch.

Birch pulled up three sheefish in three hours, cutting and cleaning the first two-foot-long one and giving the biggest portion to Mom and the smaller portion to Pup. With the exception of the scales and fins he had cut off, they didn't let any part of it go to waste. Birch was worried about the bones, but the bones didn't slow down the wolves one bit. They probably would have eaten the fins and scales too, if he had let them, but he had shoved them down the hole in the ice. Of the fish, one was a two footer, one was a three footer, and one was in between the two. Not a grand champion like he'd hoped for and had seen in the past when he was a teenager. He remembered sheefish tails sticking way out of big gunnysacks, although the official record was still only around forty-eight inches. Some years ago he had read in the paper about one of the Selawik locals cutting a sixty-five incher in half so he could get it into his freezer.

And then there are the local legends about the really big ones.

Chapter Fourteen
Boredom, Breakup, and Bear Hugs

While the warm weather was appreciated, Birch was getting antsier by the day. With the warm winds blowing in from the east, he felt the need to relocate. He was trapped. The snow had been melting fast, and the water from the melting snow and ice had started to cut channels in the stream ice. Very soon it would turn into the pretty, clear flowing stream that he had seen before freezeup last fall. A few more days like this, and it wouldn't be safe on the fjord ice either. He had loaded the freezer with sheefish fillets and didn't need to get out on the ice or go ice fishing anymore, at least not until next freezeup.

In order to keep busy, Birch loaded the snow machine and four-wheeler aboard *SASSY*, along with everything else he wanted to take with him when it was safe to get underway. And that was exactly what he was going to do as soon as he could pull anchor.

SASSY was sitting in a pool of water that had melted around the bottom of the hull, and it wouldn't be long before she was afloat. It would be awhile longer, though, before she was ice-free. In the meantime he had made a log bridge up to the top deck for access and another to the rear ramp, covering both with spruce limbs. The spruce needles would help clean the fur balls' paws, now that everything had turned to mud.

Making his way to shore, he turned the canoe over and dragged it to the rear ramp and tied it off, so it would be handy and secure in case of high winds. What other chores do I need to do? For one, I can clean the solar panels and upper deck and turrets. Birch set about heating hot water over the fire pit and went aboard to get a bucket, rags, and soap. While the water was heating, he hooked up the intake hose of the boat pump, putting the suction end in the pool of water and hosed everything down above the normal waterline, especially around the solar panels. Unlatching and uncovering hatches for the electric and water solar panels, he washed them down with soap, and then rinsed them off.

After doing the outside of *SASSY*, he started on the inside. The fur balls were nowhere to be seen. If he had a wife, he'd probably be driving her nuts. No wonder the fur balls took off. He wasn't letting them come aboard until he brushed them off. The mud balls had mixed feelings about getting too clean. They didn't really see the necessity of all this cleaning, but the brushing did sort of feel good.

As the days passed and became warmer, Birch took in his surroundings and saw that the birch branches were starting to bud and overhang the edge of the stream. The ice was gone from the stream and was now running clear again after turning muddy during breakup. The grass and bushes on the banks were turning green. To the south he saw that the ice in the fjord had melted in the shallow waters and had receded away from the shoreline but not quite enough room to maneuver around sleepers and rocks along the edge. It was a fine morning. It would be a fine day, he could tell.

Birch had two concerns that he had to face. The first was of his adopted fur balls. Would Lady and Wolf Pup want to go with him on his journey? And would it be fair to take them out of their element and environment and to travel with them on his yacht?

The second concern was whether to wait before casting off until more of the ice in the fjord had melted. If he left too soon, he faced the risk of the winds coming up and blowing the ice pack against the shore, pinning him somewhere he didn't want to be and maybe suffering damage from the ice and rocks along the shoreline.

Of the first, he knew in his heart it would be difficult for the animals. They needed to crap and pee, and he hadn't got around to teaching them how to use the toilet, toilet paper, and to flush the toilet on the ship. His fur balls were smart, but unfortunately they didn't have thumbs.

But most of all, they needed to hunt. He could supplement their diet, but he couldn't provide for their natural diet. Their natural diet had worked for them from time immemorial, and they evidently got the vitamins and nourishment needed by eating the whole of what they hunted, not just the fleshy parts of voles, birds, rabbits, moose, and caribou— all of which, oddly, where grazers.

On the first concern, he decided, after much analyzing and agonizing, that there were only two things he could do. One being he could sleep on it. The other was using his family's long-standing solution to important problems such as these. That is, there are usually a thousand different ways to handle a serious problem, and the best way was to ignore them all, and the problem would fade away. Yes, that was best, he thought, at least for the time being.

Of the second concern, he would wait another day or two. To the southeast it looked like some weather could be headed their way. In the meantime he might catch a grayling or two for lunch. He grabbed his fishing pole and headed upstream along the bank of the stream, following the wolves. When he found a likely spot, he sat down on a log and poured a cup of coffee, enjoying the spring sunshine, and told the fur balls to go play, and off they went. When he finished his coffee, he cast out in the stream and pulled in a grayling. This was a good omen, landing a fish on the first cast of spring. He took out his big knife and cut a willow branch and started making a stringer to string the fish on. Birch walked upstream a ways, checking the stream waters for signs of the big one or a more promising spot. He stopped just below a little beaver dam about a foot high. Busy little buggers, he thought. This was not here last fall. Alongside the bubbling and gurgling stream would make a nice spot for a picnic. On his second cast he pulled in a really nice grayling, just over twenty inches. Not bad. If he recalled correctly, the record grayling was twenty-four inches. Birch put the grayling on the stringer and stuck the knife in the log he was sitting on at the water's edge.

Birch was just taking in all the sunshine, thinking what a good day it was, when he glimpsed two wolves from the pack, hurtling out of the trees and across the stream, running directly at him. His whole life passed before his eyes. Just as he ducked, the wolves flew past him just as a grizzly hit him from behind, grabbing his pack in his jaws and starting to shake him like a rag doll. When the big bear let him go to fend off the wolves, he saw that his she wolf and Pup were right behind the big black wolf and the silver wolf, attacking the bear. Birch picked himself up, and like a fool, he hadn't brought his rifle. He had his pistol under his zipped-up mountain parka. Birch grabbed his big knife that he had stuck in the log and shouldered one of the wolves out of the way so he could plunge the knife into the bear, as the bear had the pup penned down. Birch stabbed the bear in the neck with all of his weight, and the bear dropped dead on top of the pup. Birch pulled and rolled the big bear off the wolf pup, and he saw that Pup wasn't hurt. The silver wolf had blood on him, but Birch couldn't get near him to see how bad he was hurt or even if it was his blood.

Lady was lying off to the side, and Pup was still lying there and shaking, but after a minute or two he was up and about. The she wolf stood up, and Birch could see she had a nasty slash across the top of her shoulders. It didn't look deep, thank God. He did not think she would need stitches, even if he had the means. Well, he did have the means, in fact, but stitching her up without giving her anesthesia would be interesting. Birch looked at the black and the silver wolves and thought, They weren't after me; they were protecting me from the grizzly. Looking directly at them eight to ten feet away, they looked directly at him when he said, "Thank guys." The silver and black whirled around and disappeared back across the stream.

While deep in thought and with the noise from the stream gurgling, he never heard the bear coming.

"Come on, Lady, we have to put something on those slashes." He let the ramp down and they went inside where Birch got the first aid kit down. "You aren't going to like this, girl," he told her as he poured some iodine on the slashes and then applied salve to each one. He was right; she did not like that one bit, but surprisingly, she held still when he told her to be still.

"Well, you guys rest up. I have work to do, and I have to get our dinner." Fat chance, he thought. He grabbed a handsaw and axe with the fur balls right on his heels. He grabbed some big baggies and sacks on the way out.

Skinning and butchering a grizzly is a ton of work, especially if you're not a pro, and Birch was far from being a pro. He thought this one was probably a medium-size bear and not one of the biggest bears, of which he was glad. The bear appeared a little on the lean side but in good shape from winter hibernation. He couldn't pick the hide up off the ground, but he was going to keep the hide and dreaded trying to tan it. As far as salvaging the meat, he pondered what to keep for him and the fur balls. Not knowing what parts were the best for cooking, he took a few of the small ribs, part of the hump for a roast, and cut off enough for a few rib steaks and one front quarter. He left the rest for those who had saved his life that he could see across the stream lying on the bank in front of the trees and brush, making no attempt to be concealed as they always had before. Well, there was one thing he could do for the pack, and that was to finish quartering the bear and placing the pieces on the rocks and grass to keep them clean and out of the gravel and dirt. I just hate it when I get gravel on my steak.

When he was through, he moved the meat he was saving for him and the fur balls downstream a ways. He set about making a make-shift travois to transport everything back to where *SASSY* was, which wasn't that far, but he wanted to take everything in one load. When he had everything loaded, he called out to the pack, "Hey guys, it's all yours." Then he sat down and poured a cup of coffee. As he sipped on the coffee and watched, one of the wolves from the pack got up and waded across the riffles and sniffed the remains of the bear, then started eating. One by one the rest ambled across and started feeding, with Birch not more than forty feet away, drinking a second cup of coffee, just watching. Birch knew that what he was presently watching and what he had just experienced was truly incredible.

For the fun of it, he scaled the grayling and cut them into pieces and put them down closer to where the pack was feeding. They hardly looked up.

Fifty degrees above and two weeks later, all the trees had leafed out and the snow had melted off. Breakup was over. He had been struggling with what he knew he had to do for the past couple of weeks, even though he couldn't really admit it to himself. But he knew and couldn't delay any longer

After the bear incident, Birch caught several grayling, and as he had done before, he cleaned and scaled several for the pack and his fur balls. Earlier he had told Lady and the pup to go play with the pack that was nearby. He could hear them playing and wrestling with the pup. Birch was all packed and ready to cast off. He had already transferred the propane from the bottles to the on-board tank and had loaded and lashed down the canoe on the main deck with the barrels. Having thought long and hard about what to do with his wolves, he had finally thought that in the long run it would be best if his fur balls stayed with the rest of the pack. He cut the grayling up and laid the pieces on the same log where the bear attacked him.

Then he said his good-byes silently to Lady, Pup, and the rest of the pack. He quietly walked back to his boat and put the rest of the grayling in the freezer, except for one he would have later, then he untied *SASSY* and cast off.

The weather looked good to the west, the direction he was headed and the only direction he could go, since he was still hemmed in by what remained of the lake ice and the shore. Still lots of ice, but there was more room to maneuver now, as it was continually melting farther away from the shore. He was using the diesel engine and keeping a close eye on the ice to port and the rocks and shore to starboard. In some places there was just enough room to get through and certainly not enough room to put up the sail. He would need open water for that. At present he was forced by the ice to hug the shoreline.

Already he was disturbing some of the birds that were in the process of migrating north and had settled in the strip of water in the fjord that wasn't covered by the ice. Along with all the birds, he already had seen two moose: one behind him and the other about a quarter of a mile ahead of him. If all the wildlife had survived the Big One, then it was only logical that there had to be other survivors like himself, somewhere, someplace. He had to set out and see if he could find any others.

It had been a couple of hours since he had cast off, and Birch was about ready to bawl. He felt like a deserter abandoning his family, sneaking away like that. He couldn't tell Lady and Pup good-bye face to face, though, and then leave them on the bank as he cast off.

As he was just passing a moose onshore, he had to throttle back and come to a stop; his eyes were so teared up he could barely see where he was going. Then he heard the familiar howls from the shoreline. He wiped his eyes and looked up, and he saw Lady and Wolf Pup heading full blast along the coastline and past the moose, who did a back flip, just like a cat, as the two wolves went around it like a pair of rockets, one to the front and one to the rear. With the wolves on past, the moose turned and watched them racing away from her for a couple more minutes before kicking out with her hind legs and rearing up, flailing her front legs long after they were gone. After a minute or two of that, she ambled off, very dignified, into the forest. He knew exactly how the moose felt when the big black and gray wolves leaped on the bear directly behind him. He never heard the bear behind him, and for the split second before the bear was on him, he thought he was lunch for the wolves and they were going to do him in.

Birch still couldn't proceed. He was laughing so hard he couldn't see. When he finally could see, he saw the two wolves down the beach perched on a fallen tree that was hanging over the water, howling their heads off. Birch eased the bow in, and using the thrusters, he swung the bow in next to the tree where Lady and Wolf Pup jumped aboard, attacking him until he was all wet from their slobber. When they eventually calmed down, he slowly eased the boat out and away from the shore and continued on their way with everyone happy and beside themselves. He was anyway.

Now, how is this going to work out?

Birch started to wonder just what would happen if they did find other humans. How would the wolves react toward others and vice versa? Well, they would just have to deal with it when and if it happened. Besides, if the newcomers couldn't get along with Lady and Wolf Pup, he would just throw the newcomers overboard.

No problem!

For the rest of the day he couldn't take a step without the fur balls being underfoot. They were not letting him out of their sight. Later on in the day, he started to look for a good place to beach for the night. The wolves needed to run for a while, and it was no inconvenience, because it was too dangerous to travel with the sun low on the horizon. He wouldn't be able to see sunken logs or rocks just below the surface until it was too late in these narrow and shallow waters between the ice and shore. Shortly, he found a little creek that flowed into the fjord and had a short gravel beach that would do nicely, he thought. He backed up into the creek, or just to the left of the creek, where it was dry and would be a good place to tie off and drop the ramp.

He told the wolves to go play while he made dinner, but they wouldn't leave his side. Birch knew they probably would like to go relieve themselves, so he went down the ramp and waited while they piddled around before they finally did piddle. While the fur balls were scouting the immediate area, they were watching him the whole time to make sure he wasn't going to run off on them again. He built a campfire, and after he had the fire going good, just for the heck of it, he took off running for the boat. When he got there the wolves were inside looking down the ramp, waiting for him. He laughed as he opened a can of potatoes and got some tinfoil, lime juice, a few other things and the fishing pole and went back outside to catch dinner.

Two casts and two arctic chars, at least that's what he thought they were. More than enough for their dinner, both of the fish were more than twenty inches, much thicker than the grayling. If they were char, then there might be salmon or some other type of fish nearby. Sheefish and grayling made their runs from deep water to the rivers after breakup. Birch knew they followed salmon in some rivers, eating the salmon eggs when they were spawning, but wasn't sure about any type of salmon running this early, though. Lady and Wolf Pup turned their noses up at the steamed potatoes, which didn't surprise Birch. Besides, he didn't make any extra potatoes for them, anyway.

After dinner, while sitting around the campfire, Birch sipped his merlot and was telling the fur balls tall tales. Lady and Wolf Pup hardly ever interrupted. It was always very pleasant having conversations with them; they might roll their eyes once in awhile, but they never called him a liar, at least to his face.

Birch started smiling and said, "I wish I had filmed that fifteen hundred-pound moose doing a backflip when you two went by it. It looked just like a spooked cat somersaulting in the air. I just know that moose needed to change its fur pants."

Chapter Fifteen
The Kobuk

Over the next couple of days, they slowly made their way along the shore of the fjord nearing the Kobuk River delta, or where it should be. The ice was thinning out the farther west he went, leaving plenty of room to maneuver. He had uncovered the solar panels, had stopped and put the sails up, and then continued searching for the main river channel in what used to be the river delta. Where the river had branched off into several channels forming the delta, it now appeared they had all dried up or had been diverted elsewhere. They continued in a west then northerly direction, following around the coastline of the delta and eventually found the hidden main channel of the Kobuk. Birch now knew how dramatically the terrain had changed the course of the river.

From the mouth of the Kobuk to the west was free of ice. Birch thought that most likely the tides had moved most of the ice out from here to the ocean. *SASSY* still had plenty of diesel fuel, but Birch decided to make his way back to Kotzebue to top off the tanks and barrels before he tried to make his way up the Kobuk. It probably would be slow going, that is, if he could even make his way up the river. He needed to make it to Noorvik and beyond to Kiana, or he wouldn't be able to rest, not knowing what became of the villages and the people in the lower part of the river. Those who lived inland stood a much better chance of surviving.

Then he thought of the Shungnak and Kobuk villages.

All the way to and from Kotzebue he was able to use the sails and not the diesel engine. Birch was surprised how well the fur balls had adapted to the roll of sailors on the high seas.

After topping off with diesel, Birch headed up the new mouth of the Kobuk River, watching the depth finder and finding that the river, so far, was more than deep enough for *SASSY*.

When Birch put the kids out on deck, they were greeted by a most aggravating screech. There was Feathers, sitting on top of the mast. The fur balls didn't quite know what to make of this newcomer and me having a friendly conversation and my inviting it in for dinner and feeding it some of our better salmon.

"You do know that if you crap on my boat, it will be into the pot with you, "chicken bones." Just mind your table manners and take that as fair warning."

It was such a nice spring day, and they all enjoyed sunning themselves while Birch piloted the boat. A few hours later they were out of the delta area and well into the river, and the going was good, but Birch thought he and the crew could take a quick picnic ashore and let the wild ones run for a while. Noorvik shouldn't be much farther.

Birch picked out a good spot, put on his hip boots, and beached the boat. The wolves didn't wait until he put the ramp down. Over the side they went, right into the mud left from ice going out and the high-water flooding that followed breakup.

After Birch tied off the boat to a nearby tree, he walked to the edge of the river, enjoying the sun, and watched a couple of ducks across the river while the Lady and Little Wolf were out on a tear.

Maybe I could get them to go for a swim in the cold water and clean the mud off before letting them back on the boat. Yeah! Good luck with that!

While the beasts were off playing, he grabbed a tarp, bucket, soap, and a towel and went topside and saw a nice little gravel bar. He went ashore and scraped out a shallow hole near the edge of the water, laid the tarp over the hole, and filled the tarp with water.

Back aboard, he made a sandwich and took a nap.

After the nap he went outside and removed his clothes and sat in the middle of the tarp and took a good bath. The water wasn't hot, but it was a lot warmer from the sun and was warm enough. He was enjoying himself and wondered where the animals were. And then there was a germ of an idea that began to evolve and grow.

Plan B. He walked to the nearby bank and sat down in the mud and lay back against the bank and completely covered himself with mud. Then he whistled and waited. He didn't have to wait long before he heard the animals splashing along the river's edge, heading his way. He was completely covered with mud several inches thick, except for his eyes. He waited until they were abreast of him, then he leaped up and shoved both of them, including himself, into the water.

He got them. Birch was so proud. Payback is good. He sneak attacked both of them real good. Scared the heck out of them. Only problem so far with plan B was now he was so cold he doubted he could make it back to the boat. He just barely made it to his royal bath on the gravel bar and lay down. Of course, both of the animals thought that was a very good idea, too, and joined him.

By the time he got all the mud off the fur balls, his bathwater wasn't fit to even stand in, much less sit in. Now he was the problem. The animals might not let him get aboard unless he got the mud off. It was back into the frigid water to quickly rinse off. You cannot imagine just how cold Alaska river water can be. If a person falls overboard, he only has a few seconds to get out before his body goes numb.

It has been a good day! He was cleaned up. The Fur Balls were cleaned up, and he hoped to catch a few grayling for dinner. Before he cast out, he momentarily looked down at the edge of water and back up as a fish broke the surface of water.

Then it started to dawn on him what he had just seen in the mud at the edge of the river.

Looking back down near where he was standing, Birch exclaimed, "If I'm the only one left on earth, then who else could be leaving footprints here on the river bank?

Yes, it was most certainly, a good day.

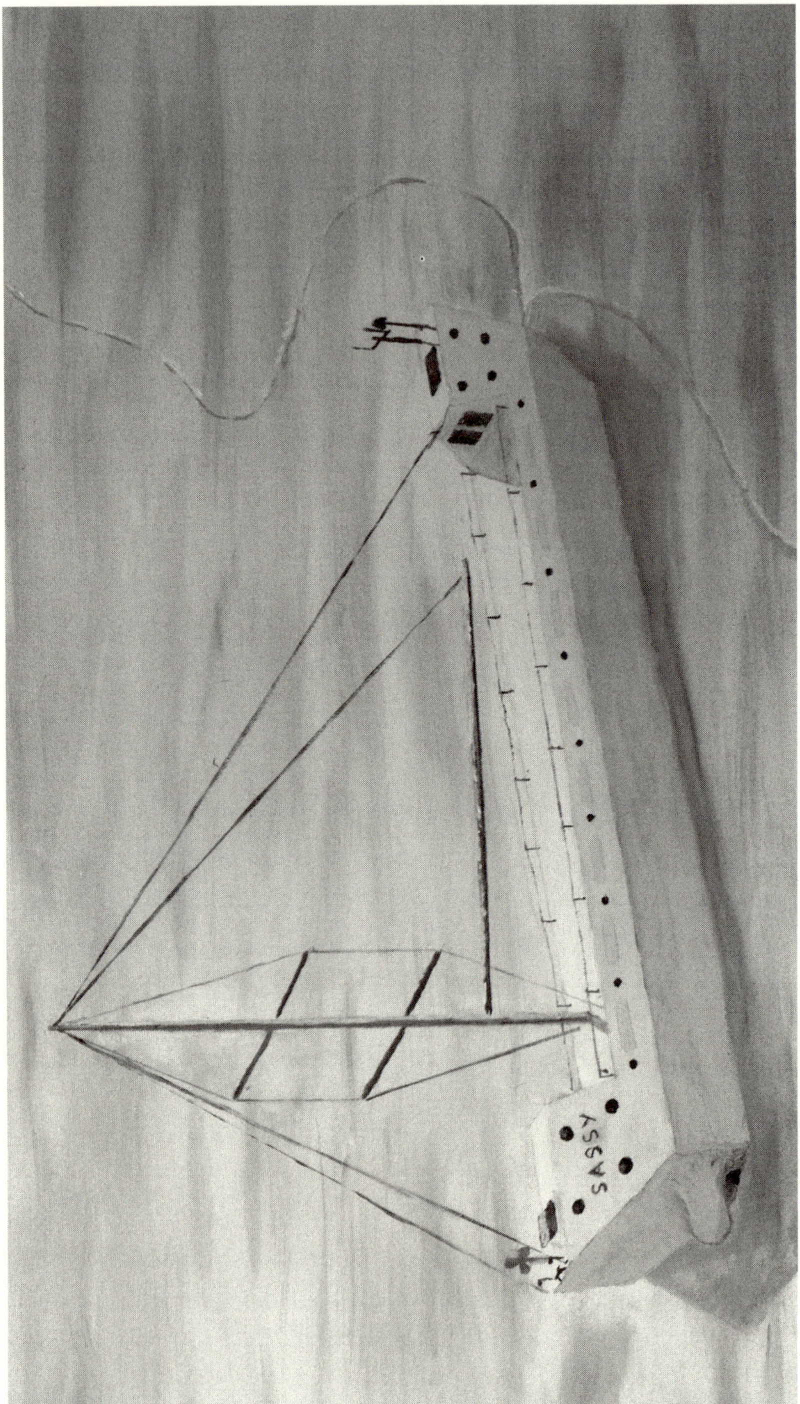

Oil painting of SASSY by author